THE UNCANNY
GASTRONOMIC

TOAST GRID.

PARAGON MINCING MACHINE.

GAME OVEN.

MORTAR AND PESTLE.

POTATO PASTY PAN.

SCALES AND WEIGHTS.

TONGUE PRESSER.

COLANDER.

BRAWN TIN.

GRAVY STRAINERS.

"ENTERPRISE" MEAT CHOPPER.

STEAK TONGS.

PATENT CASK STAND.

THE UNCANNY GASTRONOMIC

Strange Tales of the Edible Weird

Edited by
ZARA-LOUISE STUBBS

This collection first published in 2023 by
The British Library
96 Euston Road
London NW1 2DB

Selection, introduction and notes © 2023 Zara-Louise Stubbs
Volume copyright © 2023 The British Library Board

Dates attributed to each story relate to first publication.

Cataloguing in Publication Data
A catalogue record for this publication is available from the British Library

ISBN 978 0 7123 5428 8
e-ISBN 978 0 7123 6895 7

Cover design by Mauricio Villamayor with illustration by Sandra Gómez
Text design and typesetting by Tetragon, London
Printed in England by CPI Group (UK) Ltd, Croydon, CRO 4YY

CONTENTS

A DIGESTIF: ON HUMAN LOVE

To Shelley, Jackson, Carrington, Carter,
and all the other literary witches who paved the
way; your stories continue to feed us.

"Food is the prototype of all exchanges with the other, below verbal, financial, or erotic. Digestion is a kind of fleshy poetry, for metaphor begins in the body's transubstantiation of itself, while food is thesaurus of all moods and all sensations."

MAUD ELLMAN, *The Hunger Artists:*
Starving, Writing and Imprisonment (1993)

"The mouth then marks the threshold through which the other becomes part of the self, transforming the self in the process."

GITANJALI G. SHAHANI, "Writing on Food
and Literature" in *Food and Literature* (2018)

"The fact remains nonetheless that food is liable to defile."

JULIA KRISTEVA, *Powers of Horror:*
An Essay on Abjection (1941)

"'Come on,' I said. 'Eat your dinner.'
She dropped her napkin over her plate. 'It's gone.'
That seemed a sound idea to me, so I did the same and we left."

HELEN OYEYEMI, *White Is for Witching* (2009)

INTRODUCTION

An Aperitif

Each genre, in its own way, seems haunted by food. You may even go so far as to say that genres have perhaps become recognizable precisely through their styles of eating. Dystopia is typically characterized by lack, with political systems organized around widespread hunger and revolutions built to liberate foodways from the hands of oppressors. Fairy tales frequently contrast farmstead austerity with dizzyingly full tables that showcase royal or imperial decadence. Magical realism is punctuated with worlds of fabulist, frequently surreal food where emotions are a matter of flavour. Gothic novels often play host to lavish tables accompanied by—often suggestively coloured—wine fetched from the best cellar of a mysterious, dark-haired count or countess. Genre fiction, regardless of its shape, bears dark fruit.

The uncanny gastronomic takes many shapes. Any interaction that uses food to challenge the representation of a given reality, or suggests food's ability to estrange, subvert or make "Other" may be labelled as uncanny gastronomic. The uncanny gastronomic, at its core, literalizes the inherent weirdness of food, querying the many ways our appetites can begin to define our very sense of ourselves. My theorization of the uncanny gastronomic began when I started examining the fairy tale's curious obsession with eating. It would be difficult to name a fairy tale whose events does not revolve around a specific food object—pumpkin, gingerbread, beans, wheat, golden eggs—or themes of hunger and dizzying excess often in paradoxical adjacency. In the folktale and fairy tale realms, food is more than object. It is a magical helper, a lure, a trick, a marvellous technology, a harrowing scheme. Extrapolating this and thinking more widely it quickly became tempting to consider how food can be "genred"— and, as I focus on in my research, gendered accordingly. I noted the residual traces of food left behind in genre fiction and began considering how these breadcrumbs of oral storytelling could be working to connect the written text through a dual orality; that of speaking, and of eating. Texts and food both require bodies. In this sense, soma and story are naturally paired, with food acting as the bridge between the two.

The uncanny gastronomic is to some extent, an application of Freud's uncanny. Working via the understanding that the terror at the heart of the unknown functions through its simultaneous distance and similarity to our reality. In his 1919 essay entitled "The Uncanny", Freud wrote that "an uncanny effect often arises when the boundary between fantasy and reality is blurred, when we are faced with the reality of something that we have until now considered imaginary, when a symbol takes on the full function and significance of what it symbolizes, and so forth". The uncanny gastronomic occupies the gap between reality and representation, leaving genre fiction—particularly the magical realist, gothic, fairy tale and weird—as its natural residence. In this way strange gustatory interactions become a site for expressing interiority; of turning the self inside-out, and exposing the soft underbelly of the psyche by examining the contents of the stomach. Through this consideration of food as an identity builder, I began to think in a skew of Descartes' maxim; instead of "I think therefore I am", rather, "I *eat*, therefore I am". Diane Purkiss describes this paradigm, stating that a crucial "part of eating is defining food as what we are not", in a process along the lines of Julia Kristeva's theory of abjection, the borders between self and other are integral to our eating practices. This is complicated and made all the murkier when we begin to see tales of humans consuming one another—where then, do we draw the line? How do we position ourselves when our food is not in opposition, but an exact mirror of ourselves?

The works collected in *The Uncanny Gastronomic: Strange Tales of the Edible Weird* show us that, when it comes to the dark domains of appetite, we are not as safe as we imagine. This collection warns that humans can easily be toppled from the top of the food chain; that food may be as imprisoning as it is freeing and that eating as a day-to-day practice can be its own microcosm of strangeness. In these shadowy, liminal spaces are people—and more-than-human entities, creatures, and shades—waiting to be fed with the dastardliest of dishes. The driving force of each eater in these narratives is unique. Some strive to satiate hungers of the stomach, some of the mind, and others of the heart. Food, as ubiquitous as it is, has naturally pervaded all kinds of discourse. Notably, food pertains to the most divine of ritualistic numericals; that of the Trinity. Food is grown (or, in an era of mass production, manufactured), then prepared and consumed. Days are marked by the temporal necessity of eating arranged into breakfast, lunch, and dinner. Lavish meals often include (at the very least) an appetizer, a main meal, a dessert—three courses. Typically, in the Western world, food is eaten with three utensils. Eating is obsessed with the threefold. This theological nature of food extends from its numeracy to its rituals. Food is made bodily with the ritual of the eucharist's transubstantiation—Christ's body is bread; Christ's blood is wine. Globally, people practise their faith by eating (or abstaining) from certain foods, at certain times, as taught by their scriptures. Food, initially at least, seems governed by the holy. Yet, so easily in uncanny gastronomic texts, food is made the mode of monsters. What the uncanny gastronomic achieves, is the loosening of food symbols from the vines of religious discourse, and the subsequent cultivation of this spiritual thread within the soil of the occult. Of course, this switch from divine to demonic is not novel; given the context of the original sin, the movement to the darkness of food is a revisiting—a return, rather than fresh territory.

In horror, our most notorious monsters are threatening due to their appetites. These well-feared, well-recorded—and often, peculiarly well-loved—creatures implicate a fear that is core to the human condition; the anxiety of being consumed. Through horror media, the image of the wide-mouthed, hungry-eyed, insatiable entity has become synonymous with the most abject kind of terror. Yet the fear of incorporation goes beyond food. We may fear being consumed by our work, passions, loves, our families, beauty standards, social media. Food, as Maud Ellman writes, has become "metaphorically omnivorous", and therefore offers a natural mode to articulate anxieties. The myriad ways we examine food relations—through its association with politics, power, provision (or lack of), gender, sexuality, theology, space, place, and race implicate a human struggle to level with the aporia of eating. We might suggest the need and desire to eat mark the fallibility of bodies as organic mechanisms in a post-industrial, post-modern age. The need to eat carries much anxiety both personally, and politically. As does the frequent reversal of our status as humans from *eater* to *eaten*. Eating is ritual or ordered; it is pathologized in terms of eating disorders, denied due to poverty, or indulged in the context of neoliberal excess. Our associations with our bodies are configured through engagements with food, which is itself formed through the mitigating factors of media influence, access, and personal circumstance. Food is so pervasive that "ingestion" Mintz suggests, begins to function "as an arena for the acting out of moral principles". Quickly, eating transcends the borders of the solely biological to enter the philosophical arena for thinkers, writers, and readers to chew upon. In this manner, food is much more than mere fuel. It makes sense, then, for us to characterize what iconic food writer M. F. K. Fisher terms "the dark necessity of eating", in the context of other worlds, other selves. The uncanny gastronomic investigates if we can trust what we eat, or indeed, our own bodies.

The Uncanny Gastronomic gives space to the myriad kinds of strange eating present throughout literary history. It considers the ways we may police our own bodies—either at the behest of ourselves, or others—how we may be a threat to our own forms, or, indeed, the forms of others. Through its ubiquity and its necessity, food is the ultimate leverage; and therefore, an unequivocal recipe for horror. As Leonora Carrington wrote, "The person who controls the distribution of food has almost unlimited power in a society such as ours." Hunger will always be relatable. Greed will always be terrifying. The all-encompassing nature of the uncanny gastronomic means that the reader of horror, the gothic, or the weird will be well accustomed to its dark palate. In this sense, readers of the uncanny gastronomic are the same as fine diners. Reading about the edible weird functions along the same lines of fine dining. Diane Purkiss writes that "posh diners want and don't want these things; they want enough, but not too much contact with the exotica of death and decay and disgust. Hence the restaurant can offer to perform the labour of immediate interaction with the unprocessed disgusting." The uncanny gastronomic tale, then, is a thought experiment for the daring; an imagined foray into dark appetites that can keep our moral status—and our stomachs—in check.

The contents of this book are arranged in the mode of a meal; by replicating the etiquette of fine dining, I hope to make even starker the strangeness of the uncanny gastronomic by juxtaposing it with the rules of the dinner table. By contrasting supernatural, murderous, and folkloric appetites against the neat, clean hospitality expected in our day-to-day eating, this collection aims to highlight the presence of the edible weird against our ingrained, expected food rituals. In these pages, you will find tales of the strangest appetites. The collected stories, poems, and essays revolve around a plethora of hungers: for blood, cake, flesh, freedom, power, revenge, and connection. The collection is structured in four thematic sections. Each section is organized chronologically. *The Uncanny Gastronomic* ranges temporally, spanning over one hundred and sixty-six years. The earliest work included here is Edgar Allan Poe's "Berenice", originally published in 1835. The most recent is a vignette from Jim Crace's novel *The Devil's Larder* (2001). It also ranges geographically, with stories from Argentina, Italy, China as well as England and America, as well as formally, with the inclusion of an essay and several poems alongside the selected stories chosen from the horror, science fiction, gothic, magical realist and fairy tale genres.

The opening section—an appetizer, if you will—focuses on human horror. Its stories exude a suggestive strangeness. They are odd, reactive, and unnerving. This initial section invites the reader to consider the oddness of some very human—but, perhaps not always *humane*—appetites. This selection considers eating as a kaleidoscopic lens through which to view our own desires. The collection opens with a dramatic monologue from Robert Browning which ponders the length a lover will go to secure her partner. Next, an essay from food writer M. F. K. Fisher recounts a childhood anecdote that details the slippage of gastronomic pleasure to violence. This is followed by Franz Kafka's infamous "A Fasting-Artist" (aka "A Hunger Artist"), a discomforting read that investigates less the strangeness of eating, and more the personal and political elements of restriction in the light of performance. The section on human horror ends with a story from Shirley Jackson's canon, showcasing an uncanny gastronomic flavoured with her characteristically subtle domestic horror.

The second section of this collection—the main course—consults various kinds of supernatural appetites, focusing on the feeding habits of those not quite of this world. In this section you will rub shoulders with mythic legends of the uncanny gastronomic; the vampire, the werewolf, and even the devil himself. Opening with Christina Rossetti's *Goblin Market*, then being followed with works by Hume Nisbet, Saki, Damon Knight, Angela Carter, and Jim Crace, this section considers the folkloric, fantastic, and occult shades of the edible weird.

Following this course is a palate cleanser; an eerie tale from Virginia Woolf, a brief sketch that takes place at a restaurant and is threaded with a kind of unidentifiable, palpable disquiet you can sense in your stomach.

For dessert—section three—a course for those with a taste for human flesh is served. This section includes four tales on the most harrowing of uncanny gastronomic topics: cannibalism. Alongside a work from the literary legend of the weird, Algernon Blackwood, are stories from Mark Twain, Lu Xun, and Roald Dahl. Each writer approaches this most taboo eating practice from a different place and time, inflecting the motif of the man-eating entity as collective and powerful, dangerously political, and even naive and laughable. Oddly, cannibalism today, at the time of writing this introduction, is once again, in vogue. A plethora of horror films, literature, and TV shows (including HBO's *Yellow Jackets* (2021–2023), films such as *Fresh* (2022) *Bones and All* (2022) and novels such as Shalom Auslander's *Mother for Dinner* (2020) and Augustina Bazterrica's

Tender Is the Flesh (2020) all indicate that the anxieties around flesh-eating have resurfaced in recent years.

The collection concludes with a digestif, a series of stories dedicated to the uncanny gastronomic coding of human love. After opening with Edgar Allan Poe's dizzying infatuation with his deceased lover, this section begins to grow more grounded. The stories from O. Henry, Silvina Ocampo, and Italo Calvino finish the collection with a more relatable kind of longing, a desire for connection. This connection is achieved—or evaded—through food, showing the many ways in which the provision or refusal of food can perform acts of scaffolding or severance in physical and emotional contexts. In an era where social media exposure impedes on privacy and the recent (and ongoing) pandemic exemplifies the permeability of our bodies, we are rightly concerned with the borders of the self. Perhaps, together, these two phenomena have heralded a collective identity crisis; the concerns with what we do or do not take into our bodies through eating is a measure of self-identification and both bodily and psychic protection. The fear of being eaten—and of eating the inedible—lie dormant in our cultural consciousness, and therefore, our media.

The Uncanny Gastronomic wishes to display the perplexity of the edible weird. The collection aims to consider how eating—that most ordinary event which punctuates our days like clockwork—can be made so unfamiliar, so disconcerting, so newly strange. Beyond that, the collection strives to argue for food as the ultimate image of change, of anxiety, fear, and pleasure, where food is ascribed universal value. The uncanny gastronomic shows that food is not just provision; it is pleasure, politics, and power. As Gabriel García Márquez writes in *One Hundred Years of Solitude*, "The world is round, like an orange." By viewing the world through the lens of food, we can begin to approach a kaleidoscopic view of our own bodies, selves, and consciousness, and perhaps begin to question them, to reassemble, and rebuild. We can then begin to probe a little deeper—right into the flesh of things.

ZARA-LOUISE STUBBS, 2023

WORKS CITED

Carrington, Leonora, *The Hearing Trumpet* (London: Penguin, 2005). Original published 1974.

Ellmann, Maud, *The Hunger Artists: Starving, Writing and Imprisonment* (London: Virago, 1993).

Fisher, M. F. K., *The Gastronomical Me* (London: Daunt Books, 2017). Original published 1943.

Freud, Sigmund, "The Uncanny", *The Uncanny* (London: Penguin, 2003), pp. 121–162. Original published 1919.

Márquez, Gabriel García, *One Hundred Years of Solitude* (London: Penguin, 2014). Original published 1967.

Mintz, Sidney, "Sugar and morality", *Morality and Health* (New York: Routledge, 1997), pp. 173–184.

Purkiss, Diane, *English Food: A People's History* (London: William Collins, 2002).

FURTHER READING

Andrievskikh, Natalia, "Food: Sugar-Coated Fairy Tales and the Contemporary Cultures of Consumption", *The Routledge Companion to Media and Fairy-Tale Cultures*, 1st ed (London: Routledge, 2018), pp. 525–31.

Bordo, Susan, *Unbearable Weight: Feminism, Western Culture and The Body* (Berkeley: University of California Press, 1992).

Kilgour, Maggie, *From Communion to Cannibalism: An Anatomy of Metaphors of Incorporation* (Princeton: Princeton University Press, 1990).

Kristeva, Julia, *Powers of Horror: An Essay on Abjection* (New York: Columbia University Press, 1984). Original published 1980.

Newbury, Michael, "Fast Zombie/Slow Zombie: Food Writing, Horror Movies, and Agribusiness Apocalypse", *American literary history* 24.1 (2012): 87–114.

Shahani, Gitanjali G., ed., *Food and Literature* (Cambridge: Cambridge University Press, 2018).

Various, *In The Kitchen: Essays on Food and Life* (London: Daunt Books, 2020).

ACKNOWLEDGEMENTS

My thanks to Dr. Alice Hall for her advice and warmth during the PhD process so far, and for encouraging me to untangle the various aspects that make the uncanny gastronomic what it is.

I also thank Sophie Coulombeau, Nicola MacDonald, Chloe Wigston Smith, Helen Smith and the English Department at the University of York for their kindness in supporting this project, as well as for its general vibrancy and eclecticism, which continually influence my own research and critical thinking.

Thanks also to my friends and family for enduring various conversations on cannibalism, vampirism, hallucinogenic crops, and other chats about odd eating through literature and history.

Thank you to my fiancé for attending the conferences, reading the papers, and talking strange books or ghoulish appetites with me (frequently, over dinner...). Thank you to my sister for reading drafts of dense theory, and my mum for being proud of my weird little project. Your support is immeasurable. Thanks also to my dad, who showed me horror films when I was far too young.

Final thanks to the people who have shown interest in my work or encouraged me in pursuing a career in academia. Research really is a delicious place to be.

A NOTE FROM THE PUBLISHER

The original short stories reprinted in the British Library Tales of the Weird series were written and published in a period ranging across the nineteenth and twentieth centuries. There are many elements of these stories which continue to entertain modern readers; however, in some cases there are also uses of language, instances of stereotyping and some attitudes expressed by narrators or characters which may not be endorsed by the publishing standards of today. We acknowledge therefore that some elements in the stories selected for reprinting may continue to make uncomfortable reading for some of our audience. With this series British Library Publishing aims to offer a new readership a chance to read some of the rare material of the British Library's collections in an affordable paperback format, to enjoy their merits and to look back into the worlds of the past two centuries as portrayed by their writers. It is not possible to separate these stories from the history of their writing and as such the following stories are presented as they were originally published with minor edits only, made for consistency of style and sense. We welcome feedback from our readers, which can be sent to the following address:

British Library Publishing
The British Library
96 Euston Road
London, NW1 2DB
United Kingdom

AN APPETIZER: HUMAN HORROR

THE LABORATORY

Robert Browning

Robert Browning (1812–1889) was a Victorian playwright and poet, best known for his dramatic monologues. From 1836, Browning was married to Elizabeth Barrett Browning, a peer in her own right within the poetic world. Robert Browning's first works included *Pauline: A Fragment of a Confession* (1833) and *Paracelsus* (1835). Browning is perhaps best known for his poems "Porphyria's Lover" (1836) and "My Last Duchess" (1842), works that, similarly to "The Laboratory", explore the vicious underbelly of desire.

"The Laboratory" was initially published in 1844, in an issue of *Hood's Magazine and Comic Miscellany* before being collected in Browning's *Dramatic Romances and Lyrics* the following year. The poem leans into the Victorian motif of poison as the ideal tool for murderesses due to its discreet nature. The poem's narrator is a jealous woman, excitably discussing her plans to murder the women who similarly vie for her lover's affection. Browning's uncanny gastronomic is found in the dark, dusty shelves of the apothecary; in the heady scent of the "faint smokes curling whitely", lingering in the bewitching phials of "exquisite blue". It is a very human, obsessive depiction of the uncanny gastronomic. Crucially, the ingredients concocted at the behest of the narrator are to be consumed—either in food, in drink, or in a lozenge—they must be hidden in a comestible that is sweet, enticing, and too good to ignore. Browning's monologue pairs the edibility of foodstuffs with the insatiable natures of pleasure—and danger. Through the edible poison, Browning pairs the illicit character of murder and sex, the hungriness of desire, and the feeling of vying over a lover's attention as though fighting over a plate of residual crumbs.

Browning's poem is an excellent place to start, as it showcases that the uncanny gastronomic is not always about odd food, but odd intentions.

I

Now that I, tying thy glass mask tightly,
May gaze thro' these faint smokes curling whitely,
As thou pliest thy trade in this devil's-smithy—
Which is the poison to poison her, prithee?

II

He is with her; and they know that I know
Where they are, what they do: they believe my tears flow
While they laugh, laugh at me, at me fled to the drear
Empty church to pray God in for them!—I am here.

III

Grind away, moisten and mash up thy paste,
Pound at thy powder,—am I in haste?
Better sit thus, and observe thy strange things,
Than go where men wait me and dance at the King's.

IV

That in the mortar—you call it a gum?
Ah, the brave tree whence such gold oozings come!
And yonder soft phial, the exquisite blue,
Sure to taste sweetly,—is that poison too?

V

Had I but all of them, thee and thy treasures,
What a wild crowd of invisible pleasures!
To carry pure death in an earring, a casket,
A signet, a fan-mount, a fillagree-basket!

VI

Soon, at the King's, but a lozenge to give
And Pauline should have just thirty minutes to live!
To light a pastille, and Elise, with her head,
And her breast, and her arms, and her hands, should drop dead!

VII

Quick—is it finished? The colour's too grim!
Why not like the phial's, enticing and dim?
Let it brighten her drink, let her turn it and stir,
And try it and taste, ere she fix and prefer!

VIII

What a drop! She's not little, no minion like me—
That's why she ensnared him: this never will free
The soul from those masculine eyes,—say, "no!"
To that pulse's magnificent come-and-go.

IX

For only last night, as they whispered, I brought
My own eyes to bear on her so, that I thought
Could I keep them one half minute fixed, she would fall,
Shrivelled; she fell not; yet this does it all!

X

Not that I bid you spare her the pain!
Let death be felt and the proof remain;
Brand, burn up, bite into its grace—
He is sure to remember her dying face!

XI

Is it done? Take my mask off! Nay, be not morose,
It kills her, and this prevents seeing it close—
The delicate droplet, my whole fortune's fee—
If it hurts her, beside, can it ever hurt me?

XII

Now, take all my jewels, gorge gold to your fill,
You may kiss me, old man, on my mouth if you will!
But brush this dust off me, lest horror it brings
Ere I know it—next moment I dance at the King's.

THE MEASURE OF MY POWERS

M. F. K. Fisher

M. F. K. Fisher (1908–1992) was a prolific American food writer lauded for her approach to thinking and writing on food; Fisher's seminal title *The Gastronomical Me* (1943) is often thought of as the first food memoir. Fisher left America as a young woman, travelling to France at the age of 21. It was in France that Fisher began to write extensively on life, love, and travel, ultimately beginning a practice of philosophizing through the lens of food. Fisher opens *The Gastronomical Me* with a kind of treatise on the significance of food writing: "People ask me: Why do you write about food, and eating, and drinking? Why don't you write about the struggle for power and security, and about love, the way others do? They asked accusingly as if I was somehow gross, unfaithful to the honour of my craft. But it suffices to say that, like most other humans, I am hungry."* Fisher's uncanny gastronomic is just that; a very human conceptualization of food and feeling querying of what it means to be hungry.

Fisher was unapologetic in both her way of eating and representing food on the page. "The Measure of My Powers" is one of several essays with the same title that were collected in *The Gastronomical Me*. In it, Fisher reminisces about the cook her family hired during her childhood; the beautiful, intricate meals she would create, the

---

* Page xv

delight she gave to the children of the house, and the strange air of unease sensed by Fisher's grandmother. The story examines the joys—and risks—of food that does more than solely nourishes, and shows the swift slippage from pleasure to violence that frequently pervades the uncanny gastronomic.

I know a beautiful honey-colored actress who is a gourmande, in a pleasant way. She loves to cook rich hot lavish meals. She does it well, too.

She is slender, fragile, with a mute otherworldly pathos in her large azure eyes, and she likes to invite a lot of oddly assorted and usually famous people to a long table crowded with flowers, glasses, dishes of nuts, bowls of Armenian jelly and Russian relishes and Indian chutney, and beer and wine and even water, and then bring in a huge bowl of oxtail stew with dumplings. She has spent days making it, with special spices she found in Bombay or Soho or Honolulu, and she sits watching happily while it disappears. Then she disappears herself, and in a few minutes staggers to the table with a baked Alaska as big as a washtub, a thing of beauty, and a joy for about fifteen minutes.

But this star-eyed slender gourmande has a daughter about eight or nine, and the daughter *hates* her mother's sensuous dishes. In fact, she grows spindly on them. The only way to put meat on her bones is to send her to stay for a week or two with her grandmother, where she eats store ice cream for lunch, mashed potatoes for supper, hot white pap for breakfast.

"*My* daughter!" the actress cries in despair and horror. I tell her there is still hope, with the passage of time. But she, perhaps because of her beauty, pretends Time is not.

The truth is, I think, that small children have very sensitive palates. A little pepper is to them what a highly spiced curry is to us. They can stand sweetness best, perhaps, but anything sour or spiced is actually painful to them.

The ability of an adult to enjoy a subtle goulash or a red-hot enchilada or even a well-hung bird is due partly to his dulled taste buds, calloused by other such delightful ordeals and the constant stupefaction of alcohol and cigaret smoke. Young humans, not yet tough, can taste bland delight in dishes that would sicken older men.

On the other hand, it is wrong to think that children with any spirit and intelligence welcome complete monotony. I know that, because I remember most clearly a cook we had when I was about nine, named Ora.

My grandmother, who oddly seems to have been connected with whatever infantine gastronomy I knew, spent the last thirty years of her life dying of some obscure internal ailment until a paralytic stroke finished her in four days. She was a vigorous woman, tight with repressed emotions, and probably had a "nervous stomach." She spent a lot of time at sanatoria, often genuinely ill, and when she was with us we had to follow her dietary rules, probably to our benefit: no fried things or pastries, no oils, no seasonings.

Grandmother, a handsome dignified old lady, had been told by her doctors to belch whenever she felt like it, which she did... long voluptuous gargantuan belches, anywhere and any time at all, which unless you knew Grandmother would have led you to believe that our table was one of fabulous delights. And once, for a few weeks, it was. That was during Ora's sojourn in our kitchen.

Ora was a spare gray-haired woman, who kept herself to herself in a firm containment. She took her afternoons and Sundays off without incident or comment, and kept her small hot room as neat as her person. The rest of the time she spent in a kind of ecstasy in the kitchen.

She loved to cook, the way some people love to pray, or dance, or fight. She preferred to be let alone, even for the ordering of food, and made it clear that the meals were her business. They were among the best I have ever eaten… all the things we had always accepted as food, but presented in ways that baffled and delighted us.

Grandmother hated her. I don't know any real reasons, of course, after such a long time, but I think it was because Ora was not like the friendly stupid hired girls she thought were proper for middle-class kitchens. And then Ora did things to "plain good food" that made it exciting and new and delightful, which in my poor grandmother's stern ascetism meant that Ora was wrong.

"Eat what's set before you, and be thankful for it," Grandmother said often; or in other words, "Take what God has created and eat it humbly and without sinful pleasure."

Most of the things Ora brought to the table Grandmother professed to be unable to touch. Her belches grew uncompromisingly louder, and she lived on rice water and tomatoes stewed with white bread.

"The girl is ruining you," she would say to Mother when Monday's hash appeared in some new delicious camouflage. But the bills were no larger, Mother must confess.

"The children will be bilious before another week," Grandmother would remark dourly. But we were healthier than ever.

"Their table manners are getting worse," Grandmother observed between belches. And that was true, if you believed as she and unhappy millions of Anglo-Saxons have been taught to believe, that food should be consumed without comment of any kind but above all without sign of praise or enjoyment.

My little sister Anne and I had come in Ora's few weeks with us to watch every plate she served, and to speculate with excitement on what it would taste like. "Oh, *Mother*," we would exclaim in a kind of anguish of delight. "There are little stars, all made of pie crust! They have seeds on them! Oh, how beautiful! How good!"

Mother grew embarrassed, and finally stern; after all, she had been raised by Grandmother. She talked to us privately, and told us how unseemly it was for little children to make comments about food, especially when the cook could hear them. "You've never behaved this way before," she said, thereby admitting the lack of any reason to, until then.

We contented ourselves with silent glances of mutual bliss and, I really think, an increased consciousness of the possibilities of the table.

I was very young, but I can remember observing, privately of course, that meat hashed with a knife is better than meat mauled in a food-chopper; that freshly minced herbs make almost any good thing better; that chopped celery tastes different from celery in the stalk, just as carrots in thin curls and toast in crescents are infinitely more appetizing than in thick chunks and squares.

There were other less obvious things I decided, about using condiments besides salt and pepper, about the danger of monotony... things like that. But it is plain that most of my observations were connected in some way with Ora's knife.

She did almost everything with it, cut, and carved, and minced, and chopped, and even used it to turn things in the oven, as if it were part of her hand. It was a long one, with a bright curved point. She brought it with her to our house, and called it her French knife. That was one more thing Grandmother disliked about her; it was a wicked affectation to have a "French" knife, and take it everywhere as if it were alive, and spend all the spare time polishing and sharpening it.

We had an old woman named Mrs. Kemp come to the house every Saturday morning, to wash Grandmother's beautiful white hair and sometimes ours, and she and Grandmother must have talked together about Ora. Mrs. Kemp announced that she would no longer come through the kitchen to keep her appointments. She didn't like "that girl," she said. Ora scared her, always sitting so haughty sharpening that wicked knife.

So Mrs. Kemp came in the front door, and Anne and I kept our tongues politely silent and our mouths open like little starved birds at every meal, and Grandmother belched rebelliously, and I don't remember what Mother and Father did, except eat of course.

Then, one Sunday, Ora didn't come back with her usual remote severity from her day off. Mother was going to have a baby fairly soon, and Grandmother said, "You see? That girl is way above herself! She simply doesn't want to be in the house with a nurse!"

Grandmother was pleased as Punch, and that night for supper we probably had her favorite dish, steamed soda crackers with hot milk.

The next day, though, we found that Ora, instead of leaving her mother after a quiet pleasant Sunday in which the two elderly women had gone to church and then rested, had cut her into several neat pieces with the French knife.

Then she ripped a tent thoroughly to ribbons. I don't know how the tent came in... maybe she and her mother were resting in it. Anyway, it was a good thing to rip.

Then Ora cut her wrists and her own throat, expertly. The police told Father there wasn't a scratch or a nick in the knife.

Mrs. Kemp, and probably Grandmother too, felt righteous. "I just *felt* something," Mrs. Kemp would say, for a long time after Ora left.

I don't know about Father and Mother, but Anne and I were depressed. The way of dying was of only passing interest to us at our ages, but our inevitable return to ordinary sensible plain food was something to regret. We were helpless then, but we both learned from mad Ora, and now we know what to do about it, because of her.

A FASTING-ARTIST

Franz Kafka

Franz Kafka (1883–1924) was born in Prague and died in Vienna. Written in German and subsequently translated, Kafka's works are considered by many to be extremely significant to the wider twentieth-century literary canon. Kafka is mainly regarded for his strange, surrealist commentaries on both personal and socio-political paradoxes that work in the liminal space between the real and the unreal (or as some may argue, the hyperreal). Kafka's most celebrated works include *The Metamorphosis* (1915) and "In the Penal Colony" (1919) as well as the short story "A Fasting-Artist" (1922).

"A Fasting-Artist" was first published as "Ein Hungerkünstler" in the German literary magazine *Die Neue Rundschau* in 1922. The story was then posthumously republished among three others in a collection of the same name following Kafka's death in 1924. It was subsequently translated into English in 1938, over a decade and a half after its initial publication. "A Fasting-Artist" follows a man who hones his craft—his ability to fast for prolonged periods of time—and travels around Europe in an attempt to display his "art". The work blurs the spiritual and political aspects of restrictive dieting (in terms of holy fasting, and hunger striking) to comment on the limits of art, exposure, and the ethics of society's reception. "A Fasting-Artist" is a morose consideration of restriction, both in terms of appetite and in the waning interest of the voyeuristic masses, that queries the validity of self-knowledge as opposed to public perception and belief. It also works to break the gendered association between fasting and femininity.

Though often referred to as "A Hunger Artist", the title and translation which appears in this collection is J. A. Underwood's, from 1981.

I nterest in fasting as an art has declined very considerably in recent decades. Whereas it used to be well worth staging major performances in this discipline on an entrepreneurial basis, nowadays that is quite impossible. Times have changed. Then the whole city used to be involved in what the fasting-artist was doing; public participation increased from day to day of his fast; everybody wanted to see the fasting-artist at least once daily; during the later stages season-ticket holders used to sit in front of the little barred cage all day long; there was viewing at night, too, with flares to enhance the effect; on fine days the cage was carried out into the open, when it was particularly the children for whose benefit the fasting-artist was exhibited; whereas for grown-ups he was often no more than a joke with which they went along for the sake of fashion, the children used to gaze in open-mouthed wonder, for safety's sake holding one another by the hand, at the pale figure who, dressed in a black bathing-suit, ribs protruding hugely, spurned even a chair to sit in a heap of straw, and who sometimes, nodding politely, answered questions with a strained smile and even stretched his arm out between the bars for people to feel how thin he was. At other times, however, withdrew into himself completely, took no notice of anyone, not even of something so important to him as the stroke of the clock, which was the only piece of furniture in the cage, but simply stared straight ahead of him through half-closed eyes and took occasional sips from a tiny glass of water in order to wet his lips.

Apart from the spectators, who came and went, there were also permanent guards there, men chosen by the public—curiously enough they were usually butchers—who, operating in shifts of three, had the job of keeping watch on the fasting-artist day and night lest, for example, he should in some mysterious fashion contrive after all to take food. This was purely a formality, though, introduced to reassure the masses. Initiates knew perfectly well that during his fast the fasting-artist would never, under any circumstances, even under coercion, have eaten the least little thing; the dignity of his art forbade it. Of course, not all the guards were capable of understanding this, and it happened sometimes that a night shift was extremely lax about the way it kept watch, the men deliberately retiring to a remote corner and settling down to a game of cards, clearly with the intention of letting the fasting-artist enjoy a little refreshment, which it was their opinion he was able to procure from some secret source. Nothing caused the fasting-artist greater torment than guards of this sort; they made his life a misery; they made fasting appallingly difficult for him; sometimes he would overcome his weakness and sing during these night shifts, keeping it up for as long as he could in order to show the people how unjustly they suspected him. Not that it helped; they only marvelled at his skill in managing to eat even while singing. He much preferred the guards who sat down close to the bars and who, not satisfied with the auditorium's dim night lighting, kept him in the beams of the electric torches with which they had been issued by his manager. The glare did not bother him, he was unable to sleep in any case, and he could doze a little in any light and at any time, even in the crowded, noisy auditorium. He was quite prepared, given such guards, to spend the night entirely without sleep; he was prepared to joke with them, tell them stories from his much-travelled past, and listen in turn to their stories, all purely in order to keep them awake, in order to be able to demonstrate to them over and over again that he had nothing edible in the cage and that he was fasting as none of them would be capable of doing. His happiest times, though, were when morning came and they were brought, at his expense, a lavish breakfast on which they fell with the appetite of healthy men after a hard night's vigil. True, there were even some who insisted on seeing this breakfast in terms of exercising undue influence on the guards, but that was really going too far, and when asked whether they would be willing to take on the night shift purely for the job's sake, without any breakfast, they made off in a hurry, though they took their suspicions with them.

These and other suspicions, however, were an inseparable concomitant of the whole business of fasting. No one, you see, was able to stand guard over the fasting-artist continuously, day and night, for all that time, so no one could ever know at first hand whether his fast really had been continuous and complete; only the fasting-artist himself could know that, in other words only he could at the same time be a wholly satisfied spectator of his own fast. But then there was another reason why he was never satisfied: it may not even have been his fasting that had made him so extremely thin that many people had regretfully to miss his performances, the sight of him being too much for them; he may have become so thin purely out of dissatisfaction with himself. For he alone knew—not even any of the initiates knew this—how easy fasting was. It was the easiest thing in the world. He told people so, too, but they did not believe him, attributing his claim to modesty at best but more often to publicity-seeking, some even calling him a fraud who found fasting easy only because he had found an easy way of doing it and who, on top of that, had the effrontery to hint as much. All this he had to put up with, in fact over the years he had grown accustomed to it, but disappointment kept on gnawing away at him inside, and not once, on conclusion of a fast—this much had to be said for him—had he left the cage voluntarily. The manager had set a maximum fasting period of forty days; he never let a fast go beyond that, not even in big cities, and for a very good reason. Experience had shown that for about forty days, by steadily intensifying your publicity, you could fan a city's interest higher and higher, but then the audience folded and you began to record a substantial drop in popularity; there were of course minor discrepancies in this respect as between different cities and different countries, but forty days was regarded as the maximum. On the fortieth day, then, with an enthusiastic crowd filling the arena and a military band playing, the doors of the flower-garlanded cage were opened, two doctors entered the cage to carry out the necessary measurements on the fasting-artist, the results were announced to the audience through a megaphone, and finally two young ladies, delighted that the lot had fallen to them, came and tried to lead the fasting-artist out of the cage and down a couple of steps to a small table laid with a meal that had been selected in strict accordance with dietary principles. And at that point the fasting-artist always put up some resistance. He placed his skinny arms willingly enough in the ladies' helpfully outstretched hands as they bent over him, but he refused to stand up. Why, after forty days, stop now? He could have kept going for a long time, indefinitely long; why stop now when he was on his best fasting form, no, had not even reached his best fasting form? Why did they want to rob him of the glory of fasting even longer, the glory not only of becoming the greatest fasting-artist of all time, which he probably was already, but of surpassing even himself to reach inconceivable heights, for he felt his fasting potential to be unlimited. Why did this crowd that professed to admire him so much have so little patience with him; if he could keep up his fasting, why were they not prepared to keep it up too? Also he was tired, it was comfortable sitting in the straw, and they now expected him to drag himself to his feet and go and consume food, the mere thought of which provoked feelings of nausea to which he refrained with an effort from giving expression out of respect for the ladies. He looked up into the eyes of these ladies who seemed so friendly but were in reality so cruel, and he shook a head grown too heavy for its feeble neck. Then, however, events always took the same course. The manager came; silently, since the band made speech impossible, he raised his arms over the fasting-artist as if calling upon heaven to look down at its handiwork crouching in the straw, at this pitiable martyr, which incidentally the fasting-artist was, only in quite another sense; grasped the fasting-artist round his thin waist, seeking by an exaggerated carefulness of manner to suggest how frail an object he was dealing with; and handed him over—not without covertly giving him a little shake, so that the fasting-artist's legs and torso lolled about in an uncoordinated fashion—to the now deathly-pale ladies. The fasting-artist suffered all this in silence; his head lay on his chest as if it had rolled there and for no apparent reason come to rest; his body showed cavernous hollows; his legs, with the instinct of self-preservation, pressed themselves together at the knee while at the same time shuffling along in such a way as to suggest that this was not the real ground, they were still looking for that; and the whole weight of his body, which was not of course very great, lay upon one of the ladies who, casting about for help, her breath coming in gasps—this was not what she had imagined her honorary office would involve—tried at first to crane her neck as far as it would go in order at least to prevent her face from coming into contact with the fasting-artist, and subsequently, failing in this and finding that her more fortunate companion did not come to her aid but contented herself with bearing tremblingly before her the little bundle of bones that was the fasting-artist's other hand, burst into tears amid the delighted laughter of the audience and had to be relieved by an attendant who had been placed in readiness well before. Then came the meal, with the manager spooning a little food into the almost comatose fasting-artist, chatting gaily the while in order to divert attention from the fasting-artist's condition; after that there was even a toast to the audience, allegedly proposed by the fasting-artist in a whispered communication to the manager; the band sanctioned each piece of business with a tremendous flourish, everybody dispersed, and no one had any right to feel dissatisfied with what he had seen; no one, that is, except the fasting-artist, and him alone.

He lived in this way, with regular, brief rest periods, for many years, an apparently brilliant success, held in universal esteem, yet spending most of the time in a mood of gloom that was made gloomier still by people's inability to take it seriously. How was one to cheer the man up? What more did he want? And, when some kind-hearted soul did take pity on him and tried to explain that his sadness was probably a by-product of his fasting, it sometimes happened, particularly if the current fast was well-advanced, that the fasting-artist would reply with a furious tantrum and to everyone's alarm begin rattling the bars of his cage like an animal. For fits of this kind, however, the manager had a punishment he was not loath to impose. He apologized to the assembled audience on the fasting-artist's behalf, admitting that only the irritability engendered by fasting and not immediately comprehensible to the well-fed could in any way excuse such behaviour; went on, while on the subject, to speak of the fasting-artist's claim, which also called for some explanation, that he was capable of fasting for much longer than he did; praised the high aspiration, excellent intentions, and enormous self-denial that were undoubtedly implicit in that claim; then, however, sought to refute the claim by the simple enough means of producing photographs, which were at the same time on sale, that showed the fasting-artist on the fortieth day of a fast, lying in bed almost dead of exhaustion. This distortion of the truth, familiar though it was to the fasting-artist, always exasperated him afresh. What was the effect of premature termination of his fast was here being represented as its cause! There was no combating that kind of stupidity; it was all-embracing. Up to that point he always clung to the bars, listening eagerly and in good faith to what the manager had to say, but when the photographs came out he invariably relaxed his grip and with a sigh sank back into the straw, whereupon the audience, reassured, was once more able to approach and view him.

When witnesses of such scenes looked back on them a year or two later, they were often puzzled by their own behaviour. For by then the change already referred to had taken place. It happened almost overnight; there may have been deeper reasons, but who was interested in discovering them; anyway, the fasting-artist, accustomed to adulation, suddenly found himself abandoned by the pleasure-seeking masses, who elected to pour into other shows. His manager went chasing round half Europe with him one more time to see whether the old interest was not still to be found here and there; all to no avail; as if by some process of collusion, what amounted almost to a distaste for exhibition fasting had set in everywhere. In reality, of course, it cannot have supervened so abruptly, and indeed, thinking back, one began to recall a number of premonitory symptoms that at the time, in the euphoria of success, had been insufficiently noted and inadequately dealt with, but by then it was too late to do anything about them. Of course, fasting was bound to make a comeback one day, like everything else, but that was no consolation to the living. What was the fasting-artist to do now? A man who had been cheered by thousands could not appear as a mere sideshow at village fairs, and as far as taking up another profession was concerned the fasting-artist was not only too old but above all too fanatically dedicated to fasting. So, discharging his manager and associate in a quite unique career, he signed on with a big circus; consideration for his own feelings prompted him to leave the terms of the contract unread.

A big circus with its vast numbers of people, animals, and items of equipment forever balancing and supplementing one another can find a use for anybody at any time, even a fasting-artist—if suitably modest in his requirements, of course—on top of which, in this particular instance it was not only the fasting-artist himself who was being engaged but also his long-famous name; indeed, it being a peculiarity of this art that a practitioner's skills do not diminish with advancing age, one could not even say that this was a case of a superannuated artist, past his prime, seeking refuge in a leisurely circus job; on the contrary, the fasting-artist declared—and there was every reason to believe him—that he was fasting as well as ever, in fact he even claimed that, if they let him have his way—as they had no hesitation in promising to do—the day was yet to come when he would really give the world something to wonder at, although in view of the mood of the time, which in his enthusiasm the fasting-artist was prone to overlook, this claim of his provoked no more than a smile from the experts.

Deep down, however, even the fasting-artist retained his sense of proportion, accepting as perfectly natural the fact that he and his cage were not, for example, given star billing and put in the centre of the ring but were placed outside in what was nevertheless a most accessible position in the vicinity of the stables. Large, brightly-painted signs surrounded the cage, announcing what was to be seen there. When during the intervals the audience thronged towards the stables to see the animals it was almost inevitable that they passed the fasting-artist and that people stopped for a moment; they might have stayed with him longer had not the passageway been a narrow one and the pressure of those coming along behind, for whom this constituted an inexplicable hold-up on the way to their desired goal, ruled out a more extended and leisurely look. This was also the reason why the fasting-artist, though he looked forward eagerly to these visits as justifying his existence, also trembled at the prospect of them. At first he had hardly been able to wait for interval time; he had feasted his eyes on the advancing throng—only to bow all too soon, since even the most stubborn, almost deliberate self-deception was not proof against the lessons of experience, to the conviction that, every single time, at least as far as intentions were concerned, it was yet another lot *en route* to the stables. Moreover that view of them from a distance was always the most beautiful in memory. Because as soon as they drew level with him his ears were assailed by the shouting and scolding of the two factions that formed and re-formed continually: those on the one hand—for the fasting-artist they were soon the more embarrassing faction of the two—who wished to contemplate him at their ease, not out of any appreciation of what he was doing but out of a spiteful whim, and those who for the moment hankered only after the stables. Once the main body had gone by there came the stragglers, but they, with nothing to prevent them from lingering for as long as they liked, strode rapidly past, almost without a sideways glance, in order to be in time to see the animals. And it was an all-too-infrequent treat when a father chanced along with his children, pointed to the fasting-artist, explained in detail what was involved here, and told them of similar but incomparably more magnificent performances that he had attended years before, and when the children, although as a result of their inadequate preparation both academically and at the hands of life they still stood there uncomprehending—what was fasting to them?—nevertheless revealed in the brightness of their inquisitive eyes a glimpse of fresh, more generous times to come. Possibly it was true, the fasting-artist used then to say to himself sometimes: everything would be that little bit better were his pitch not quite so close to the stables. It made the choice too easy for people, to say nothing of the fact that the smells emanating from the stables, the animals' restlessness during the night, the carrying past of pieces of raw meat for the carnivores, and the cries at feeding-time were all deeply offensive to him and weighed permanently on his mind. To lodge a complaint with the management, however, was more than he dared; after all, it was the animals he had to thank for the vast number of visitors, among whom there might just be the odd one for him, and there was no knowing where he would be hidden away if he attempted to remind them of his existence and consequently of the fact that, when all was said and done, he was no more than an obstacle on the way to the stables.

A minor obstacle, admittedly, and growing smaller all the time. People became accustomed to the strangeness, in this day and age, of anyone's seeking to claim attention for a fasting-artist, and with that his fate was sealed. Fast as he might—and he did so as only he knew how—nothing could save him now; people passed him by. You try explaining fasting to someone! Unless a person feels it he can never be made to understand it. The beautiful signs became soiled and illegible, they were torn down, and no one thought to replace them; the little board showing the number of days fasted, which had at first been kept scrupulously up to date, had for a long time now indicated the same figure, even this small task having become a burden to the staff after the first few weeks; and so, although the fasting-artist fasted on, just as he had once dreamt of doing, and even succeeded without difficulty in accomplishing precisely what he had then said he would accomplish, no one was counting the days, no one, not even the fasting-artist himself, knew the scale of his achievement to date, and his heart grew heavy. And when, as happened at one point, a passing idler stopped in front of the cage, ridiculed the old figure, and spoke of fraud, it was in a sense the stupidest lie that indifference and innate malice could contrive since it was not the fasting-artist who was cheating, he was doing an honest job, it was the world that was cheating him of his reward.

Many more days went by, however, and there came an end to that, too. A foreman, noticing the cage one day, asked the attendants why a perfectly good cage was allowed to stand around unused, full of rotten straw; no one knew the answer until one man, his memory jogged by the little board with the numbers on it, recalled the fasting-artist. They turned the straw over with sticks and found the fasting-artist underneath. "You still fasting, mate?" the foreman asked. "Aren't you ever going to stop?" "Forgive me," the fasting-artist whispered, addressing them all, though only the foreman, with his ear to the bars, could hear. "Of course," the foreman said, putting a finger to his temple to indicate to his men what sort of state the fasting-artist was in. "Of course we forgive you." "I always wanted you to admire my fasting," the fasting-artist said. "And so we do," the foreman said obligingly. "But you shouldn't admire it," the fasting-artist said. "Well, all right, we don't," said the foreman, "but why shouldn't we?" "Because I have to fast, I can't help it," the fasting-artist said. "Well, I'm blowed," said the foreman, "and why can't you help it?" "Because," the fasting-artist began, lifting his head a little and, with lips pursed as if for a kiss, speaking right into the foreman's ear lest anything be lost, "because I've never been able to find the kind of nourishment I like. If I had found it, believe you me, I'd not have made this fuss but would have eaten my fill the same as you and everyone else." Those were his last words, but his shattered gaze retained the firm if no longer proud conviction that he was fasting yet.

"All right, deal with this mess!" the foreman said, and they buried the fasting-artist together with the straw. Into the cage they now put a young panther. It was a palpable relief even to the most stolid to see this savage animal thrashing about in the cage that had been bleakly lifeless for so long. He lacked nothing. The food he liked was brought to him by his keepers without a second thought; even freedom he did not appear to miss; that noble body, endowed almost to bursting-point with all it required, seemed to carry its very freedom around with it—somewhere in the teeth, apparently; and sheer delight at being alive made such a torch of the beast's breath that the spectators had difficulty in holding their ground against it. With a conscious effort, however, they crowded round the cage and, once there, would not budge.

LIKE MOTHER USED TO MAKE

Shirley Jackson

Shirley Jackson (1916–1965) is an iconic figure of American horror. Jackson's tales of unease continue to capture the public's imagination, with arguably her most famous novels, *The Haunting of Hill House* (1959) and *We Always Lived in the Castle* (1962) both adapted for the screen in 2018, over half a century after their initial publications.

Jackson's fictional works are famous for her particular brand of creeping, domestic uncanny. Much of Jackson's work is thought to have been informed by her own experiences; with her fictionalized memoir *The Life Among the Savages* (1953) cementing Jackson's creative attention to examining the tension between homemaking and horror in her narratives. In Jackson's texts, houses, objects, and the spirits—both alive and dead—that haunt them are foregrounded; domestic spaces—workplaces, homes, and in some cases, grocery stores exist as semi-sentient characters as much as settings. For Jackson, the home is coded as psychological; kitchens are spaces of uncontrollable violence: Eleanor's descent is marked by an obsession with her "cup of stars" in *The Haunting of Hill House*. In *We Have Always Lived in the Castle*, mushrooms show that cooking is a domestic double for witchcraft, and the dinner table stages the tension between offers of nourishment and acts of brutality.

"Like Mother Used to Make" was published in Jackson's first collection of short stories, *The Lottery and Other Stories* (1948) which has gone on to achieve cult classic status. The story pays close attention to the idiosyncratic nature of our homemaking—and cooking—rituals with starkly precise prose. Jackson probes into these idiosyncrasies, experimenting with and querying the role of the domestic as an all-powerful identity and meaning-maker, ultimately collapsing the assertion that home is a place of refuge.

David Turner, who did everything in small quick movements, hurried from the bus stop down the avenue toward his street. He reached the grocery on the corner and hesitated; there had been something. Butter, he remembered with relief; this morning, all the way up the avenue to his bus stop, he had been telling himself butter, don't forget butter coming home tonight, when you pass the grocery remember butter. He went into the grocery and waited his turn, examining the cans on the shelves. Canned pork sausage was back, and corned-beef hash. A tray full of rolls caught his eye, and then the woman ahead of him went out and the clerk turned to him.

"How much is butter?" David asked cautiously.

"Eighty-nine," the clerk said easily.

"Eighty-nine?" David frowned.

"That's what it is," the clerk said. He looked past David at the next customer.

"Quarter of a pound, please," David said. "And a half-dozen rolls."

Carrying his package home he thought, I really ought not to trade there any more; you'd think they'd know me well enough to be more courteous.

There was a letter from his mother in the mailbox. He stuck it into the top of the bag of rolls and went upstairs to the third floor. No light in Marcia's apartment, the only other apartment on the floor. David turned to his own door and unlocked it, snapping on the light as he came in the door. Tonight, as every night when he came home, the apartment looked warm and friendly and good; the little foyer, with the neat small table and four careful chairs, and the bowl of little marigolds against the pale green walls David had painted himself; beyond, the kitchenette, and beyond that, the big room where David read and slept and the ceiling of which was a perpetual trouble to him; the plaster was falling in one corner and no power on earth could make it less noticeable. David consoled himself for the plaster constantly with the thought that perhaps if he had not taken an apartment in an old brown-stone the plaster would not be falling, but then, too, for the money he paid he could not have a foyer and a big room and a kitchenette, anywhere else.

He put his bag down on the table and put the butter away in the refrigerator and the rolls in the breadbox. He folded the empty bag and put it in a drawer in the kitchenette. Then he hung his coat in the hall closet and went into the big room, which he called his living-room, and lighted the desk light. His word for the room, in his own mind, was "charming." He had always been partial to yellows and browns, and he had painted the desk and the bookcases and the end tables himself, had even painted the walls, and had hunted around the city for the exact tweedish tan drapes he had in mind. The room satisfied him: the rug was a rich dark brown that picked up the darkest thread in the drapes, the furniture was almost yellow, the cover on the studio couch and the lampshades were orange. The rows of plants on the window sills gave the touch of green the room needed; right now David was looking for an ornament to set on the end table, but he had his heart set on a low translucent green bowl for more marigolds, and such things cost more than he could afford, after the silverware.

He could not come into this room without feeling that it was the most comfortable home he had ever had; tonight, as always, he let his eyes move slowly around the room, from couch to drapes to bookcase, imagined the green bowl on the end table, and sighed as he turned to the desk. He took his pen from the holder, and a sheet of the neat notepaper sitting in one of the desk cubbyholes, and wrote carefully: "Dear Marcia, don't forget you're coming for dinner tonight. I'll expect you about six." He signed the note with a "*D*" and picked up the key to Marcia's apartment which lay in the flat pencil tray on his desk. He had a key to Marcia's apartment because she was never home when her laundryman came, or when the man came to fix the refrigerator or the telephone or the windows, and someone had to let them in because the landlord was reluctant to climb three flights of stairs with the pass key. Marcia had never suggested having a key to David's apartment, and he had never offered her one; it pleased him to have only one key to his home, and that safely in his own pocket; it had a pleasant feeling to him, solid and small, the only way into his warm fine home.

He left his front door open and went down the dark hall to the other apartment. He opened the door with his key and turned on the light. This apartment was not agreeable for him to come into; it was exactly the same as his: foyer, kitchenette, living-room, and it reminded him constantly of his first day in his own apartment, when the thought of the careful homemaking to be done had left him very close to despair. Marcia's home was bare and at random; an upright piano a friend had given her recently stood crookedly, half in the foyer, because the little room was too narrow and the big room was too cluttered for it to sit comfortably anywhere; Marcia's bed was unmade and a pile of dirty laundry lay on the floor. The window had been open all day and papers had blown wildly around the floor. David closed the window, hesitated over the papers, and then moved away quickly. He put the note on the piano keys and locked the door behind him.

In his own apartment he settled down happily to making dinner. He had made a little pot roast for dinner the night before; most of it was still in the refrigerator and he sliced it in fine thin slices and arranged it on a plate with parsley. His plates were orange, almost the same color as the couch cover, and it was pleasant to him to arrange a salad, with the lettuce on the orange plate, and the thin slices of cucumber. He put coffee on to cook, and sliced potatoes to fry, and then, with his dinner cooking agreeably and the window open to lose the odor of the frying potatoes, he set lovingly to arranging his table. First, the table-cloth, pale green, of course. And the two fresh green napkins. The orange plates and the precise cup and saucer at each place. The plate of rolls in the center, and the odd salt and pepper shakers, like two green frogs. Two glasses—they came from the five-and-ten, but they had thin green bands around them—and finally, with great care, the silverware. Gradually, tenderly, David was buying himself a complete set of silverware; starting out modestly with a service for two, he had added to it until now he had well over a service for four, although not quite a service for six, lacking salad forks and soup spoons. He had chosen a sedate, pretty pattern, one that would be fine with any sort of table setting, and each morning he gloried in a breakfast that started with a shining silver spoon for his grapefruit, and had a compact butter knife for his toast and a solid heavy knife to break his eggshell, and a fresh silver spoon for his coffee, which he sugared with a particular spoon meant only for sugar. The silverware lay in a tarnish-proof box on a high shelf all to itself, and David lifted it down carefully to take out a service for two. It made a lavish display set out on the table—knives, forks, salad forks, more forks for the pie, a spoon to each place, and the special serving pieces—the sugar spoon, the large serving spoons for the potatoes and the salad, the fork for the meat, and the pie fork. When the table held as much silverware as two people could possibly use he put the box back on the shelf and stood back, checking everything and admiring the table, shining and clean. Then he went into his living-room to read his mother's letter and wait for Marcia.

The potatoes were done before Marcia came, and then suddenly the door burst open and Marcia arrived with a shout and fresh air and disorder. She was a tall handsome girl with a loud voice, wearing a dirty raincoat, and she said, "*I* didn't forget, Davie, I'm just late as usual. What's for dinner? You're not mad, are you?"

David got up and came over to take her coat. "I left a note for you," he said.

"Didn't see it," Marcia said. "Haven't been home. Something smells good."

"Fried potatoes," David said. "Everything's ready."

"Golly." Marcia fell into a chair to sit with her legs stretched out in front of her and her arms hanging. "I'm tired," she said. "It's cold out."

"It was getting colder when I came home," David said. He was putting dinner on the table, the platter of meat, the salad, the bowl of fried potatoes. He walked quietly back and forth from the kitchenette to the table, avoiding Marcia's feet. "I don't believe you've been here since I got my silverware," he said.

Marcia swung around to the table and picked up a spoon. "It's beautiful," she said, running her finger along the pattern. "Pleasure to eat with it."

"Dinner's ready," David said. He pulled her chair out for her and waited for her to sit down.

Marcia was always hungry; she put meat and potatoes and salad on her plate without admiring the serving silver, and started to eat enthusiastically. "Everything's beautiful," she said once. "Food is wonderful, Davie."

"I'm glad you like it," David said. He liked the feel of the fork in his hand, even the sight of the fork moving up to Marcia's mouth.

Marcia waved her hand largely. "I mean everything," she said, "furniture, and nice place you have here, and dinner, and everything."

"I *like* things this way," David said.

"I know you do." Marcia's voice was mournful. "Someone should teach me, I guess."

"You *ought* to keep your home neater," David said. "You ought to get curtains at least, and keep your windows shut."

"I never remember," she said. "Davie, you are the most *wonderful* cook." She pushed her plate away, and sighed.

David blushed happily. "I'm glad you like it," he said again, and then he laughed. "I made a pie last night."

"A pie." Marcia looked at him for a minute and then she said, "Apple?"

David shook his head, and she said, "Pineapple?" and he shook his head again, and, because he could not wait to tell her, said, "Cherry."

"My *God*!" Marcia got up and followed him into the kitchen and looked over his shoulder while he took the pie carefully out of the breadbox. "Is this the first pie you ever made?"

"I've made two before," David admitted, "but this one turned out better than the others."

She watched happily while he cut large pieces of pie and put them on other orange plates, and then she carried her own plate back to the table, tasted the pie, and made wordless gestures of appreciation. David tasted his pie and said critically, "I think it's a little sour. I ran out of sugar."

"It's perfect," Marcia said. "I always loved a cherry pie really *sour*. This isn't sour enough, even."

David cleared the table and poured the coffee, and as he was setting the coffeepot back on the stove Marcia said, "My doorbell's ringing." She opened the apartment door and listened, and they could both hear the ringing in her apartment. She pressed the buzzer in David's apartment that opened the downstairs door, and far away they could hear heavy footsteps starting up the stairs. Marcia left the apartment door open and came back to her coffee. "Landlord, most likely," she said. "I didn't pay my rent again." When the footsteps reached the top of the last staircase Marcia yelled, "Hello?" leaning back in her chair to see out the door into the hall. Then she said, "Why, Mr. Harris." She got up and went to the door and held out her hand. "Come in," she said.

"I just thought I'd stop by," Mr. Harris said. He was a very large man and his eyes rested curiously on the coffee cups and empty plates on the table. "I don't want to interrupt your dinner."

"*That's* all right," Marcia said, pulling him into the room. "It's just Davie. Davie, this is Mr. Harris, he works in my office. This is Mr. Turner."

"How do you do," David said politely, and the man looked at him carefully and said, "How do you do?"

"Sit down, sit down," Marcia was saying, pushing a chair forward. "Davie, how about another cup for Mr. Harris?"

"Please don't bother," Mr. Harris said quickly, "I just thought I'd stop by."

While David was taking out another cup and saucer and getting a spoon down from the tarnish-proof silverbox, Marcia said, "You like homemade pie?"

"Say," Mr. Harris said admiringly, "I've forgotten what homemade pie *looks* like."

"Davie," Marcia called cheerfully, "how about cutting Mr. Harris a piece of that pie?"

Without answering, David took a fork out of the silverbox and got down an orange plate and put a piece of pie on it. His plans for the evening had been vague; they had involved perhaps a movie if it were not too cold out, and at least a short talk with Marcia about the state of her home; Mr. Harris was settling down in his chair and when David put the pie down silently in front of him he stared at it admiringly for a minute before he tasted it.

"Say," he said finally, "this is certainly some pie." He looked at Marcia. "This is really *good* pie," he said.

"You like it?" Marcia asked modestly. She looked up at David and smiled at him over Mr. Harris' head. "I haven't made but two, three pies before," she said.

David raised a hand to protest, but Mr. Harris turned to him and demanded, "Did you ever eat any better pie in your life?"

"I don't think Davie liked it much," Marcia said wickedly, "I think it was too sour for him."

"I *like* a sour pie," Mr. Harris said. He looked suspiciously at David. "A cherry pie's *got* to be sour."

"I'm glad you like it, anyway," Marcia said. Mr. Harris ate the last mouthful of pie, finished his coffee, and sat back. "*I'm* sure glad I dropped in," he said to Marcia.

David's desire to be rid of Mr. Harris had slid imperceptibly into an urgency to be rid of them both; his clean house, his nice silver, were not meant as vehicles for the kind of fatuous banter Marcia and Mr. Harris were playing at together; almost roughly he took the coffee cup away from the arm Marcia had stretched across the table, took it out to the kitchenette and came back and put his hand on Mr. Harris' cup.

"Don't bother, Davie, honestly," Marcia said. She looked up, smiling again, as though she and David were conspirators against Mr. Harris. "I'll do them all tomorrow, honey," she said.

"Sure," Mr. Harris said. He stood up. "Let them wait. Let's go in and sit down where we can be comfortable."

Marcia got up and led him into the living-room and they sat down on the studio couch. "Come on in, Davie," Marcia called.

The sight of his pretty table covered with dirty dishes and cigarette ashes held David. He carried the plates and cups and silverware into the kitchenette and stacked them in the sink and then, because he could not endure the thought of their sitting there any longer, with the dirt gradually hardening on them, he tied an apron on and began to wash them carefully. Now and then, while he was washing them and drying them and putting them away, Marcia would call to him, sometimes, "Davie, what *are* you doing?" or, "Davie, won't you stop all that and come sit down?" Once she said, "Davie, I don't want you to wash all those dishes," and Mr. Harris said, "Let him work, he's happy."

David put the clean yellow cups and saucers back on the shelves— by now, Mr. Harris' cup was unrecognizable; you could not tell, from the clean rows of cups, which one he had used or which one had been stained with Marcia's lipstick or which one had held David's coffee which he had finished in the kitchenette—and finally, taking the tarnish-proof box down, he put the silverware away. First the forks all went together into the little grooves which held two forks each—later, when the set was complete, each groove would hold four forks—and then the spoons, stacked up neatly one on top of another in their own grooves, and the knives in even order, all facing the same way, in the special tapes in the lid of the box. Butter knives and serving spoons and the pie knife all went into their own places, and then David put the lid down on the lovely shining set and put the box back on the shelf. After wringing out the dishcloth and hanging up the dish towel and taking off his apron he was through, and he went slowly into the living-room. Marcia and Mr. Harris were sitting close together on the studio couch, talking earnestly.

"My *father's* name was James," Marcia was saying as David came in, as though she were clinching an argument. She turned around when David came in and said, "Davie, you were so nice to do all those dishes yourself."

"That's all right," David said awkwardly. Mr. Harris was looking at him impatiently.

"I should have helped you," Marcia said. There was a silence, and then Marcia said, "Sit down, Davie, won't you?"

David recognized her tone; it was the one hostesses used when they didn't know what else to say to you, or when you had come too early or stayed too late. It was the tone he had expected to use on Mr. Harris.

"James and I were just talking about..." Marcia began and then stopped and laughed. "What *were* we talking about?" she asked, turning to Mr. Harris.

"Nothing much," Mr. Harris said. He was still watching David.

"Well," Marcia said, letting her voice trail off. She turned to David and smiled brightly and then said, "Well," again.

Mr. Harris picked up the ashtray from the end table and set it on the couch between himself and Marcia. He took a cigar out of his pocket and said to Marcia, "Do you mind cigars?" and when Marcia shook her head he unwrapped the cigar tenderly and bit off the end. "Cigar smoke's good for plants," he said thickly, around the cigar, as he lighted it, and Marcia laughed.

David stood up. For a minute he thought he was going to say something that might start, "Mr. Harris, I'll thank you to..." but what he actually said, finally, with both Marcia and Mr. Harris looking at him, was, "Guess I better be getting along, Marcia."

Mr. Harris stood up and said heartily, "Certainly have enjoyed meeting you." He held out his hand and David shook hands limply.

"Guess I better be getting along," he said again to Marcia, and she stood up and said, "I'm sorry you have to leave so soon."

"Lots of work to do," David said, much more genially than he intended, and Marcia smiled at him again as though they were conspirators and went over to the desk and said, "Don't forget your key."

Surprised, David took the key of her apartment from her, said good night to Mr. Harris, and went to the outside door.

"Good night, Davie honey," Marcia called out, and David said "Thanks for a simply *wonderful* dinner, Marcia," and closed the door behind him.

He went down the hall and let himself into Marcia's apartment; the piano was still awry, the papers were still on the floor, the laundry scattered, the bed unmade. David sat down on the bed and looked around. It was cold, it was dirty, and as he thought miserably of his own warm home he heard faintly down the hall the sound of laughter and the scrape of a chair being moved. Then, still faintly, the sound of his radio. Wearily, David leaned over and picked up a paper from the floor, and then he began to gather them up one by one.

A MAIN COURSE: SUPERNATURAL APPETITES

1862

GOBLIN MARKET

Christina Rossetti

Christina Georgina Rossetti (1830–1894) initially wrote under the pseudonym Ellen Alleyne and is now known as Christina Rossetti. Rossetti's literary talent, along with her brother Dante Gabriel Rossetti's artistic success, positioned the Rossetti family as synonymous with the Pre-Raphaelite movement and the wider art and culture of their time. A late twentieth-century revival in readership and critical engagement with Rossetti's work has cemented her reputation as one of the best poets of her era. Rossetti is now celebrated as one of the best female poets to have written in English. Much of Rossetti's poetry and stories are characterized as romantic and are frequently religious in theme.

"Goblin Market" was thought to have been composed in 1859 and was first published in *Goblin Market and Other Poems* (1862). The narrative poem is arguably Rossetti's most famous work. It narrates the tale of two sisters, Lizzie and Laura, and their encounters with a strange night-time market run by goblins. The plethora of goods available are described in vivid detail, the precise attention to colour and texture creating a dizzying litany of fruits "all ripe together". In line with their folkloric counterparts, Rossetti's goblin men do not run their market out of philanthropy. As the descriptions of the fruit move from appealing to excessive, the poem teases the risks of indulging in the fairy tale lure of food, suggesting the willpower it takes to resist a forbidden feast. The "Goblin Market" is a pivotal example of the uncanny gastronomic. The nocturnal peddling is a literary and moral experiment with the limits of food as symbol. Rossetti imagines this as inherently gendered, with the suggestions of violence implicating insatiable hunger as parallel to sexual desire. Rossetti's centring of female relationships as integral to collective and personal strength makes comment on the specific power—and importance—of sisterhood in the face of danger.

Morning and evening
Maids heard the goblins cry:
"Come buy our orchard fruits,
Come buy, come buy:
Apples and quinces,
Lemons and oranges,
Plump unpeck'd cherries,
Melons and raspberries,
Bloom-down check'd peaches,
Swart-headed mulberries,
Wild free-born cranberries,
Crab-apples, dewberries,
Pine-apples, blackberries,
Apricots, strawberries;—
All ripe together
In summer weather,—
Morns that pass by,
Fair eves that fly;
Come buy, come buy:
Our grapes fresh from the vine,
Pomegranates full and fine,
Dates and sharp bullaces,
Rare pears and greengages,

Damsons and bilberries,
Taste them and try:
Currants and gooseberries,
Bright-fire-like barberries,
Figs to fill your mouth,
Citrons from the South,
Sweet to tongue and sound to eye;
Come buy, come buy."

Evening by evening
Among the brookside rushes,
Laura bow'd her head to hear,
Lizzie veil'd her blushes:
Crouching close together
In the cooling weather,
With clasping arms and cautioning lips,
With tingling cheeks and finger tips.
"Lie close," Laura said,
Pricking up her golden head:
"We must not look at goblin men,
We must not buy their fruits:
Who knows upon what soil they fed
Their hungry thirsty roots?"
"Come buy," call the goblins
Hobbling down the glen.

"Oh," cried Lizzie, "Laura, Laura,
You should not peep at goblin men."
Lizzie cover'd up her eyes,
Cover'd close lest they should look;

Laura rear'd her glossy head,
And whisper'd like the restless brook:
"Look, Lizzie, look, Lizzie,
Down the glen tramp little men.
One hauls a basket,
One bears a plate,
One lugs a golden dish
Of many pounds weight.
How fair the vine must grow
Whose grapes are so luscious;
How warm the wind must blow
Through those fruit bushes."
"No," said Lizzie, "No, no, no;
Their offers should not charm us,
Their evil gifts would harm us."
She thrust a dimpled finger
In each ear, shut eyes and ran:
Curious Laura chose to linger
Wondering at each merchant man.
One had a cat's face,
One whisk'd a tail,
One tramp'd at a rat's pace,
One crawl'd like a snail,
One like a wombat prowl'd obtuse and furry,
One like a ratel tumbled hurry skurry.
She heard a voice like voice of doves
Cooing all together:
They sounded kind and full of loves
In the pleasant weather.

Laura stretch'd her gleaming neck
Like a rush-imbedded swan,
Like a lily from the beck,
Like a moonlit poplar branch,
Like a vessel at the launch
When its last restraint is gone.

Backwards up the mossy glen
Turn'd and troop'd the goblin men,
With their shrill repeated cry,
"Come buy, come buy."
When they reach'd where Laura was
They stood stock still upon the moss,
Leering at each other,
Brother with queer brother;
Signalling each other,
Brother with sly brother.
One set his basket down,
One rear'd his plate;
One began to weave a crown
Of tendrils, leaves, and rough nuts brown
(Men sell not such in any town);
One heav'd the golden weight
Of dish and fruit to offer her:
"Come buy, come buy," was still their cry.
Laura stared but did not stir,
Long'd but had no money:
The whisk-tail'd merchant bade her taste
In tones as smooth as honey,
The cat-faced purr'd,

The rat-faced spoke a word
Of welcome, and the snail-paced even was heard;
One parrot-voiced and jolly
Cried "Pretty Goblin" still for "Pretty Polly;"—
One whistled like a bird.

But sweet-tooth Laura spoke in haste:
"Good folk, I have no coin;
To take were to purloin:
I have no copper in my purse,
I have no silver either,
And all my gold is on the furze
That shakes in windy weather
Above the rusty heather."
"You have much gold upon your head,"
They answer'd all together:
"Buy from us with a golden curl."
She clipp'd a precious golden lock,
She dropp'd a tear more rare than pearl,
Then suck'd their fruit globes fair or red:
Sweeter than honey from the rock,
Stronger than man-rejoicing wine,
Clearer than water flow'd that juice;
She never tasted such before,
How should it cloy with length of use?
She suck'd and suck'd and suck'd the more
Fruits which that unknown orchard bore;
She suck'd until her lips were sore;
Then flung the emptied rinds away
But gather'd up one kernel stone,

And knew not was it night or day
As she turn'd home alone.

Lizzie met her at the gate
Full of wise upbraidings:
"Dear, you should not stay so late,
Twilight is not good for maidens;
Should not loiter in the glen
In the haunts of goblin men.
Do you not remember Jeanie,
How she met them in the moonlight,
Took their gifts both choice and many,
Ate their fruits and wore their flowers
Pluck'd from bowers
Where summer ripens at all hours?
But ever in the noonlight
She pined and pined away;
Sought them by night and day,
Found them no more, but dwindled and grew grey;
Then fell with the first snow,
While to this day no grass will grow
Where she lies low:
I planted daisies there a year ago
That never blow.
You should not loiter so."
"Nay, hush," said Laura:
"Nay, hush, my sister:
I ate and ate my fill,
Yet my mouth waters still;
Tomorrow night I will

Buy more;" and kiss'd her:
"Have done with sorrow;
I'll bring you plums tomorrow
Fresh on their mother twigs,
Cherries worth getting;
You cannot think what figs
My teeth have met in,
What melons icy-cold
Piled on a dish of gold
Too huge for me to hold,
What peaches with a velvet nap,
Pellucid grapes without one seed:
Odorous indeed must be the mead
Whereon they grow, and pure the wave they drink
With lilies at the brink,
And sugar-sweet their sap."

Golden head by golden head,
Like two pigeons in one nest
Folded in each other's wings,
They lay down in their curtain'd bed:
Like two blossoms on one stem,
Like two flakes of new-fall'n snow,
Like two wands of ivory
Tipp'd with gold for awful kings.
Moon and stars gaz'd in at them,
Wind sang to them lullaby,
Lumbering owls forbore to fly,
Not a bat flapp'd to and fro
Round their rest:

Cheek to cheek and breast to breast
Lock'd together in one nest.

Early in the morning
When the first cock crow'd his warning,
Neat like bees, as sweet and busy,
Laura rose with Lizzie:
Fetch'd in honey, milk'd the cows,
Air'd and set to rights the house,
Kneaded cakes of whitest wheat,
Cakes for dainty mouths to eat,
Next churn'd butter, whipp'd up cream,
Fed their poultry, sat and sew'd;
Talk'd as modest maidens should:
Lizzie with an open heart,
Laura in an absent dream,
One content, one sick in part;
One warbling for the mere bright day's delight,
One longing for the night.

At length slow evening came:
They went with pitchers to the reedy brook;
Lizzie most placid in her look,
Laura most like a leaping flame.
They drew the gurgling water from its deep;
Lizzie pluck'd purple and rich golden flags,
Then turning homeward said: "The sunset flushes
Those furthest loftiest crags;
Come, Laura, not another maiden lags.
No wilful squirrel wags,

The beasts and birds are fast asleep."
But Laura loiter'd still among the rushes
And said the bank was steep.

And said the hour was early still
The dew not fall'n, the wind not chill;
Listening ever, but not catching
The customary cry,
"Come buy, come buy,"
With its iterated jingle
Of sugar-baited words:
Not for all her watching
Once discerning even one goblin
Racing, whisking, tumbling, hobbling;
Let alone the herds
That used to tramp along the glen,
In groups or single,
Of brisk fruit-merchant men.

Till Lizzie urged, "O Laura, come;
I hear the fruit-call but I dare not look:
You should not loiter longer at this brook:
Come with me home.
The stars rise, the moon bends her arc,
Each glowworm winks her spark,
Let us get home before the night grows dark:
For clouds may gather
Though this is summer weather,
Put out the lights and drench us through;
Then if we lost our way what should we do?"

Laura turn'd cold as stone
To find her sister heard that cry alone,
That goblin cry,
"Come buy our fruits, come buy."
Must she then buy no more such dainty fruit?
Must she no more such succous pasture find,
Gone deaf and blind?
Her tree of life droop'd from the root:
She said not one word in her heart's sore ache;
But peering thro' the dimness, nought discerning,
Trudg'd home, her pitcher dripping all the way;
So crept to bed, and lay
Silent till Lizzie slept;
Then sat up in a passionate yearning,
And gnash'd her teeth for baulk'd desire, and wept
As if her heart would break.

Day after day, night after night,
Laura kept watch in vain
In sullen silence of exceeding pain.
She never caught again the goblin cry:
"Come buy, come buy;"—
She never spied the goblin men
Hawking their fruits along the glen:
But when the noon wax'd bright
Her hair grew thin and grey;
She dwindled, as the fair full moon doth turn
To swift decay and burn
Her fire away.

One day remembering her kernel-stone
She set it by a wall that faced the south;
Dew'd it with tears, hoped for a root,
Watch'd for a waxing shoot,
But there came none;
It never saw the sun,
It never felt the trickling moisture run:
While with sunk eyes and faded mouth
She dream'd of melons, as a traveller sees
False waves in desert drouth
With shade of leaf-crown'd trees,
And burns the thirstier in the sandful breeze.

She no more swept the house,
Tended the fowls or cows,
Fetch'd honey, kneaded cakes of wheat,
Brought water from the brook:
But sat down listless in the chimney-nook
And would not eat.

Tender Lizzie could not bear
To watch her sister's cankerous care
Yet not to share.
She night and morning
Caught the goblins' cry:
"Come buy our orchard fruits,
Come buy, come buy;"—
Beside the brook, along the glen,
She heard the tramp of goblin men,
The yoke and stir

Poor Laura could not hear;
Long'd to buy fruit to comfort her,
But fear'd to pay too dear.
She thought of Jeanie in her grave,
Who should have been a bride;
But who for joys brides hope to have
Fell sick and died
In her gay prime,
In earliest winter time
With the first glazing rime,
With the first snow-fall of crisp winter time.

Till Laura dwindling
Seem'd knocking at Death's door:
Then Lizzie weigh'd no more
Better and worse;
But put a silver penny in her purse,
Kiss'd Laura, cross'd the heath with clumps of furze
At twilight, halted by the brook:
And for the first time in her life
Began to listen and look.

Laugh'd every goblin
When they spied her peeping:
Came towards her hobbling,
Flying, running, leaping,
Puffing and blowing,
Chuckling, clapping, crowing,
Clucking and gobbling,
Mopping and mowing,

Full of airs and graces,
Pulling wry faces,
Demure grimaces,
Cat-like and rat-like,
Ratel- and wombat-like,
Snail-paced in a hurry,
Parrot voiced and whistler,
Helter skelter, hurry skurry,
Chattering like magpies,
Fluttering like pigeons,
Gliding like fishes,—
Hugg'd her and kiss'd her:
Squeez'd and caress'd her:
Stretch'd up their dishes,
Panniers, and plates:
"Look at our apples
Russet and dun,
Bob at our cherries,
Bite at our peaches,
Citrons and dates,
Grapes for the asking,
Pears red with basking
Out in the sun,
Plums on their twigs;
Pluck them and suck them,
Pomegranates, figs."—

"Good folk," said Lizzie,
Mindful of Jeanie:
"Give me much and many:" —

Held out her apron,
Toss'd them her penny.
"Nay, take a seat with us,
Honour and eat with us,"
They answer'd grinning:
"Our feast is but beginning.
Night yet is early,
Warm and dew-pearly,
Wakeful and starry:
Such fruits as these
No man can carry:
Half their bloom would fly,
Half their dew would dry,
Half their flavour would pass by.
Sit down and feast with us,
Be welcome guest with us,
Cheer you and rest with us."—
"Thank you," said Lizzie: "But one waits
At home alone for me:
So without further parleying,
If you will not sell me any
Of your fruits though much and many,
Give me back my silver penny
I toss'd you for a fee."—
They began to scratch their pates,
No longer wagging, purring,
But visibly demurring,
Grunting and snarling.
One call'd her proud,
Cross-grain'd, uncivil;

Their tones wax'd loud,
Their looks were evil.
Lashing their tails
They trod and hustled her,
Elbow'd and jostled her,
Claw'd with their nails,
Barking, mewing, hissing, mocking,
Tore her gown and soil'd her stocking,
Twitch'd her hair out by the roots,
Stamp'd upon her tender feet,
Held her hands and squeez'd their fruits
Against her mouth to make her eat.

White and golden Lizzie stood,
Like a lily in a flood,—
Like a rock of blue-vein'd stone
Lash'd by tides obstreperously,—
Like a beacon left alone
In a hoary roaring sea,
Sending up a golden fire,—
Like a fruit-crown'd orange-tree
White with blossoms honey-sweet
Sore beset by wasp and bee,—
Like a royal virgin town
Topp'd with gilded dome and spire
Close beleaguer'd by a fleet
Mad to tug her standard down.

One may lead a horse to water,
Twenty cannot make him drink.

Though the goblins cuff'd and caught her,
Coax'd and fought her,
Bullied and besought her,
Scratch'd her, pinch'd her black as ink,
Kick'd and knock'd her,
Maul'd and mock'd her,
Lizzie utter'd not a word;
Would not open lip from lip
Lest they should cram a mouthful in:
But laugh'd in heart to feel the drip
Of juice that syrupp'd all her face,
And lodg'd in dimples of her chin,
And streak'd her neck which quaked like curd.
At last the evil people,
Worn out by her resistance,
Flung back her penny, kick'd their fruit
Along whichever road they took,
Not leaving root or stone or shoot;
Some writh'd into the ground,
Some div'd into the brook
With ring and ripple,
Some scudded on the gale without a sound,
Some vanish'd in the distance.

In a smart, ache, tingle,
Lizzie went her way;
Knew not was it night or day;
Sprang up the bank, tore thro' the furze,
Threaded copse and dingle,
And heard her penny jingle

86

Bouncing in her purse,—
Its bounce was music to her ear.
She ran and ran
As if she fear'd some goblin man
Dogg'd her with gibe or curse
Or something worse:
But not one goblin scurried after,
Nor was she prick'd by fear;
The kind heart made her windy-paced
That urged her home quite out of breath with haste
And inward laughter.

She cried, "Laura," up the garden,
"Did you miss me?
Come and kiss me.
Never mind my bruises,
Hug me, kiss me, suck my juices
Squeez'd from goblin fruits for you,
Goblin pulp and goblin dew.
Eat me, drink me, love me;
Laura, make much of me;
For your sake I have braved the glen
And had to do with goblin merchant men."

Laura started from her chair,
Flung her arms up in the air,
Clutch'd her hair:
"Lizzie, Lizzie, have you tasted
For my sake the fruit forbidden?
Must your light like mine be hidden,

Your young life like mine be wasted,
Undone in mine undoing,
And ruin'd in my ruin,
Thirsty, canker'd, goblin-ridden?"—
She clung about her sister,
Kiss'd and kiss'd and kiss'd her:
Tears once again
Refresh'd her shrunken eyes,
Dropping like rain
After long sultry drouth;
Shaking with aguish fear, and pain,
She kiss'd and kiss'd her with a hungry mouth.

Her lips began to scorch,
That juice was wormwood to her tongue,
She loath'd the feast:
Writhing as one possess'd she leap'd and sung,
Rent all her robe, and wrung
Her hands in lamentable haste,
And beat her breast.
Her locks stream'd like the torch
Borne by a racer at full speed,
Or like the mane of horses in their flight,
Or like an eagle when she stems the light
Straight toward the sun,
Or like a caged thing freed,
Or like a flying flag when armies run.

Swift fire spread through her veins, knock'd at her heart,
Met the fire smouldering there

And overbore its lesser flame;
She gorged on bitterness without a name:
Ah! fool, to choose such part
Of soul-consuming care!
Sense fail'd in the mortal strife:
Like the watch-tower of a town
Which an earthquake shatters down,
Like a lightning-stricken mast,
Like a wind-uprooted tree
Spun about,
Like a foam-topp'd waterspout
Cast down headlong in the sea,
She fell at last;
Pleasure past and anguish past,
Is it death or is it life?

Life out of death.
That night long Lizzie watch'd by her,
Counted her pulse's flagging stir,
Felt for her breath,
Held water to her lips, and cool'd her face
With tears and fanning leaves:
But when the first birds chirp'd about their eaves,
And early reapers plodded to the place
Of golden sheaves,
And dew-wet grass
Bow'd in the morning winds so brisk to pass,
And new buds with new day
Open'd of cup-like lilies on the stream,
Laura awoke as from a dream,

Laugh'd in the innocent old way,
Hugg'd Lizzie but not twice or thrice;
Her gleaming locks show'd not one thread of grey,
Her breath was sweet as May
And light danced in her eyes.

Days, weeks, months, years
Afterwards, when both were wives
With children of their own;
Their mother-hearts beset with fears,
Their lives bound up in tender lives;
Laura would call the little ones
And tell them of her early prime,
Those pleasant days long gone
Of not-returning time:
Would talk about the haunted glen,
The wicked, quaint fruit-merchant men,
Their fruits like honey to the throat
But poison in the blood;
(Men sell not such in any town):
Would tell them how her sister stood
In deadly peril to do her good,
And win the fiery antidote:
Then joining hands to little hands
Would bid them cling together,
"For there is no friend like a sister
In calm or stormy weather;
To cheer one on the tedious way,
To fetch one if one goes astray,
To lift one if one totters down,
To strengthen whilst one stands."

THE VAMPIRE MAID

Hume Nisbet

James Hume Nisbet (1849–1923) was a Scottish artist and writer who often went by Hume Nisbet. Nisbet travelled to Australia in his young adulthood and began practising painting, drawing, and writing during his time abroad. Nisbet focused on painting after returning to London, acting as the art master of Edinburgh's Watt Institution and School of Art for several years. Unfortunately, his art career was not particularly lucrative and Nisbet refocused his attention on writing, publishing novels and several collections of ghost stories including *The Haunted Station* (1894), *Paths of the Dead* (1899) and *Stories Weird and Wonderful* (1900).

"The Vampire Maid" (1900) is a story that continues the late nineteenth century's fascination with the literary vampire, following John Polidori's "The Vampyre" (1819), Sheridan La Fanu's *Carmilla* (1872) and just three years after Bram Stoker's *Dracula* (1897).

The novella takes place in the northwest of England. An unnamed male narrator comes across a cottage on the moors after walking for many days. The narrator is entranced by "the weird charms of [the] landlady's daughter, Ariadne Brunnell"; the name of the daughter is an early allusion to claustrophobia, danger, and labyrinthine entrapment. Nisbet toys with the nature of the home and the comfortable abode, querying the motives behind a household's unmitigated welcoming of a stranger. Having found a home and hearth, the tale uses the lens of the vampiric to query the laws of hospitality; being intertwined with rituals of eating, etiquette, and notions of the self and Other.

It was the exact kind of abode that I had been looking after for weeks, for I was in that condition of mind when absolute renunciation of society was a necessity. I had become diffident of myself, and wearied of my kind. A strange unrest was in my blood; a barren dearth in my brains. Familiar objects and faces had grown distasteful to me. I wanted to be alone.

This is the mood which comes upon every sensitive and artistic mind when the possessor has been overworked or living too long in one groove. It is Nature's hint for him to seek pastures new; the sign that a retreat has become needful.

If he does not yield, he breaks down and becomes whimsical and hypochondriacal, as well as hypercritical. It is always a bad sign when a man becomes over-critical and censorious about his own or other people's work, for it means that he is losing the vital portions of work, freshness and enthusiasm.

Before I arrived at the dismal stage of criticism I hastily packed up my knapsack, and taking the train to Westmoreland I began my tramp in search of solitude, bracing air and romantic surroundings.

Many places I came upon during that early summer wandering that appeared to have almost the required conditions, yet some petty drawback prevented me from deciding. Sometimes it was the scenery that I did not take kindly to. At other places I took sudden antipathies to the landlady or landlord, and felt I would abhor them before a week was spent under their charge. Other places which might have suited me I could not have, as they did not want a lodger. Fate was driving me to this Cottage on the Moor, and no once can resist destiny.

One day I found myself on a wide and pathless moor near the sea. I had slept the night before at a small hamlet, but that was already eight miles in my rear, and since I had turned my back upon it I had not seen any signs of humanity; I was alone with a fair sky above me, a balmy ozone-filled wind blowing over the stony and heather-clad mounds, and nothing to disturb my meditations.

How far the moor stretched I had no knowledge; I only knew that by keeping in a straight line I would come to the ocean cliffs, then perhaps after a time arrive at some fishing village.

I had provisions in my knapsack, and being young did not fear a night under the stars. I was inhaling the delicious summer air and once more getting back the vigour and happiness I had lost; my city-dried brains were becoming again juicy.

Thus hour after hour slid past me, with the paces, until I had covered about fifteen miles since morning, when I saw before me in the distance a solitary stone-built cottage with roughly slated roof. "I'll camp there if possible," I said to myself as I quickened my steps towards it.

To one in search of a quiet, free life, nothing could have possibly been more suitable than this cottage. It stood on the edge of lofty cliffs, with its front door facing the moor and the back-yard wall overlooking the ocean. The sound of the dancing waves struck upon my ears like a lullaby as I drew near; how they would thunder when the autumn gales came on and the sea-birds fled shrieking to the shelter of the sedges.

A small garden spread in front, surrounded by a dry-stone wall just high enough for one to lean lazily upon when inclined. This garden was a flame of colour, scarlet predominating, with those other soft shades that cultivated poppies take on in their blooming, for this was all that the garden grew.

As I approached, taking notice of this singular assortment of poppies, and the orderly cleanness of the windows, the front door opened and a woman appeared who impressed me at once favourably as she leisurely came along the pathway to the gate, and drew it back as if to welcome me.

She was of middle age, and when young must have been remarkably good-looking. She was tall and still shapely, with smooth clear skin, regular features and a calm expression that at once gave me a sensation of rest.

To my inquiries she said that she could give me both a sitting and bedroom, and invited me inside to see them. As I looked at her smooth black hair, and cool brown eyes, I felt that I would not be too particular about the accommodation. With such a landlady, I was sure to find what I was after here.

The rooms surpassed my expectation, dainty white curtains and bedding with the perfume of lavender about them, a sitting-room homely yet cosy without being crowded. With a sigh of infinite relief I flung down my knapsack and clinched the bargain.

She was a widow with one daughter, whom I did not see the first day, as she was unwell and confined to her own room, but on the next day she was somewhat better, and then we met.

The fare was simple, yet it suited me exactly for the time, delicious milk and butter with homemade scones, fresh eggs and bacon; after a hearty tea I went early to bed in a condition of perfect content with my quarters.

Yet happy and tired out as I was I had by no means a comfortable night. This I put down to the strange bed. I slept certainly, but my sleep was filled with dreams so that I woke late and unrefreshed; a good walk on the moor, however, restored me, and I returned with a fine appetite for breakfast.

Certain conditions of mind, with aggravating circumstances, are required before even a young man can fall in love at first sight, as Shakespeare has shown in his Romeo and Juliet. In the city, where many fair faces passed me every hour, I had remained like a stoic, yet no sooner did I enter the cottage after that morning walk than I succumbed instantly before the weird charms of my landlady's daughter, Ariadne Brunnell.

She was somewhat better this morning and able to meet me at breakfast, for we had our meals together while I was their lodger. Ariadne was not beautiful in the strictly classical sense, her complexion being too lividly white and her expression too set to be quite pleasant at first sight; yet, as her mother had informed me, she had been ill for some time, which accounted for that defect. Her features were not regular, her hair and eyes seemed too black with that strangely white skin, and her lips too red for any except the decadent harmonies of an Aubrey Beardsley.

Yet my fantastic dreams of the preceding night, with my morning walk, had prepared me to be enthralled by this modern poster-like invalid.

The loneliness of the moor, with the singing of the ocean, had gripped my heart with a wistful longing. The incongruity of those flaunting and evanescent poppy flowers, dashing their giddy tints in the face of that sober heath, touched me with a shiver as I approached the cottage, and lastly that weird embodiment of startling contrasts completed my subjugation.

She rose from her chair as her mother introduced her, and smiled while she held out her hand. I clasped that soft snowflake, and as I did so a faint thrill tingled over me and rested on my heart, stopping for the moment its beating.

This contact seemed also to have affected her as it did me; a clear flush, like a white flame, lighted up her face, so that it glowed as if an alabaster lamp had been lit; her black eyes became softer and more humid as our glances crossed, and her scarlet lips grew moist. She was a living woman now, while before she had seemed half a corpse.

She permitted her white slender hand to remain in mine longer than most people do at an introduction, and then she slowly withdrew it, still regarding me with steadfast eyes for a second or two afterwards.

Fathomless velvety eyes these were, yet before they were shifted from mine they appeared to have absorbed all my willpower and made me her abject slave. They looked like deep dark pools of clear water, yet they filled me with fire and deprived me of strength. I sank into my chair almost as languidly as I had risen from my bed that morning.

Yet I made a good breakfast, and although she hardly tasted anything, this strange girl rose much refreshed and with a slight glow of colour on her cheeks, which improved her so greatly that she appeared younger and almost beautiful.

I had come here seeking solitude, but since I had seen Ariadne it seemed as if I had come for her only. She was not very lively; indeed, thinking back, I cannot recall any spontaneous remark of hers; she answered my questions by monosyllables and left me to lead in words: yet she was insinuating and appeared to lead my thoughts in her direction and speak to me with her eyes. I cannot describe her minutely, I only know that from the first glance and touch she gave me I was bewitched and could think of nothing else.

It was a rapid, distracting, and devouring infatuation that possessed me; all day long I followed her about like a dog, every night I dreamed of that white glowing face, those steadfast black eyes, those moist scarlet lips, and each morning I rose more languid than I had been the day before. Sometimes I dreamt that she was kissing me with those red lips, while I shivered at the contact of her silky black tresses as they covered my throat; sometimes that we were floating in the air, under the moonlight, her arms about me and her long hair enveloping us both like an inky cloud, while I lay supine and helpless.

She went with me after breakfast on that first day to the moor, and before we came back I had spoken my love and received her assent. I held her in my arms and had taken her kisses in answer to mine, nor did I think it strange that all this had happened so quickly. She was mine, or rather I was hers, without a pause. I told her it was fate that had sent me to her, for I had no doubts about my love, and she replied that I had restored her to life.

Acting upon Ariadne's advice, and also from a natural shyness, I did not inform her mother how quickly matters had progressed between us, yet although we both acted as circumspectly as possible, I had no doubt Mrs. Brunnell could see how engrossed we were in each other. Lovers are not unlike ostriches in their modes of concealment. I was not afraid of asking Mrs. Brunnell for her daughter, for she already showed her partiality towards me, and had bestowed upon me some confidences regarding her own position in life, and I therefore knew that, so far as social position was concerned, there could be no real objection to our marriage. They lived in this lonely spot for the sake of their health, and kept no servant because they could not get any to take service so far away from other humanity.

My coming had been opportune and welcome to both mother and daughter.

For the sake of decorum, however, I resolved to delay my confession for a week or two and trust to some favourable opportunity of doing it discreetly.

Meantime Ariadne and I passed our time in a thoroughly idle and lotus-eating style. Each night I retired to bed meditating starting work next day, each morning I rose languid from those disturbing dreams with no thought for anything outside my love. She grew stronger every day, while I appeared to be taking her place as the invalid, yet I was more frantically in love than ever, and only happy when with her. She was my lode-star, my only joy—my life.

We did not go great distances, for I liked best to lie on the dry heath and watch her glowing face and intense eyes while I listened to the surging of the distant waves. It was love made me lazy, I thought, for unless a man has all he longs for beside him, he is apt to copy the domestic cat and bask in the sunshine.

I had been enchanted quickly. My disenchantment came as rapidly, although it was long before the poison left my blood.

One night, about a couple of weeks after my coming to the cottage, I had retired after a delicious moonlight walk with Ariadne. The night was warm and the moon at the full, therefore I left my bedroom window open to let in what little air there was.

I was more than usually fagged out, so that I had only strength enough to remove my boots and coat before I flung myself wearily on the coverlet and fell almost instantly asleep without tasting the nightcap draught that was constantly placed on the table, and which I had always before drained thirstily.

I had a ghastly dream this night. I thought I saw a monster bat, with the face and tresses of Ariadne, fly into the open window and fasten its white teeth and scarlet lips on my arm. I tried to beat the horror away, but could not, for I seemed chained down and thralled also with drowsy delight as the beast sucked my blood with a gruesome rapture.

I looked out dreamily and saw a line of dead bodies of young men lying on the floor, each with a red mark on their arms, on the same part where the vampire was then sucking me, and I remembered having seen and wondered at such a mark on my own arm for the past fortnight. In a flash I understood the reason of my strange weakness, and at the same moment a sudden prick of pain roused me from my dreamy pleasure.

The vampire in her eagerness had bitten a little too deeply that night, unaware that I had not tasted the drugged draught. As I woke I saw her fully revealed by the midnight moon, with her black tresses flowing loosely, and with her red lips glued to my arm. With a shriek of horror I dashed her backwards, getting one last glimpse of her savage eyes, glowing white face and blood-stained red lips; then I rushed out to the night, moved on by my fear and hatred, nor did I pause in my mad flight until I had left miles between me and that accursed Cottage on the Moor.

GABRIEL-ERNEST

Saki

Hector Hugh Munroe (1870–1916) published works as both H. H. Munro and Saki. Saki's writing places classic supernatural motifs within biting commentaries of Edwardian culture to create witty tales of spirited satire and suspense. Saki was said to be inspired by Lewis Carroll and Oscar Wilde, and his own novel, *The Unbearable Bassington* is written in a style that precedes that of Evelyn Waugh.

"Gabriel-Ernest" was first featured in 1909, in *The Westminster Gazette*, before being collected in *Reginald in Russia* the following year. The story has since been featured in numerous collections, including *Unnatural Creatures* (2013), an anthology edited by the celebrated fantasy writer Neil Gaiman. "Gabriel-Ernest" is a classic supernatural take on the uncanny gastronomic. Surrounding the mystery of a "strange-eyed, strange-tongued youth", the short story emphasizes the disconcerting mix of the playful nature and unrestrainable impulse of youth that solidifies in the eerie image of a threatening child.

By drawing on an infamous figure of European folklore, Saki stretches the meaning of the *enfant terrible*, to ponder the consequences of perceiving childhood and viciousness as mutually exclusive conditions. By doing this, Saki re-establishes the wood as a place where the uncanny gastronomic reigns and predator-prey relations are inverted to create new and disturbing hierarchies. Doubling—a key motif of the uncanny—is used to elaborate on the risk of unseen and unthinkable dangers that haunt the English woods of noblemen and women.

"There is a wild beast in your woods," said the artist Cunningham, as he was being driven to the station. It was the only remark he had made during the drive, but as Van Cheele had talked incessantly his companion's silence had not been noticeable.

"A stray fox or two and some resident weasels. Nothing more formidable," said Van Cheele. The artist said nothing.

"What did you mean about a wild beast?" said Van Cheele later, when they were on the platform.

"Nothing. My imagination. Here is the train," said Cunningham.

That afternoon Van Cheele went for one of his frequent rambles through his woodland property. He had a stuffed bittern in his study, and knew the names of quite a number of wild flowers, so his aunt had possibly some justification in describing him as a great naturalist. At any rate, he was a great walker. It was his custom to take mental notes of everything he saw during his walks, not so much for the purpose of assisting contemporary science as to provide topics for conversation afterwards. When the bluebells began to show themselves in flower he made a point of informing every one of the fact; the season of the year might have warned his hearers of the likelihood of such an occurrence, but at least they felt that he was being absolutely frank with them.

What Van Cheele saw on this particular afternoon was, however, something far removed from his ordinary range of experience. On a shelf of smooth stone overhanging a deep pool in the hollow of an oak coppice a boy of about sixteen lay asprawl, drying his wet brown limbs luxuriously in the sun. His wet hair, parted by a recent dive, lay close to his head, and his light-brown eyes, so light that there was an almost tigerish gleam in them, were turned towards Van Cheele with a certain lazy watchfulness. It was an unexpected apparition, and Van Cheele found himself engaged in the novel process of thinking before he spoke. Where on earth could this wild-looking boy hail from? The miller's wife had lost a child some two months ago, supposed to have been swept away by the mill-race, but that had been a mere baby, not a half-grown lad.

"What are you doing there?" he demanded.

"Obviously, sunning myself," replied the boy.

"Where do you live?"

"Here, in these woods."

"You can't live in the woods," said Van Cheele.

"They are very nice woods," said the boy, with a touch of patronage in his voice.

"But where do you sleep at night?"

"I don't sleep at night; that's my busiest time."

Van Cheele began to have an irritated feeling that he was grappling with a problem that was eluding him.

"What do you feed on?" he asked.

"Flesh," said the boy, and he pronounced the word with slow relish, as though he were tasting it.

"Flesh! What flesh?"

"Since it interests you, rabbits, wild-fowl, hares, poultry, lambs in their season, children when I can get any; they're usually too well locked in at night, when I do most of my hunting. It's quite two months since I tasted child-flesh."

Ignoring the chaffing nature of the last remark Van Cheele tried to draw the boy on the subject of possible poaching operations.

"You're talking rather through your hat when you speak of feeding on hares." (Considering the nature of the boy's toilet the simile was hardly an apt one.) "Our hillside hares aren't easily caught."

"At night I hunt on four feet," was the somewhat cryptic response.

"I suppose you mean that you hunt with a dog?" hazarded Van Cheele.

The boy rolled slowly over on to his back, and laughed a weird low laugh, that was pleasantly like a chuckle and disagreeably like a snarl.

"I don't fancy any dog would be very anxious for my company, especially at night."

Van Cheele began to feel that there was something positively uncanny about the strange-eyed, strange-tongued youngster.

"I can't have you staying in these woods," he declared authoritatively.

"I fancy you'd rather have me here than in your house," said the boy.

The prospect of this wild, nude animal in Van Cheele's primly ordered house was certainly an alarming one.

"If you don't go I shall have to make you," said Van Cheele.

The boy turned like a flash, plunged into the pool, and in a moment had flung his wet and glistening body halfway up the bank where Van Cheele was standing. In an otter the movement would not have been remarkable; in a boy Van Cheele found it sufficiently startling. His foot slipped as he made an involuntary backward movement, and he found himself almost prostrate on the slippery weed-grown bank, with those tigerish yellow eyes not very far from his own. Almost instinctively he half raised his hand to his throat. The boy laughed again, a laugh in which the snarl had nearly driven out the chuckle, and then, with another of his astonishing lightning movements, plunged out of view into a yielding tangle of weed and fern.

"What an extraordinary wild animal!" said Van Cheele as he picked himself up. And then he recalled Cunningham's remark, "There is a wild beast in your woods."

Walking slowly homeward, Van Cheele began to turn over in his mind various local occurrences which might be traceable to the existence of this astonishing young savage.

Something had been thinning the game in the woods lately, poultry had been missing from the farms, hares were growing unaccountably scarcer, and complaints had reached him of lambs being carried off bodily from the hills. Was it possible that this wild boy was really hunting the countryside in company with some clever poacher dog? He had spoken of hunting "four footed" by night, but then, again, he had hinted strangely at no dog caring to come near him, "especially at night." It was certainly puzzling. And then, as Van Cheele ran his mind over the various depredations that had been committed during the last month or two, he came suddenly to a dead stop, alike in his walk and his speculations. The child missing from the mill two months ago—the accepted theory was that it had tumbled into the mill-race and been swept away; but the mother had always declared she had heard a shriek on the hill side of the house, in the opposite direction from the water. It was unthinkable, of course, but he wished that the boy had not made that uncanny remark about child-flesh eaten two months ago. Such dreadful things should not be said even in fun.

Van Cheele, contrary to his usual wont, did not feel disposed to be communicative about his discovery in the wood. His position as a parish councillor and justice of the peace seemed somehow compromised by the fact that he was harbouring a personality of such doubtful repute on his property; there was even a possibility that a heavy bill of damages for raided lambs and poultry might be laid at his door. At dinner that night he was quite unusually silent.

"Where's your voice gone to?" said his aunt. "One would think you had seen a wolf."

Van Cheele, who was not familiar with the old saying, thought the remark rather foolish; if he *had* seen a wolf on his property his tongue would have been extraordinarily busy with the subject.

At breakfast next morning Van Cheele was conscious that his feeling of uneasiness regarding yesterday's episode had not wholly disappeared, and he resolved to go by train to the neighbouring cathedral town hunt up Cunningham, and learn from him what he had really seen that had prompted the remark about a wild beast in the woods. With this resolution taken, his usual cheerfulness partially returned, and he hummed a bright little melody as he sauntered to the morning-room for his customary cigarette. As he entered the room the melody made way abruptly for a pious invocation. Gracefully asprawl on the ottoman, in an attitude of almost exaggerated repose, was the boy of the woods. He was drier than when Van Cheele had last seen him, but no other alteration was noticeable in his toilet.

"How dare you come here?" asked Van Cheele furiously.

"You told me I was not to stay in the woods," said the boy calmly.

"But not to come here. Supposing my aunt should see you!"

And with a view to minimizing that catastrophe Van Cheele hastily obscured as much of his unwelcome guest as possible under the folds of a *Morning Post*. At that moment his aunt entered the room.

"This is a poor boy who has lost his way—and lost his memory. He doesn't know who he is or where he comes from," explained Van Cheele desperately, glancing apprehensively at the waif's face to see whether he was going to add inconvenient candour to his other savage propensities.

Miss Van Cheele was enormously interested.

"Perhaps his underlinen is marked," she suggested.

"He seems to have lost most of that, too," said Van Cheele, making frantic little grabs at the *Morning Post* to keep it in its place.

A naked homeless child appealed to Miss Van Cheele as warmly as a stray kitten or derelict puppy would have done.

"We must do all we can for him," she decided, and in a very short time a messenger, dispatched to the rectory, where a pageboy was kept, had returned with a suit of pantry clothes, and the necessary accessories of shirt, shoes, collar, etc. Clothed, clean, and groomed, the boy lost none of his uncanniness in Van Cheele's eyes, but his aunt found him sweet.

"We must call him something till we know who he really is," she said. "Gabriel-Ernest, I think; those are nice suitable names."

Van Cheele agreed, but he privately doubted whether they were being grafted on to a nice suitable child. His misgivings were not diminished by the fact that his staid and elderly spaniel had bolted out of the house at the first incoming of the boy, and now obstinately remained shivering and yapping at the farther end of the orchard, while the canary, usually as vocally industrious as Van Cheele himself, had put itself on an allowance of frightened cheeps. More than ever he was resolved to consult Cunningham without loss of time.

As he drove off to the station his aunt was arranging that Gabriel-Ernest should help her to entertain the infant members of her Sunday-school class at tea that afternoon.

Cunningham was not at first disposed to be communicative.

"My mother died of some brain trouble," he explained, "so you will understand why I am averse to dwelling on anything of an impossibly fantastic nature that I may see or think that I have seen."

"But what *did* you see?" persisted Van Cheele.

"What I thought I saw was something so extraordinary that no really sane man could dignify it with the credit of having actually happened. I was standing, the last evening I was with you, half-hidden in the hedgegrowth by the orchard gate, watching the dying glow of the sunset. Suddenly I became aware of a naked boy, a bather from some neighbouring pool, I took him to be, who was standing out on the bare hillside also watching the sunset. His pose was so suggestive of some wild faun of Pagan myth that I instantly wanted to engage him as a model, and in another moment I think I should have hailed him. But just then the sun dipped out of view, and all the orange and pink slid out of the landscape, leaving it cold and grey. And at the same moment an astounding thing happened—the boy vanished too!"

"What! vanished away into nothing?" asked Van Cheele excitedly.

"No; that is the dreadful part of it," answered the artist; "on the open hillside where the boy had been standing a second ago, stood a large wolf, blackish in colour, with gleaming fangs and cruel, yellow eyes. You may think—"

But Van Cheele did not stop for anything as futile as thought. Already he was tearing at top speed towards the station. He dismissed the idea of a telegram. "Gabriel-Ernest is a werewolf" was a hopelessly inadequate effort at conveying the situation, and his aunt would think it was a code message to which he had omitted to give her the key. His one hope was that he might reach home before sundown. The cab which he chartered at the other end of the railway journey bore him with what seemed exasperating slowness along the country roads, which were pink and mauve with the flush of the sinking sun.

His aunt was putting away some unfinished jams and cake when he arrived.

"Where is Gabriel-Ernest?" he almost screamed.

"He is taking the little Toop child home," said his aunt. "It was getting so late, I thought it wasn't safe to let it go back alone. What a lovely sunset, isn't it?"

But Van Cheele, although not oblivious of the glow in the western sky, did not stay to discuss its beauties. At a speed for which he was scarcely geared he raced along the narrow lane that led to the home of the Toops. On one side ran the swift current of the mill-stream, on the other rose the stretch of bare hillside. A dwindling rim of red sun showed still on the skyline, and the next turning must bring him in view of the ill-assorted couple he was pursuing. Then the colour went suddenly out of things, and a grey light settled itself with a quick shiver over the landscape. Van Cheele heard a shrill wail of fear, and stopped running.

Nothing was ever seen again of the Toop child or Gabriel-Ernest, but the latter's discarded garments were found lying in the road, so it was assumed that the child had fallen into the water, and that the boy had stripped and jumped in, in a vain endeavour to save it. Van Cheele and some workmen who were near by at the time testified to having heard a child scream loudly just near the spot where the clothes were found. Mrs. Toop, who had eleven other children, was decently resigned to her bereavement, but Miss Van Cheele sincerely mourned her lost foundling. It was on her initiative that a memorial brass was put up in the parish church to "Gabriel-Ernest, an unknown boy, who bravely sacrificed his life for another."

Van Cheele gave way to his aunt in most things, but he flatly refused to subscribe to the Gabriel-Ernest memorial.

TO SERVE MAN

Damon Knight

Damon Knight (1922–2002) was an American writer and editor of science fiction. Knight both worked and contributed across various sci-fi publications and was considered a respected literary critic of genre fiction. "To Serve Man" debuted in the November 1950 issue of *Galaxy Science Fiction*. The story has had a consistently positive reception and has since been collected and reprinted in *The Best of Damon Knight* (1976) and various other anthologies of celebrated science fiction tales. "To Serve Man" was adapted for the screen, becoming the basis for season three, episode twenty-four of the popular sci-fi series *The Twilight Zone* in 1962. Notably, in 2001, the story was awarded a Hugo Award for the best short story in the year of its release. The story has also inspired food writers, with the release of *To Serve Man: A Cookbook for People* (1976) cementing the tale's uncanny gastronomic status.

Knight's story is a science fiction take on the strangeness of eating; it exists as a commentary on international—even interstellar—relations and the complicated politics around power and foodways. It draws upon the conceptualization of aliens as Other and sardonically plays upon the "eat or be eaten" paradigm that is frequently projected onto extra-terrestrial beings in the cultural imagination. The science fiction angle provides the opportunity to consider the uncanny gastronomic on a uniquely universal scale; to ponder the culture of war, austerity, and the complex balance of coexisting as not only a dynamic of human-food relations but as a negotiation of the more-than-human.

The Kanamit were not very pretty, it's true. They looked something like pigs and something like people, and that is not an attractive combination. Seeing them for the first time shocked you; that was their handicap. When a thing with the countenance of a fiend comes from the stars and offers a gift, you are disinclined to accept.

I don't know what we expected interstellar visitors to look like—those who thought about it at all, that is. Angels, perhaps, or something too alien to be really awful. Maybe that's why we were all so horrified and repelled when they landed in their great ships and we saw what they really were like.

The Kanamit were short and very hairy—thick, bristly brown-gray hair all over their abominably plump bodies. Their noses were snoutlike and their eyes small, and they had thick hands of three fingers each. They wore green leather harness and green shorts, but I think the shorts were a concession to our notions of public decency. The garments were quite modishly cut, with slash pockets and half-belts in the back. The Kanamit had a sense of humor, anyhow; their clothes proved it.

There were three of them at this session of the U.N., and I can't tell you how queer it looked to see them there in the middle of a solemn Plenary Session—three fat piglike creatures in green harness and shorts, sitting at the long table below the podium, surrounded by the packed arcs of delegates from every nation. They sat correctly upright, politely watching each speaker. Their flat ears drooped over the earphones. Later on, I believe, they learned every human language, but at this time they knew only French and English.

They seemed perfectly at ease—and that, along with their humor, was a thing that tended to make me like them. I was in the minority; I didn't think they were trying to put anything over. They said quite simply that they wanted to help us and I believed it. As a U.N. translator, of course, my opinion didn't matter, but I thought they were the best thing that ever happened to Earth.

The delegate from Argentina got up and said that his government was interested by the demonstration of a new cheap power source, which the Kanamit had made at the previous session, but that the Argentine government could not commit itself as to its future policy without a much more thorough examination.

It was what all the delegates were saying, but I had to pay particular attention to Senor Valdes, because he tended to sputter and his diction was bad. I got through the translation all right, with only one or two momentary hesitations, and then switched to the Polish-English line to hear how Gregori was doing with Janciewicz. Janciewicz was the cross Gregori had to bear, just as Valdes was mine.

Janciewicz repeated the previous remarks with a few ideological variations, and then the Secretary-General recognized the delegate from France, who introduced Dr. Denis Leveque, the criminologist, and a great deal of complicated equipment was wheeled in.

Dr. Leveque remarked that the question in many people's minds had been aptly expressed by the delegate from the U.S.S.R. at the preceding session, when he demanded, "What is the motive of the

Kanamit? What is their purpose in offering us these unprecedented gifts, while asking nothing in return?"

The doctor then said, "At the request of several delegates and with the full consent of our guests, the Kanamit, my associates and I have made a series of tests upon the Kanamit with the equipment which you see before you. These tests will now be repeated."

A murmur ran through the chamber. There was a fusillade of flashbulbs, and one of the TV cameras moved up to focus on the instrument board of the doctor's equipment. At the same time, the huge television screen behind the podium lighted up, and we saw the blank faces of two dials, each with its pointer resting at zero, and a strip of paper tape with a stylus point resting against it.

The doctor's assistants were fastening wires to the temples of one of the Kanamit, wrapping a canvas-covered rubber tube around his forearm, and taping something to the palm of his right hand.

In the screen, we saw the paper tape begin to move while the stylus traced a slow zigzag pattern along it. One of the needles began to jump rhythmically; the other flipped over and stayed there, wavering slightly.

"These are the standard instruments for testing the truth of a statement," said Dr. Leveque. "Our first object, since the physiology of the Kanamit is unknown to us, was to determine whether or not they react to these tests as human beings do. We will now repeat one of the many experiments which was made in the endeavor to discover this."

He pointed to the first dial. "This instrument registers the subject's heart-beat. This shows the electrical conductivity of the skin in the palm of his hand, a measure of perspiration, which increases under stress. And this—" pointing to the tape-and-stylus device— "shows the pattern and intensity of the electrical waves emanating from his brain. It has been shown, with human subjects, that all these readings vary markedly depending upon whether the subject is speaking the truth."

He picked up two large pieces of cardboard, one red and one black. The red one was a square about a meter on a side; the black was a rectangle a meter and a half long. He addressed himself to the Kanama:

"Which of these is longer than the other?"

"The red," said the Kanama.

Both needles leaped wildly, and so did the line on the unrolling tape.

"I shall repeat the question," said the doctor. "Which of these is longer than the other?"

"The black," said the creature.

This time the instruments continued in their normal rhythm.

"How did you come to this planet?" asked the doctor.

"Walked," replied the Kanama.

Again the instruments responded, and there was a subdued ripple of laughter in the chamber.

"Once more," said the doctor, "how did you come to this planet?"

"In a spaceship," said the Kanama, and the instruments did not jump.

The doctor again faced the delegates. "Many such experiments were made," he said, "and my colleagues and myself are satisfied that the mechanisms are effective. Now," he turned to the Kanama, "I shall ask our distinguished guest to reply to the question put at the last session by the delegate of the U.S.S.R., namely, what is the motive of the Kanamit people in offering these great gifts to the people of Earth?"

The Kanama rose. Speaking this time in English, he said, "On my planet there is a saying, 'There are more riddles in a stone than in a philosopher's head.' The motives of intelligent beings, though they may at times appear obscure, are simple things compared to the complex workings of the natural universe. Therefore I hope that the people of Earth will understand, and believe, when I tell you that our mission upon your planet is simply this—to bring to you the peace and plenty which we ourselves enjoy, and which we have in the past brought to other races throughout the galaxy. When your world has no more hunger, no more war, no more needless suffering, that will be our reward."

And the needles had not jumped once.

The delegate from the Ukraine jumped to his feet, asking to be recognized, but the time was up and the Secretary-General closed the session.

I met Gregori as we were leaving the U.N. chamber. His face was red with excitement. "Who promoted that circus?" he demanded.

"The tests looked genuine to me," I told him.

"A circus!" he said vehemently. "A second-rate farce! If they were genuine, Peter, why was debate stifled?"

"There'll be time for debate tomorrow surely."

"Tomorrow the doctor and his instruments will be back in Paris. Plenty of things can happen before tomorrow. In the name of sanity, man, how can anybody trust a thing that looks as if it ate the baby?"

I was a little annoyed. I said, "Are you sure you're not more worried about their politics than their appearance?"

He said, "Bah," and went away.

The next day reports began to come in from government laboratories all over the world where the Kanamit's power source was being tested. They were wildly enthusiastic. I don't understand such things myself, but it seemed that those little metal boxes would give more electrical power than an atomic pile, for next to nothing and nearly forever. And it was said that they were so cheap to manufacture that everybody in the world could have one of his own. In the early afternoon there were reports that seventeen countries had already begun to set up factories to turn them out.

The next day the Kanamit turned up with plans and specimens of a gadget that would increase the fertility of any arable land by sixty to one hundred per cent. It speeded the formation of nitrates in the soil, or something. There was nothing in the headlines but the Kanamit any more. The day after that, they dropped their bombshell.

"You now have potentially unlimited power and increased food supply," said one of them. He pointed with his three-fingered hand to an instrument that stood on the table before him. It was a box on a tripod, with a parabolic reflector on the front of it. "We offer you today a third gift which is at least as important as the first two."

He beckoned to the TV men to roll their cameras into closeup position. Then he picked up a large sheet of cardboard covered with drawings and English lettering. We saw it on the large screen above the podium; it was all clearly legible.

"We are informed that this broadcast is being relayed through-out your world," said the Kanama. "I wish that everyone who has equipment for taking photographs from television screens would use it now."

The Secretary-General leaned forward and asked a question sharply, but the Kanama ignored him.

"This device," he said, "projects a field in which no explosive, of whatever nature, can detonate."

There was an uncomprehending silence.

The Kanama said, "It cannot now be suppressed. If one nation has it, all must have it." When nobody seemed to understand, he explained bluntly, "There will be no more war."

That was the biggest news of the millennium, and it was perfectly true. It turned out that the explosions the Kanama was talking about included gasoline and Diesel explosions. They had simply made it impossible for anybody to mount or equip a modern army.

We could have gone back to bows and arrows, of course, but that wouldn't have satisfied the military. Not after having atomic bombs and all the rest. Besides, there wouldn't be any reason to make war. Every nation would soon have everything.

Nobody ever gave another thought to those lie-detector experiments, or asked the Kanamit what their politics were. Gregori was put out; he had nothing to prove his suspicions.

I quit my job with the U.N. a few months later, because I foresaw that it was going to die under me anyhow. U.N. business was booming at the time, but after a year or so there was going to be nothing for it to do. Every nation on Earth was well on the way to being completely self-supporting; they weren't going to need much arbitration.

I accepted a position as translator with the Kanamit Embassy, and it was there that I ran into Gregori again. I was glad to see him, but I couldn't imagine what he was doing there.

"I thought you were on the opposition," I said. "Don't tell me you're convinced the Kanamit are all right."

He looked rather shamefaced. "They're not what they look, anyhow," he said.

It was as much of a concession as he could decently make, and I invited him down to the embassy lounge for a drink. It was an intimate kind of place, and he grew confidential over the second daiquiri.

"They fascinate me," he said. "I hate them instinctively on sight still—that hasn't changed, but I can evaluate it. You were right, obviously; they mean us nothing but good. But do you know—" he leaned across the table—"the question of the Soviet delegate was never answered."

I am afraid I snorted.

"No, really," he said. "They told us what they wanted to do—'to bring to you the peace and plenty which we ourselves enjoy.' But they didn't say *why*."

"Why do missionaries—"

"Hogwash!" he said angrily. "Missionaries have a religious motive. If these creatures do own a religion, they haven't once mentioned it. What's more, they didn't send a missionary group, they sent a diplomatic delegation—a group representing the will and policy of their whole people. Now just what have the Kanamit, as a people or a nation, got to gain from our welfare?"

I said, "Cultural—"

"Cultural cabbage-soup! No, it's something less obvious than that, something obscure that belongs to their psychology and not to ours. But trust me, Peter, there is no such thing as a completely disinterested altruism. In one way or another, they have something to gain."

"And that's why you're here," I said, "to try to find out what it is?"

"Correct. I wanted to get on one of the ten-year exchange groups to their home planet, but I couldn't; the quota was filled a week after they made the announcement. This is the next best thing. I'm studying their language, and you know that language reflects the basic assumptions of the people who use it. I've got a fair command of the spoken lingo already. It's not hard, really, and there are hints in it. I'm sure I'll get the answer eventually."

"More power," I said, and we went back to work.

I saw Gregori frequently from then on, and he kept me posted about his progress. He was highly excited about a month after that first meeting; said he'd got hold of a book of the Kanamit's and was trying to puzzle it out. They wrote in ideographs, worse than Chinese, but he was determined to fathom it if it took him years. He wanted my help.

Well, I was interested in spite of myself, for I knew it would be a long job. We spent some evenings together, working with material from Kanamit bulletin-boards and so forth, and the extremely limited English-Kanamit dictionary they issued the staff. My conscience bothered me about the stolen book, but gradually I became absorbed by the problem. Languages are my field, after all. I couldn't help being fascinated.

We got the title worked out in a few weeks. It was "How to Serve Man," evidently a handbook they were giving out to new Kanamit members of the embassy staff. They had new ones in, all the time now, a shipload about once a month; they were opening all kinds of research laboratories, clinics and so on. If there was anybody on Earth besides Gregori who still distrusted those people he must have been somewhere in the middle of Tibet.

It was astonishing to see the changes that had been wrought in less than a year. There were no more standing armies, no more shortages, no unemployment. When you picked up a newspaper you didn't see "H-BOMB" or "V-2" leaping out at you; the news was always good. It was a hard thing to get used to. The Kanamit were working on human biochemistry, and it was known around the embassy that they were nearly ready to announce methods of making our race taller and stronger and healthier—practically a race of supermen—and they had a potential cure for heart disease and cancer.

I didn't see Gregori for a fortnight after we finished working out the title of the book; I was on a long-overdue vacation in Canada. When I got back, I was shocked by the change in his appearance.

"What on Earth is wrong, Gregori?" I asked. "You look like the very devil."

"Come down to the lounge."

I went with him, and he gulped a stiff Scotch as if he needed it.

"Come on, man, what's the matter?" I urged.

"The Kanamit have put me on the passenger list for the next exchange ship," he said. "You, too, otherwise I wouldn't be talking to you."

"Well," I said, "but—"

"They're not altruists."

"What do you mean?"

"What I told you," he said. "They're not altruists."

I tried to reason with him. I pointed out they'd made Earth a paradise compared to what it was before. He only shook his head.

Then I said, "Well, what about those lie-detector tests?"

"A farce," he replied, without heat. "I said so at the time, you fool. They told the truth, though, as far as it went."

"And the book?" I demanded, annoyed. "What about that—'How to Serve Man'? That wasn't put there for you to read. They *mean* it. How do you explain that?"

"I've read the first paragraph of that book," he said. "Why do you suppose I haven't slept for a week?"

I said, "Well?" and he smiled that curious, twisted smile, as if he really wanted to cry instead.

"It's a cookbook," he said.

THE COMPANY OF WOLVES

Angela Carter

Referred to fondly as a "white witch" by fairy tale scholar Cristina Bacchilega, Angela Carter is a name synonymous with the feminist fairy tale movement. Carter is the pseudonym of Angela Olive Stalker (1940–1992), a writer who was at the helm of the twentieth-century renaissance of the fairy tale, collecting and reworking numerous narratives to frequently dark, seductive effect. Carter was also known for her original works including novels such as *The Magic Toyshop* (1967), *The Passion of New Eve* (1977) and *Nights at the Circus* (1984). Carter is perhaps best known for her *Virago Book of Fairy Tales* series and the short story collection *The Bloody Chamber* (1979), which is frequently taught in literature classes in British secondary schools.

Writer, critic, and historian Marina Warner describes Carter's approach to fairy tale retelling as a process of "put[ting] new wine in old bottles so that they would explode: the old bottles were necessary to the pyrotechnics". "The Company of Wolves" was published in Carter's collection of short stories, *The Bloody Chamber*. Heavily inspired by the tale of Little Red Riding Hood, the narrative is a patchwork of various encounters with wolves in the woods. It is a tale of viciousness and desire, and an experiment in unexpected endings. Greedy wolves and the consumption of human flesh feature heavily in Carter's short stories. This is thought to be part of the reclamation of the usual reading of Little Red Riding Hood, where the attack on the young girl is often read as a representation of sexual violence. It acts as a classic example of Carter's version of the uncanny gastronomic, a kind of "re-fanging" of the fairy tale heroine where the woman-as-meat association is queried and repackaged through the lens of female empowerment, often through images of violence or confident sexuality.

One beast and only one howls in the woods by night.

The wolf is carnivore incarnate and he's as cunning as he is ferocious; once he's had a taste of flesh then nothing else will do.

At night, the eyes of wolves shine like candle flames, yellowish, reddish, but that is because the pupils of their eyes fatten on darkness and catch the light from your lantern to flash it back to you—red for danger; if a wolf's eyes reflect only moonlight, then they gleam a cold and unnatural green, a mineral, a piercing colour. If the benighted traveller spies those luminous, terrible sequins stitched suddenly on the black thickets, then he knows he must run, if fear has not struck him stock-still.

But those eyes are all you will be able to glimpse of the forest assassins as they cluster invisibly round your smell of meat as you go through the wood unwisely late. They will be like shadows, they will be like wraiths, grey members of a congregation of nightmare; hark! his long, wavering howl... an aria of fear made audible.

The wolfsong is the sound of the rending you will suffer, in itself a murdering.

It is winter and cold weather. In this region of mountain and forest, there is now nothing for the wolves to eat. Goats and sheep are locked up in the byre, the deer departed for the remaining pasturage on the southern slopes—wolves grow lean and famished.

There is so little flesh on them that you could count the starveling ribs through their pelts, if they gave you time before they pounced. Those slavering jaws; the lolling tongue; the rime of saliva on the grizzled chops—of all the teeming perils of the night and the forest, ghosts, hobgoblins, ogres that grill babies upon gridirons, witches that fatten their captives in cages for cannibal tables, the wolf is worst for he cannot listen to reason.

You are always in danger in the forest, where no people are. Step between the portals of the great pines where the shaggy branches tangle about you, trapping the unwary traveller in nets as if the vegetation itself were in a plot with the wolves who live there, as though the wicked trees go fishing on behalf of their friends—step between the gateposts of the forest with the greatest trepidation and infinite precautions, for if you stray from the path for one instant, the wolves will eat you. They are grey as famine, they are as unkind as plague.

The grave-eyed children of the sparse villages always carry knives with them when they go out to tend the little flocks of goats that provide the homesteads with acrid milk and rank, maggoty cheeses. Their knives are half as big as they are, the blades are sharpened daily.

But the wolves have ways of arriving at your own hearthside. We try and try but sometimes we cannot keep them out. There is no winter's night the cottager does not fear to see a lean, grey, famished snout questing under the door, and there was a woman once bitten in her own kitchen as she was straining the macaroni.

Fear and flee the wolf; for, worst of all, the wolf may be more than he seems.

There was a hunter once, near here, that trapped a wolf in a pit. This wolf had massacred the sheep and goats; eaten up a mad old man who used to live by himself in a hut halfway up the mountain and sing to Jesus all day; pounced on a girl looking after the sheep, but she made such a commotion that men came with rifles and scared him away and tried to track him into the forest but he was cunning and easily gave them the slip. So this hunter dug a pit and put a duck in it, for bait, all alive-oh; and he covered the pit with straw smeared with wolf dung. Quack, quack! went the duck and a wolf came slinking out of the forest, a big one, a heavy one, he weighed as much as a grown man and the straw gave way beneath him—into the pit he tumbled. The hunter jumped down after him, slit his throat, cut off all his paws for a trophy.

And then no wolf at all lay in front of the hunter but the bloody trunk of a man, headless, footless, dying, dead.

A witch from up the valley once turned an entire wedding party into wolves because the groom had settled on another girl. She used to order them to visit her, at night, from spite, and they would sit and howl around her cottage for her, serenading her with their misery.

Not so very long ago, a young woman in our village married a man who vanished clean away on her wedding night. The bed was made with new sheets and the bride lay down in it; the groom said, he was going out to relieve himself, insisted on it, for the sake of decency, and she drew the coverlet up to her chin and she lay there. And she waited and she waited and then she waited again—surely he's been gone a long time? Until she jumps up in bed and shrieks to hear a howling, coming on the wind from the forest.

That long-drawn, wavering howl has, for all its fearful resonance, some inherent sadness in it, as if the beasts would love to be less beastly if only they knew how and never cease to mourn their own condition. There is a vast melancholy in the canticles of the wolves, melancholy infinite as the forest, endless as these long nights of winter and yet that ghastly sadness, that mourning for their own, irremediable appetites, can never move the heart for not one phrase in it hints at the possibility of redemption; grace could not come to the wolf from its own despair, only through some external mediator, so that, sometimes, the beast will look as if he half welcomes the knife that despatches him.

The young woman's brothers searched the outhouses and the haystacks but never found any remains so the sensible girl dried her eyes and found herself another husband not too shy to piss into a pot who spent the nights indoors. She gave him a pair of bonny babies and all went right as a trivet until, one freezing night, the night of the solstice, the hinge of the year when things do not fit together as well as they should, the longest night, her first good man came home again.

A great thump on the door announced him as she was stirring the soup for the father of her children and she knew him the moment she lifted the latch to him although it was years since she'd worn black for him and now he was in rags and his hair hung down his back and never saw a comb, alive with lice.

"Here I am again, missus," he said. "Get me my bowl of cabbage and be quick about it."

Then her second husband came in with wood for the fire and when the first one saw she'd slept with another man and, worse, clapped his red eyes on her little children who'd crept into the kitchen to see what all the din was about, he shouted: "I wish I were a wolf again, to teach this whore a lesson!" So a wolf he instantly became and tore off the eldest boy's left foot before he was chopped up with the hatchet they used for chopping logs. But when the wolf lay bleeding and gasping its last, the pelt peeled off again and he was just as he had been, years ago, when he ran away from his marriage bed, so that she wept and her second husband beat her.

They say there's an ointment the Devil gives you that turns you into a wolf the minute you rub it on. Or, that he was born feet first and had a wolf for his father and his torso is a man's but his legs and genitals are a wolf's. And he has a wolf's heart.

Seven years is a werewolf's natural span but if you burn his human clothing you condemn him to wolfishness for the rest of his life, so old wives hereabouts think it some protection to throw a hat or an apron at the werewolf, as if clothes made the man. Yet by the eyes, those phosphorescent eyes, you know him in all his shapes; the eyes alone unchanged by metamorphosis.

Before he can become a wolf, the lycanthrope strips stark naked. If you spy a naked man among the pines, you must run as if the Devil were after you.

It is midwinter and the robin, the friend of man, sits on the handle of the gardener's spade and sings. It is the worst time in all the year for wolves but this strong-minded child insists she will go off through the wood. She is quite sure the wild beasts cannot harm her although, well-warned, she lays a carving knife in the basket her mother has packed with cheeses. There is a bottle of harsh liquor distilled from brambles; a batch of flat oatcakes baked on the hearthstone; a pot or two of jam. The flaxen-haired girl will take these delicious gifts to a reclusive grandmother so old the burden of her years is crushing her to death. Granny lives two hours' trudge through the winter woods; the child wraps herself up in her thick shawl, draws it over her head. She steps into her stout wooden shoes; she is dressed and ready and it is Christmas Eve. The malign door of the solstice still swings upon its hinges but she has been too much loved ever to feel scared.

Children do not stay young for long in this savage country. There are no toys for them to play with so they work hard and grow wise but this one, so pretty and the youngest of her family, a little late-comer, had been indulged by her mother and the grandmother who'd knitted her the red shawl that, today, has the ominous if brilliant look of blood on snow. Her breasts have just begun to swell; her hair is like lint, so fair it hardly makes a shadow on her pale forehead; her cheeks are an emblematic scarlet and white and she has just started her woman's bleeding, the clock inside her that will strike, henceforward, once a month.

She stands and moves within the invisible pentacle of her own virginity. She is an unbroken egg; she is a sealed vessel; she has inside her a magic space the entrance to which is shut tight with a plug of membrane; she is a closed system; she does not know how to shiver. She has her knife and she is afraid of nothing.

Her father might forbid her, if he were home, but he is away in the forest, gathering wood, and her mother cannot deny her.

The forest closed upon her like a pair of jaws.

There is always something to look at in the forest, even in the middle of winter—the huddled mounds of birds, succumbed to the lethargy of the season, heaped on the creaking boughs and too forlorn to sing; the bright frills of the winter fungi on the blotched trunks of the trees; the cuneiform slots of rabbits and deer, the herringbone tracks of the birds, a hare as lean as a rasher of bacon streaking across the path where the thin sunlight dapples the russet brakes of last year's bracken.

When she heard the freezing howl of a distant wolf, her practised hand sprang to the handle of her knife, but she saw no sign of a wolf at all, nor of a naked man, neither, but then she heard a clattering among the brushwood and there sprang on to the path a fully clothed one, a very handsome young one, in the green coat and wideawake hat of a hunter, laden with carcasses of game birds. She had her hand on her knife at the first rustle of twigs but he laughed with a flash of white teeth when he saw her and made her a comic yet flattering little bow; she'd never seen such a fine fellow before, not among the rustic clowns of her native village. So on they went together, through the thickening light of the afternoon.

Soon they were laughing and joking like old friends. When he offered to carry her basket, she gave it to him although her knife was in it because he told her his rifle would protect them. As the day darkened, it began to snow again; she felt the first flakes settle on her eyelashes but now there was only half a mile to go and there would be a fire, and hot tea, and a welcome, a warm one, surely, for the dashing huntsman as well as for herself.

This young man had a remarkable object in his pocket. It was a compass. She looked at the little round glass face in the palm of his hand and watched the wavering needle with a vague wonder. He assured her this compass had taken him safely through the wood on his hunting trip because the needle always told him with perfect accuracy where the north was. She did not believe it; she knew she should never leave the path on the way through the wood or else she would be lost instantly. He laughed at her again; gleaming trails of spittle clung to his teeth. He said, if he plunged off the path into the forest that surrounded them, he could guarantee to arrive at her grandmother's house a good quarter of an hour before she did, plotting his way through the undergrowth with his compass, while she trudged the long way, along the winding path.

I don't believe you. Besides, aren't you afraid of the wolves?

He only tapped the gleaming butt of his rifle and grinned.

Is it a bet? he asked her. Shall we make a game of it? What will you give me if I get to your grandmother's house before you?

What would you like? she asked disingenuously.

A kiss.

Commonplaces of a rustic seduction; she lowered her eyes and blushed.

He went through the undergrowth and took her basket with him but she forgot to be afraid of the beasts, although now the moon was rising, for she wanted to dawdle on her way to make sure the handsome gentleman would win his wager.

Grandmother's house stood by itself a little way out of the village. The freshly falling snow blew in eddies about the kitchen garden and the young man stepped delicately up the snowy path to the door as if he were reluctant to get his feet wet, swinging his bundle of game and the girl's basket and humming a little tune to himself.

There is a faint trace of blood on his chin; he has been snacking on his catch.

He rapped upon the panels with his knuckles.

Aged and frail, granny is three-quarters succumbed to the mortality the ache in her bones promises her and almost ready to give in entirely. A boy came out from the village to build up her hearth for the night an hour ago and the kitchen crackles with busy firelight. She has her Bible for company, she is a pious old woman. She is propped up on several pillows in the bed set into the wall peasant-fashion, wrapped up in the patchwork quilt she made before she was married, more years ago than she cares to remember. Two china spaniels with liver-coloured blotches on their coats and black noses sit on either side of the fireplace. There is a bright rug of woven rags on the pantiles. The grandfather clock ticks away her eroding time.

We keep the wolves outside by living well.

He rapped upon the panels with his hairy knuckles.

It is your granddaughter, he mimicked in a high soprano.

Lift up the latch and walk in, my darling.

You can tell them by their eyes, eyes of a beast of prey, nocturnal, devastating eyes as red as a wound; you can hurl your Bible at him and your apron after, granny, you thought that was a sure prophylactic against these infernal vermin... now call on Christ and his mother and all the angels in heaven to protect you but it won't do you any good.

His feral muzzle is sharp as a knife; he drops his golden burden of gnawed pheasant on the table and puts down your dear girl's basket, too. Oh, my God, what have you done with her?

Off with his disguise, that coat of forest-coloured cloth, the hat with the feather tucked into the ribbon; his matted hair streams down his white shirt and she can see the lice moving in it. The sticks in the hearth shift and hiss; night and the forest has come into the kitchen with darkness tangled in its hair.

He strips off his shirt. His skin is the colour and texture of vellum. A crisp stripe of hair runs down his belly, his nipples are ripe and dark as poison fruit but he's so thin you could count the ribs under his skin if only he gave you the time. He strips off his trousers and she can see how hairy his legs are. His genitals, huge. Ah! huge.

The last thing the old lady saw in all this world was a young man, eyes like cinders, naked as a stone, approaching her bed.

The wolf is carnivore incarnate.

When he had finished with her, he licked his chops and quickly dressed himself again, until he was just as he had been when he came through her door. He burned the inedible hair in the fireplace and wrapped the bones up in a napkin that he hid away under the bed in the wooden chest in which he found a clean pair of sheets. These he carefully put on the bed instead of the tell-tale stained ones he stowed away in the laundry basket. He plumped up the pillows and shook out the patchwork quilt, he picked up the Bible from the floor, closed it and laid it on the table. All was as it had been before except that grandmother was gone. The sticks twitched in the grate, the clock ticked and the young man sat patiently, deceitfully beside the bed in granny's nightcap.

Rat-a-tap-tap.

Who's there, he quavers in granny's antique falsetto.

Only your granddaughter.

So she came in, bringing with her a flurry of snow that melted in tears on the tiles, and perhaps she was a little disappointed to see only her grandmother sitting beside the fire. But then he flung off the blanket and sprang to the door, pressing his back against it so that she could not get out again.

The girl looked round the room and saw there was not even the indentation of a head on the smooth cheek of the pillow and how, for the first time she'd seen it so, the Bible lay closed on the table. The tick of the clock cracked like a whip. She wanted her knife from her basket but she did not dare reach for it because his eyes were fixed upon her—huge eyes that now seemed to shine with a unique, interior light, eyes the size of saucers, saucers full of Greek fire, diabolic phosphorescence.

What big eyes you have.

All the better to see you with.

No trace at all of the old woman except for a tuft of white hair that had caught in the bark of an unburned log. When the girl saw that, she knew she was in danger of death.

Where is my grandmother?

There's nobody here but we two, my darling.

Now a great howling rose up all around them, near, very near, as close as the kitchen garden, the howling of a multitude of wolves; she knew the worst wolves are hairy on the inside and she shivered, in spite of the scarlet shawl she pulled more closely round herself as if it could protect her although it was as red as the blood she must spill.

Who has come to sing us carols, she said.

Those are the voices of my brothers, darling; I love the company of wolves. Look out of the window and you'll see them.

Snow half-caked the lattice and she opened it to look into the garden. It was a white night of moon and snow; the blizzard whirled round the gaunt, grey beasts who squatted on their haunches among the rows of winter cabbage, pointing their sharp snouts to the moon and howling as if their hearts would break. Ten wolves; twenty wolves—so many wolves she could not count them, howling in concert as if demented or deranged. Their eyes reflected the light from the kitchen and shone like a hundred candles.

It is very cold, poor things, she said; no wonder they howl so.

She closed the window on the wolves' threnody and took off her scarlet shawl, the colour of poppies, the colour of sacrifices, the colour of her menses, and, since her fear did her no good, she ceased to be afraid.

What shall I do with my shawl?

Throw it on the fire, dear one. You won't need it again.

She bundled up her shawl and threw it on the blaze, which instantly consumed it. Then she drew her blouse over her head; her small breasts gleamed as if the snow had invaded the room.

What shall I do with my blouse?

Into the fire with it, too, my pet.

The thin muslin went flaring up the chimney like a magic bird and now off came her skirt, her woollen stockings, her shoes, and on to the fire they went, too, and were gone for good. The firelight shone through the edges of her skin; now she was clothed only in her untouched integument of flesh. This dazzling, naked she combed out her hair with her fingers; her hair looked white as the snow outside. Then went directly to the man with red eyes in whose unkempt mane the lice moved; she stood up on tiptoe and unbuttoned the collar of his shirt.

What big arms you have.

All the better to hug you with.

Every wolf in the world now howled a prothalamion outside the window as she freely gave the kiss she owed him.

What big teeth you have!

She saw how his jaw began to slaver and the room was full of the clamour of the forest's Liebestod but the wise child never flinched, even when he answered:

All the better to eat you with.

The girl burst out laughing; she knew she was nobody's meat. She laughed at him full in the face, she ripped off his shirt for him and flung it into the fire, in the fiery wake of her own discarded clothing. The flames danced like dead souls on Walpurgisnacht and the old bones under the bed set up a terrible clattering but she did not pay them any heed.

Carnivore incarnate, only immaculate flesh appeases him.

She will lay his fearful head on her lap and she will pick out the lice from his pelt and perhaps she will put the lice into her mouth and eat them, as he will bid her, as she would do in a savage marriage ceremony.

The blizzard will die down.

The blizzard died down, leaving the mountains as randomly covered with snow as if a blind woman had thrown a sheet over them, the upper branches of the forest pines limed, creaking, swollen with the fall.

Snowlight, moonlight, a confusion of paw-prints.

All silent, all still.

Midnight; and the clock strikes. It is Christmas Day, the were-wolves' birthday, the door of the solstice stands wide open; let them all sink through.

See! sweet and sound she sleeps in granny's bed, between the paws of the tender wolf.

2 0 0 1

#54

from *The Devil's Larder*

Jim Crace

Jim Crace (1946–) is an English writer known for his inventive and varying fiction. His novels have received a myriad of awards, including the Whitbread Novel Award (*Quarantine* (1997)), The National Book Critics Circle (*Being Dead* (1999)) and he has been shortlisted for the Booker Prize twice with *Quarantine* and *Harvest* (2013). Crace cites magical realism as a large inspiration for his work, favouring novels by authors Italo Calvino and Gunter Grass.

The Devil's Larder (2001) is a novel in sixty-four numbered vignettes that centre and celebrate food as strange and essential, yet elusive. Deftly crossing generic, temporal and culinary borders, the sections of the book consider whistling waiters, a search to identify the secret ingredients of a mysterious soup, a man whose stomach begins to grow root vegetables, and a woman who consumes her husband's ashes. By considering the endless ways that we can relate to food, Crace shows that there are as many modes for food to be uncanny as there are different ingredients. #54 focuses on mushrooms. Mushrooms as a literary motif have sprouted into the popular imagination in recent years, notably in the weird fiction of Jeff Vandermeer's *Ambergris Trilogy* (2020), Aliyah Whitley's *The Beauty* (2014), Silvia Moreno-Garcia's *Mexican Gothic* (2022) and An Yu's *Ghost Music* (2022). Crace's #54 uses mushrooms to consider ideas of contamination and infection, sin and blasphemy, fabricated emotion, and delirious excess. Playing on the natural growing environment of mushrooms—in the dark, damp, depths—Crace's tale follows the night-time ramblings of an unexpected forager.

The devil wanders with his straw sack at night through the meadows and the woods behind the town. He's there, we're told, to plant the mushrooms that he's raised in hell, where there's no light to green them, so that the gatherers who come at dawn, against the wisdoms of the countryside, can satisfy their appetites for sickeners or conjurers or fungi smelling of dead flesh and tasting of nothing when they're cooked. He feeds them disappointments, nightmares, fevers, indigestion, fear. He lets them breakfast on his spite.

The mushroom devil has been seen from time to time. Courting couples seeking privacy in some deep undergrowth have heard his foot snap stems behind them or sensed him creeping by their cars, a mocking voyeur hoping to disrupt their love. Those midnight wanderers who search for mysteries and gods when all the bars have shut have told how he has come so close that he has stunned them with his breath. He shows himself to children, too. They run out of the woods and fields, their punnets empty, their bikes abandoned, with the devil at their tails.

Those foolish ones who stand and stare report his backing gait, his clumsiness. He has the odours of a kennel, plus boiled eggs, scorched hair and sweat, they say. They cannot capture him. He will not talk or give his name. He slips away, enveloped by the unresisting darkness. But first he holds his open sack for them to see and smell the rootless puffballs and the chanterelles, the honey funguses, the magic heads, the ceps, the shagcaps, boletes, morels, the inky dicks, which he will push into the earth that night like unconvincing garden ornaments.

Sometimes they only see his stooping back and watch his white hands coming from his sack.

I, too, have met the devil in the woods. I, too, have seen the mushrooms in his bag, lolling like eviscerated parts, meringues of human tissue, sweetbreads, smelling of placenta and decay. To tell the truth, these mushrooms baffle me. I've eaten them in many of their forms, I've tried the best, but always I am bored by them. The moment that you take them from the earth, they're dull. The moment that you place them in your mouth, they let you down. I've always thought they were expensive and absurd. If they've been planted by the devil, then he is making fun of us.

So I was curious when he and I crossed paths. I followed him. He let me follow him, for he is not afraid of us. He turned his back on me and didn't care. I watched his antics in the night. I watched his white hands and his sack. And I can tell you, he has fooled you yet again. The devil is not emptying his sack, but filling it. He does not plant. He picks, he picks, he picks. That's why his back is bent. He is the one who wants the mushrooms for himself. His greed is stronger than his spite. He thinks the mushrooms are too good for us. We'd not appreciate the poisons or the tangs that they provide, their blasphemies. We are too dull and timid for the magic and the flesh. He roams the woods and meadows when it's dark to satisfy himself. He knows which mushrooms to pull up. The ones he leaves for us are flavourless.

A PALATE
CLEANSER

THE WATERING PLACE

Virginia Woolf

Virginia Woolf (1882–1941) was a key figure in twentieth-century literature. As a novelist, diarist and critic, Woolf was at the centre of the modernist movement. Known for her use of stream-of-consciousness and intensely interior narratives, Woolf's canon is highly respected by readers and critics alike. Alongside her most famous novels, *Mrs. Dalloway* (1925), *To the Lighthouse* (1927) and *The Waves* (1931) and non-fiction works such as *A Room of One's Own* (1929) and the essay "On Being Ill" (1926), Woolf wrote many "sketches" in her diaries. These sketches were often returned to later, as inspiration for scenes in her novels.

"The Watering Place" is thought to be one of the final things Woolf composed before her death in March 1941. The sketch lingers on a snippet of dinner table conversation in a restaurant in a seaside town. The consistent return to the smell of fish that lingers throughout the town is suggestive of the narrator's rapt attentiveness, revulsion, and potential obsession. Smell is often a literary suggestion of foreboding; stenches lingering where they should not frequently implicate the presence of a similarly unwanted—or even contaminative—entity. Food is not consumed on the page; rather the narrator muses about the large quantities of food that must have been eaten before the story begins. Woolf's uncanny gastronomic exists in the shadow of actual food, in the odour that exudes from it and the conversations around it. The ending sentences describing the dark seaside at night heighten the strange power of the water in this town, which is perhaps made bleaker still when one considers the events that lead to Woolf's death.

Like all seaside towns it was pervaded by the smell of fish. The toy shops were full of shells, varnished, hard yet fragile. Even the inhabitants had a shelly look—a frivolous look as if the real animal had been extracted on the point of a pin and only the shell remained. The old men on the parade were shells. Their gaiters, their riding breeches, their spy glasses seemed to make them into toys. They could no more have been real sailors or real sportsmen than the shells stuck onto the rims of photograph frames and looking-glasses could have lain in the depths of the sea. The women too, with their trousers and their little high heeled shoes and their raffia bags and their pearl necklaces seemed shells of real women who go out in the morning to buy household stores.

At one o'clock this frail varnished shell fish population clustered together in the restaurant. The restaurant had a fishy smell, the smell of a smack that has drawn up nets full of sprats and herrings. The consumption of fish in that dining room must have been enormous. The smell pervaded even the room that was marked Ladies on the first landing. This room was separated by a door only into two compartments. On the one side of the door the claims of nature were gratified; and on the other, at the washing table, at the looking-glass, nature was disciplined by art. Three young ladies had reached this second stage of the daily ritual. They were exerting their rights upon improving nature, subduing her, with their powder puffs and little red tablets. As they did so they talked; but their talk was interrupted as by the surge of an indrawing tide; and then the tide withdrew and one was heard saying:

"I never did care about her—the simpering little thing... Bert never did care about big women... Ave you seen him since he's been back?... His eyes... they're so blue... Like pools... Gert's too... Both ave the same eyes... You look down into them... They've both got the same teeth... Are He's got such beautiful white teeth... Gert has em too... But his are a bit crooked... when he smiles..."

The water gushed... The tide foamed and withdrew. It uncovered next: "But he had ought to be more careful. If he's caught doing it, he'll be courtmartialled..." Here came a great gush of water from the next compartment. The tide in the watering place seems to be for ever drawing and withdrawing. It uncovers these little fish; it sluices over them. It withdraws, and there are the fish again, smelling very strong of some queer fishy smell that seems to permeate the whole watering place.

But at night the town looks quite ethereal. There is a white glow on the horizon. There are hoops and coronets in the streets. The town has sunk down into the water. And the skeleton only is picked out in fairy lamps.

DESSERT:
A TASTE FOR
HUMAN FLESH

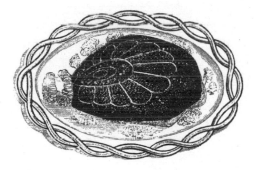

CANNIBALISM IN THE CARS

Mark Twain

Mark Twain (1835–1910)—real name Samuel Langhorne Clemens—was a much-lauded journalist, academic, and writer of non-fiction, stories, and novels. Twain gained renown for his travel writing in works such as *The Innocents Abroad* (1869) and *Life on the Mississippi* (1883). Following his success in travel writing, Twain published several novels, including *The Adventures of Tom Sawyer* (1876) and *Adventures of Huckleberry Finn* (1895), now regarded as classics of children's literature. Twain's writing is known for its wit, dryness, and a strong sense of politics, and for frequently pondering the human grappling with adventure and the supreme power of nature. "Cannibalism in the Cars" first appeared in the November 1868 issue of *The Broadway Annual*, a literary periodical that ran briefly between 1867 and 1868. It was subsequently included in a later collection of Twain's work, *Sketches New and Old* (1875). "Cannibalism in the Cars" is a humorously twisted assessment of the trustworthiness of the anecdote. Twain's approach to the uncanny gastronomic is to endow it with a sense of mystery and suggestion; it exists in the liminal space between exaggerated truth and reality, working to emphasize the power of a well-told story. The tale makes a mockery of grand oratory in the face of genuine danger, deriding the political tendency to use language to obscure grotesque reality. By connecting eating and orality, Twain presents the mouth as the ultimate human locus of power—both as the site of eating and the site of speech.

I visited St. Louis lately, and on my way west, after changing cars at Terre Haute, Indiana, a mild, benevolent-looking gentleman of about forty-five, or may be fifty, came in at one of the way-stations and sat down beside me. We talked together pleasantly on various subjects for an hour, perhaps, and I found him exceedingly intelligent and entertaining. When he learned that I was from Washington, he immediately began to ask questions about various public men, and about Congressional affairs; and I saw very shortly that I was conversing with a man who was perfectly familiar with the ins and outs of political life at the Capital, even to the ways and manners, and customs of procedure of Senators and Representatives in the Chambers of the National Legislature. Presently two men halted near us for a single moment, and one said to the other:

"Harris, if you'll do that for me, I'll never forget you, my boy."

My new comrade's eyes lighted pleasantly. The words had touched upon a happy memory, I thought. Then his face settled into thoughtfulness—almost into gloom. He turned to me and said, "Let me tell you a story; let me give you a secret chapter of my life—a chapter that has never been referred to by me since its events transpired. Listen patiently, and promise that you will not interrupt me."

I said I would not, and he related the following strange adventure, speaking sometimes with animation, sometimes with melancholy, but always with feeling and earnestness.

THE STRANGER'S NARRATIVE

"On the 19th of December, 1853, I started from St. Louis on the evening train bound for Chicago. There were only twenty-four passengers, all told. There were no ladies and no children. We were in excellent spirits, and pleasant acquaintanceships were soon formed. The journey bade fair to be a happy one; and no individual in the party, I think, had even the vaguest presentiment of the horrors we were soon to undergo.

"At 11 P.M. it began to snow hard. Shortly after leaving the small village of Welden, we entered upon that tremendous prairie solitude that stretches its leagues on leagues of houseless dreariness far away towards the Jubilee Settlements. The winds, unobstructed by trees or hills, or even vagrant rocks, whistled fiercely across the level desert, driving the falling snow before it like spray from the crested waves of a stormy sea. The snow was deepening fast; and we knew, by the diminished speed of the train, that the engine was ploughing through it with steadily increasing difficulty. Indeed, it almost came to a dead halt sometimes, in the midst of great drifts that piled themselves like colossal graves across the track. Conversation began to flag. Cheerfulness gave place to grave concern. The possibility of being imprisoned in the snow, on the bleak prairie, fifty miles from any house, presented itself to every mind, and extended its depressing influence over every spirit.

"At two o'clock in the morning I was aroused out of an uneasy slumber by the ceasing of all motion about me. The appalling truth flashed upon me instantly—we were captives in a snowdrift! 'All hands to the rescue!' Every man sprang to obey. Out into the wild night, the pitchy darkness, the billowy snow, the driving storm, every soul leaped, with the consciousness that a moment lost now might bring destruction to us all. Shovels, hands, boards—anything, every-thing that could displace snow, was brought into instant requisition. It was a weird picture, that small company of frantic men fighting the banking snows, half in the blackest shadow and half in the angry light of the locomotive's reflector.

"One short hour sufficed to prove the utter uselessness of our efforts. The storm barricaded the track with a dozen drifts while we dug one away. And worse than this, it was discovered that the last grand charge the engine had made upon the enemy had broken the fore-and-aft shaft of the driving-wheel! With a free track before us we should still have been helpless. We entered the car wearied with labor, and very sorrowful. We gathered about the stoves, and gravely canvassed our situation. We had no provisions whatever—in this lay our chief distress. We could not freeze, for there was a good supply of wood in the tender. This was our only comfort. The discussion ended at last in accepting the disheartening decision of the conductor, viz., that it would be death for any man to attempt to travel fifty miles on foot through snow like that. We could not send for help; and even if we could, it could not come. We must submit, and await, as patiently as we might, succor or starvation! I think the stoutest heart there felt a momentary chill when those words were uttered.

"Within the hour conversation subsided to a low murmur here and there about the car, caught fitfully between the rising and falling of the blast; the lamps grew dim; and the majority of the castaways settled themselves among the flickering shadows to think to forget the present, if they could—to sleep, if they might.

"The eternal night—it surely seemed eternal to us—wore its lagging hours away at last, and the cold grey dawn broke in the east. As the light grew stronger the passengers began to stir and give signs of life, one after another, and each in turn pushed his slouched hat up from his forehead, stretched his stiffened limbs, and glanced out at the windows upon the cheerless prospect. It was cheerless indeed!—not a living thing visible anywhere, not a human habitation; nothing but a vast white desert; uplifted sheets of snow drifting hither and thither before the wind—a world of eddying flakes shutting out the firmament above.

"All day we moped about the cars, saying little, thinking much. Another lingering dreary night—and hunger.

"Another dawning—another day of silence, sadness, wasting hunger, hopeless watching for succor that could not come. A night of restless slumber, filled with dreams of feasting—wakings distressed with the gnawings of hunger.

"The fourth day came and went—and the fifth! Five days of dreadful imprisonment! A savage hunger looked out at every eye. There was in it a sign of awful import—the foreshadowing of a something that was vaguely shaping itself in every heart—a something which no tongue dared yet to frame into words.

"The sixth day passed—the seventh dawned upon as gaunt and haggard and hopeless a company of men as ever stood in the shadow of death. It must out now! That thing which had been growing up in every heart was ready to leap from every lip at last! Nature had been taxed to the utmost—she must yield. RICHARD H. GASTON, of Minnesota, tall, cadaverous, and pale, rose up. All knew what was coming. All prepared—every emotion, every semblance of excitement was smothered—only a calm, thoughtful seriousness appeared in the eyes that were lately so wild.

"'Gentlemen,—It cannot be delayed longer! The time is at hand! We must determine which of us shall die to furnish food for the rest!'

"MR. JOHN J. WILLIAMS, of Illinois, rose and said: 'Gentlemen,—I nominate the Rev. James Sawyer, of Tennessee.'

"MR. WM. R. ADAMS, of Indiana, said: 'I nominate Mr. Daniel Slote, of New York.'

"MR. CHARLES J. LANGDON: 'I nominate Mr. Samuel A. Bowen, of St. Louis.'

"MR. SLOTE: 'Gentlemen,—I desire to decline in favor of Mr. John A. Van Nostrand, Jun., of New Jersey.'

"MR. GASTON: 'If there be no objection, the gentleman's desire will be acceded to.'

"MR. VAN NOSTRAND objecting, the resignation of Mr. Slote was rejected. The resignations of Messrs. Sawyer and Bowen were also offered, and refused upon the same grounds.

"MR. A. L. BASCOM, of Ohio: 'I move that the nominations now close, and that the House proceed to an election by ballot.'

"MR. SAWYER: 'Gentlemen,—I protest earnestly against these proceedings. They are, in every way, irregular and unbecoming. I must beg to move that they be dropped at once, and that we elect a chairman of the meeting and proper officers to assist him, and then we can go on with the business before us understandingly.'

"MR. BELL, of Iowa: 'Gentlemen,—I object. This is no time to stand upon forms and ceremonious observances. For more than seven days we have been without food. Every moment we lose in idle discussion increases our distress. I am satisfied with the nominations that have been made—every gentleman present is, I believe—and I, for one, do not see why we should not proceed at once to elect one or more of them. I wish to offer a resolution—'

"MR. GASTON: 'It would be objected to, and have to lie over one day under the rules, thus bringing about the very delay you wish to avoid. The gentleman from New Jersey—'

"MR. VAN NOSTRAND: 'Gentlemen,—I am a stranger among you; I have not sought the distinction that has been conferred upon me, and I feel a delicacy—'

"MR. MORGAN, of Alabama (interrupting): 'I move the previous question.'

"The motion was carried, and further debate shut off, of course. The motion to elect officers was passed, and under it Mr. Gaston was chosen chairman, Mr. Blake secretary, Messrs. Holcomb, Dyer, and Baldwin, a committee on nominations, and Mr. R. M. Howland, purveyor, to assist the committee in making selections.

"A recess of half an hour was then taken, and some little caucussing followed. At the sound of the gavel the meeting reassembled, and the committee reported in favor of Messrs. George Ferguson, of Kentucky, Lucien Herrman, of Louisiana, and W. Messick, of Colorado, as candidates. The report was accepted.

"MR. ROGERS, of Missouri: 'Mr. President,—The report being properly before the House now, I move to amend it by substituting for the name of Mr. Herman that of Mr. Lucius Harris, of St. Louis, who is well and honorably known to us all. I do not wish to be understood as casting the least reflection upon the high character and standing of the gentleman from Louisiana—far from it. I respect and esteem him as much as any gentleman here present possibly can; but none of us can be blind to the fact that he has lost more flesh during the week that we have lain here than any among us—none of us can be blind to the fact that the committee has been derelict in its duty, either through negligence or a graver fault, in thus offering for our suffrages a gentleman who, however pure his own motives may be, has really less nutriment in him—'

"THE CHAIR: 'The gentleman from Missouri will take his seat. The Chair cannot allow the integrity of the Committee to be questioned save by the regular course, under the rules. What action will the House take upon the gentleman's motion?'

"MR. HALLIDAY, of Virginia: 'I move to further amend the report by substituting Mr. Harvey Davis, of Oregon, for Mr. Messick. It may be urged by gentlemen that the hardships and privations of a frontier life have rendered Mr. Davis tough; but, gentlemen, is this a time to cavil at toughness? is this a time to be fastidious concerning trifles? is this a time to dispute about matters of paltry significance? No, gentlemen, bulk is what we desire—substance, weight, bulk— these are the supreme requisites now—not talent, not genius, not education. I insist upon my motion.'

"MR. MORGAN (excitedly): 'Mr. Chairman,—I do most strenuously object to this amendment. The gentleman from Oregon is old, and furthermore is bulky only in bone—not in flesh. I ask the gentleman from Virginia if it is soup we want instead of solid sustenance? if he would delude us with shadows? if he would mock our suffering with an Oregonian spectre? I ask him if he can look upon the anxious faces around him, if he can gaze into our sad eyes, if he can listen to the beating of our expectant hearts, and still thrust this famine-stricken fraud upon us? I ask him if he can think of our desolate state, of our past sorrows, of our dark future, and still unpityingly foist upon us this wreck, this ruin, this tottering swindle, this gnarled and blighted and sapless vagabond from Oregon's inhospitable shores? Never!' (Applause.)

"The amendment was put to vote, after a fiery debate, and lost. Mr. Harris was substituted on the first amendment. The balloting then began. Five ballots were held without a choice. On the sixth, Mr. Harris was elected, all voting for him but himself. It was then moved that his election should be ratified by acclamation, which was lost, in consequence of his again voting against himself.

"MR. RADWAY moved that the House now take up the remaining candidates, and go into an election for breakfast. This was carried.

"On the first ballot there was a tie, half the members favoring one candidate on account of his youth, and half favoring the other on account of his superior size. The President gave the casting vote for the latter, Mr. Messick. This decision created considerable dissatisfaction among the friends of Mr. Ferguson, the defeated candidate, and there was some talk of demanding a new ballot; but in the midst of it, a motion to adjourn was carried, and the meeting broke up at once.

"The preparations for supper diverted the attention of the Ferguson faction from the discussion of their grievance for a long time, and then, when they would have taken it up again, the happy announcement that Mr. Harris was ready, drove all thought of it to the winds.

"We improvised tables by propping up the backs of car-seats, and sat down with hearts full of gratitude to the finest supper that had blessed our vision for seven torturing days. How changed we were from what we had been a few short hours before! Hopeless, sad-eyed misery, hunger, feverish anxiety, desperation, then—thankfulness, serenity, joy too deep for utterance now. That I know was the cheeriest hour of my eventful life. The wind howled, and blew the snow wildly about our prison-house, but they were powerless to distress us any more. I liked Harris. He might have been better done, perhaps, but I am free to say that no man ever agreed with me better than Harris, or afforded me so large a degree of satisfaction. Messick was very well, though rather high-flavored, but for genuine nutritiousness and delicacy of fibre, give me Harris. Messick had his good points—I will not attempt to deny it, nor do I wish to do it—but he was no more fitted for breakfast than a mummy would be, sir—not a bit. Lean? why, bless me!—and tough? Ah, he was very tough! You could not imagine it,—you could never imagine anything like it."

"Do you mean to tell me that—"

"Do not interrupt me, please. After breakfast we elected a man by the name of Walker, from Detroit, for supper. He was very good. I wrote his wife so afterwards. He was worthy of all praise. I shall always remember Walker. He was a little rare, but very good. And then the next morning we had Morgan, of Alabama, for breakfast. He was one of the finest men I ever sat down to,—handsome educated, refined, spoke several languages fluently—a perfect gentleman—he was a perfect gentleman, and singularly juicy. For supper we had that Oregon patriarch, and he *was* a fraud, there is no question about it—old, scraggy, tough, nobody can picture the reality. I finally said, gentlemen, you can do as you like, but *I* will wait for another election. And Grimes, of Illinois, said, 'Gentlemen, *I* will wait also. When you elect a man that has *something* to recommend him, I shall be glad to join you again.' It soon became evident that there was general dissatisfaction with Davis, of Oregon, and so, to preserve the good-will that had prevailed so pleasantly since we had had Harris, an election was called, and the result of it was that Baker, of Georgia, was chosen. He was splendid! Well, well—after that we had Doolittle and Hawkins, and McElroy (there was some complaint about McElroy, because he was uncommonly short and thin), and Penrod, and two Smiths, and Bailey (Bailey had a wooden leg, which was clear loss, but he was otherwise good), and an Indian boy, and an organ grinder, and a gentleman by the name of Buckminster—a poor stick of a vagabond that wasn't any good for company and no account for breakfast. We were glad we got him elected before relief came."

"And so the blessed relief *did* come at last?"

"Yes, it came one bright, sunny morning, just after election. John Murphy was the choice, and there never was a better, I am willing to testify; but John Murphy came home with us, in the train that came to succor us, and lived to marry the widow Harris—"

"Relict of—"

"Relict of our first choice. He married her, and is happy and respected and prosperous yet. Ah, it was like a novel, sir—it was like a romance. This is my stopping-place, sir; I must bid you good-by. Any time that you can make it convenient to tarry a day or two with me, I shall be glad to have you. I like you, sir; I have conceived an affection for you. I could like you as well as I liked Harris himself, sir. Good day, sir, and a pleasant journey."

He was gone. I never felt so stunned, so distressed, so bewildered in my life. But in my soul I was glad he was gone. With all his gentleness of manner and his soft voice, I shuddered whenever he turned his hungry eye upon me; and when I heard that I had achieved his perilous affection, and that I stood almost with the late Harris in his esteem, my heart fairly stood still!

I was bewildered beyond description. I did not doubt his word; I could not question a single item in a statement so stamped with the earnestness of truth as his; but its dreadful details overpowered me, and threw my thoughts into hopeless confusion. I saw the conductor looking at me. I said, "Who is that man?"

"He was a member of Congress once, and a good one. But he got caught in a snowdrift in the cars, and like to been starved to death. He got so frost-bitten and frozen up generally, and used up for want of something to eat, that he was sick and out of his head two or three months afterwards. He is all right now, only he is a monomaniac, and when he gets on that old subject he never stops till he has eat up that whole car-load of people he talks about. He would have finished the crowd by this time, only he had to get out here. He has got their names as pat as A, B, C. When he gets them all eat up but himself, he always says:—'Then the hour for the usual election for breakfast having arrived, and there being no opposition, I was duly elected, after which, there being no objections offered, I resigned. Thus I am here.'"

I felt inexpressibly relieved to know that I had only been listening to the harmless vagaries of a madman instead of the genuine experiences of a bloodthirsty cannibal.

THE PRICE OF
WIGGINS'S ORGY

Algernon Blackwood

Algernon Blackwood (1869–1951) was—and remains, posthumously—a prolific figure in literary circles. As a journalist, broadcaster, and fiction writer, his interest in the supernatural reached across both written and oral art forms. Blackwood's status as a connoisseur of the literary strange was immortalized upon his return to England when he published his first collection *The Empty House* (1906) and subsequently he began to write full-time. Readers may note the influence of his previous occupations on his work, having worked as a farmer in Canada, in a hotel, and as a reporter in New York. Blackwood's fiction is infused with images of the natural, the strangeness at the heart of the rural, secret sects, and the subversion of the known.

Perhaps combining (and critiquing) his experience of the agricultural and service industries, in "The Price of Wiggins's Orgy" Blackwood positions the restaurant as a strange expanse on which to stage the juxtaposition between frivolity and austerity, of sensory overwhelm, of the curious exposure one might feel whilst dining alone. Whilst Blackwood is known primarily as a writer of ghost stories and mysteries, "The Price of Wiggins's Orgy" (first appearing in Blackwood's 1910 collection, *The Lost Valley and Other Stories*) is a realist tale that considers the routes of wealth, exclusivity and the peaks of excess with grotesque effect. Whilst lacking spirits, wendi-gos, or horned gods, "The Price of Wiggins's Orgy" depicts perhaps a more tangible horror that lurks closer to home. Blackwood's dining room is one of whispered dangers and creeping risks, unnavigable etiquettes, and unexpected role reversals that show the fiendish nature of the food industry.

I t happened to be a Saturday when Samuel Wiggins drew the first cash sum on account of his small legacy—some twenty pounds, ten in gold and ten in notes. It felt in his pocket like a bottled-up prolongation of life. Never before had he seen so many dreams within practical reach. It produced in him a kind of high and elusive exaltation of the spirit. From time to time he put his hand down to make the notes crackle and let his fingers play through the running sovereigns as children play through sand.

For twenty years he had been secretary to a philanthropist interested in feeding—feeding the poor. Soup kitchens had been the keynote of those twenty years, the distribution of victuals his sole objective. And now he had his reward—a legacy of £100 a year for the balance of his days.

To him it was riches. He wore a shortish frock-coat, a low, spreading collar, a black made-up tie, and boots with elastic sides. On this particular day he wore also a new pair of rather bright yellow leather gloves. He was unmarried, over forty, bald, plump in the body, and possessed of a simple and emotional heart almost childlike. His brown eyes shone in a face that was wrinkled and dusty—all his dreams driven inwards by the long years of uninspired toil for another.

For the first time in his life, released from the dingy purlieus of soup kitchens and the like, he wandered towards evening among the gay and lighted streets of the "West End"—Piccadilly Circus where the flaming lamps positively hurt the eyes, and Leicester Square. It was bewildering and delightful, this freedom. It went to his head. Yet he ought to have known better.

"I'm going to dine at a restaurant tonight, by Jove," he said to himself, thinking of the gloomy boarding-house where he usually sat between a missionary and a typewriter. He fingered his money. "I'm going to celebrate my legacy. I've earned it." The thought of a motor-car flashed absurdly through his mind; it was followed by another: a holiday in Spain, Italy, Hungary—one of those sunny countries where music was cheap, in the open air, and of the romantic kind he loved. These thoughts show the kind of exaltation that possessed him.

"It's nearly, though not quite, £2 a week," he repeated to himself for the fiftieth time, reflecting upon his legacy. "I simply can't believe it!"

After indecision that threatened to be endless, he turned at length through the swinging glass doors of a big and rather gorgeous restaurant. Only once before in his life had he dined at a big London restaurant—a Railway Hotel! Passing with some hesitation through the gaudy *café* where a number of foreigners sat drinking at little marble tables, he entered the main dining-room, long, lofty, and already thronged. Here the light and noise and movement dazed him considerably, and for the life of him he could not decide upon a table. The people all looked so prosperous and important; the waiters so like gentlemen in evening dress—the kind that came to the philanthropist's table. The roar of voices, eating, knives and forks, rose about him and filled him with a certain dismay. It was all rather overwhelming.

"I should have liked a smaller place better," he murmured, "but still—" And again he fingered his money to gain confidence.

The choice of a table was intimidating, for he was absurdly retiring, was Wiggins; more at home with papers and the reports of philanthropic societies; his holidays spent in a boarding-house at Worthing with his sister and her invalid husband. Then relief came in the form of a sub-head waiter who, spying his helplessness, inquired with a bland grandeur of manner if he "looked perhaps for some one?"

"Oh, a table, thanks, only a table—"

The man, washing his hands in mid-air, swept down the crowded aisles and found one without the least difficulty. It emerged from nowhere so easily that Wiggins felt he had been a fool not to discover it alone. He wondered if he ought to tip the man half-a-crown now or later, but, before he could decide, another occupied his place, bland and smiling, with black eyes and plush-like hair, bending low before him and holding out a large pink programme.

He examined it, feeling that he ought to order dishes with outlandish names just to show that he knew his way about. Before he could steady his eye upon a single line, however, a third waiter, very youthful, suggested in broken English that Wiggins should leave his hat, coat and umbrella elsewhere. This he did willingly, though without grace or dispatch, for the yellow gloves stuck ridiculously to his hands. Then he sat down and turned to the menu again.

It was a very ordinary restaurant really, in spite of the vast height of the gilded ceiling, the scale of its sham magnificence and the excessive glitter of its hundred lights. The menu, disguised by various expensive and *recherché* dishes (which when ordered were invariably found to be "off"), was even more ordinary than the hall. But to the dazed Wiggins the words looked like a series of death-sentences printed in different languages, but all meaning the same thing: *order me—or die!* That waiter standing over him was the executioner. Unless he speedily ordered something really worth the proprietor's while to provide, the head waiter would be summoned and he, Wiggins, would be beheaded. Those stars against certain cheap dishes meant that they could only be ordered by privileged persons, and those crosses—

"This is *vairy* nice this sevening, sir," said the waiter, suddenly bending and pointing with a dirty finger to a dish that Wiggins found buried in a list uncommonly like "Voluntary Subscriptions" in his reports. It was entitled "Lancashire Hot-Pot... 2/0"—two shillings, not two pounds, as he first imagined! He leaped at it.

"Yes, thanks; that'll do, then—for tonight," he said, and the waiter ambled away indifferently, looking all round the room in search of sympathy.

By degrees, however, the other recovered his self-possession, and realized that to spend his legacy on mere Hot-Pot was to admit he knew not the values of life. He called the plush-headed waiter back and with a rush of words ordered some oysters, soup, a fried sole, and half a partridge to follow.

"Then ze 'Ot-Pot, sir?" queried the man, with respect.

"I'll see about that later."

For he was already wondering what he should drink, knowing nothing of wines and vintages. At luncheon with the philanthropist he sometimes had a glass of sherry; at Worthing with his sister he drank beer. But now he wanted something really good, something generous that would help him to celebrate. He would have ordered champagne as a conciliation to the waiter, now positively obsequious, but some one had told him once that there was not enough champagne in the world to go round, and that hotels and restaurants were supplied with "something rather bad." Burgundy, he felt, would be more the thing—rich, sunny, full-bodied.

He studied the wine-card till his head swam. A waiter, while he was thus engaged, sidled up and watched him from an angle. Wiggins, looking up distractedly at the same moment, caught his eye. Whew! It was the Head Waiter himself, a man of quite infinite presence, who at once bowed himself forward, and with a gentle but commanding manner drew his attention to the wines he could "especially recommend." Something in the man's face struck him momentarily as familiar—vaguely familiar—then passed.

Now Wiggins, as has been said, did not know one wine from another; but the spirit of his foolish pose fairly had him by the throat at last, and each time this condescending individual indicated a new vintage he shook his head knowingly and shrugged his shoulders with the air of a connoisseur. This pantomime continued for several minutes.

"Something *really* good, you know," he mumbled after a while, determined to justify himself in the eyes of this high official who was taking such pains. "A rare wine—er—with body in it." Then he added, with a sudden impulse of confidence, "It's Saturday night, remember!" And he smiled knowingly, making a gesture that a man of the world was meant to understand.

Why he should have said this remains a mystery. Perhaps it was a semi-apologetic reference to the supposed habit of men to indulge themselves on a Saturday because they need not rise early to work next day. Perhaps it was meant in some way to excuse all the trouble he was giving. In any case, there can be no question that the manner of the Head Waiter instantly changed in a subtle way difficult to describe, and from mere official politeness passed into deferential attention. He bowed slightly. He increased his distance by an inch or two. Wiggins, noticing it and slightly bewildered, repeated his remark, for want of something to say more than anything else. "It's

Saturday night, of course," he repeated, murmuring, yet putting more meaning into the words than they could reasonably hold.

"As Monsieur says," the man replied, with a marked respect in his tone not there before; "and we—close early."

"Of course," said the other, gaining confidence pleasantly, "you close early."

He had quite forgotten the fact, even if he ever knew it, but he spoke with decision. Glancing up from the wine-list, he caught the man's eye; then instantly lowered his gaze, for the Head Waiter was staring at him in a fixed and curious manner that seemed unnecessary. And once again that passing touch of familiarity appeared upon the features and was gone.

"Monsieur is here for the first time, if I may ask?" came next.

"Er—yes, I am," he replied, thinking all this attention a trifle excessive.

"Ah, *pardon*, of course, I understand," the Head Waiter added softly. "A new—a recent member, then—?"

A little non-plussed, a little puzzled, Wiggins agreed with a nod of the head. He did not know that head waiters referred to customers as "members." For an instant it occurred to him that possibly he was being mistaken for somebody else. It was really—but at that moment the oysters arrived. The Head Waiter said something in rapid Italian to his subordinate—something that obviously increased that plush-headed person's desire to please—bent over with his best manner to murmur, "And I will get monsieur the wine he will like, the right kind of wine!"—and was gone.

It was a new and delightful sensation. Wiggins, feeling proud, pleased and important under the effect of this excellent service and attention, turned to his oysters. The wine would come presently. And, meanwhile, the music had begun...

II

He began to enjoy himself thoroughly, and the wine—still, fragrant, soft—soon ran in his veins and drove out the last vestige of his absurd shyness. Behind the palm trees, somewhere out of sight, the orchestra played soothingly, and if the selections were somewhat bizarre it made no difference to him. He drank in the sound just as he drank in the wine—eagerly. Both fed the consciousness that he was enjoying himself, and the Danse Macabre gave him as much pleasure as did the Bohème, the Strauss Waltz, or Donizetti. Everything—wine, music, food, people—served to intensify his interest *in himself.* He examined his face in the big mirrors and realized what a dog he was and what a good time he was having. He watched the other customers, finding them splendid and distinguished. The whole place was really fine—he would come again and again, always ordering the same wine, for it was certainly an unusual wine, as the Head Waiter had called it, "the right kind." The price of it he never asked, for in his pocket lay the price of a whole case. His hand slipped down to finger the sovereigns—hot and slippery now—and the notes, somewhat moist and crumpled... The needles of the big staring clock meanwhile swung onwards...

Thus, aided by the tactful and occasional superintendence of the Head Waiter from a distance, the evening passed along in a happy rush of pleasurable emotion. The half-partridge had vanished, and Wiggins, toyed now with a wonderful-looking "sweet"—the most expensive he could find. He did not eat much of it, but liked to see it on his plate. The wine helped things enormously. He had ordered another half-bottle some time ago, delighted to find that it exhilarated without confusing him. And every one else in the place was enjoying himself in the same way. He was thrilled to discover this.

Only one thing jarred a little. A very big man, with a round, clean-shaven face inclined to fatness, stared at him more than he cared about from a table in the corner diagonally across the room. He had only come in half-an-hour ago. His face was somehow or other dog-like—something between a boar-hound and a pup, Wiggins thought. Each time he looked up the fellow's large and rather fierce eyes were fixed upon him, then lingeringly withdrawn. It was unpleasant to be stared at in this way by an offensive physiognomy.

But most of the time he was too full of personal visions conjured up by the wine to trouble long about external matters. His head was simply brimming over with thoughts and ideas—about himself, about soup-kitchens, feeding the poor, the change of life effected by the legacy, and a thousand other details. Once or twice, however, in sharp, clear moments when the tide of alcohol ebbed a little, other questions assailed him: Why should the Head Waiter have become so obsequious and attentive? What was it in his face that seemed familiar? What was there about the remark "It's Saturday evening" to change his manner? And—what was it about the dinner, the restaurant and the music that seemed just a little out of the ordinary?

Or was he merely thinking nonsense? And was it his imagination that this man stared so oddly? The alcohol rushed deliciously in his veins.

The vague uneasiness, however, was a passing matter, for the orchestra was tearing madly through a Csardas, and his thoughts and feelings were swept away in the wild rhythm. He drank his bottle out and ordered another. Was it the second or the third? He could not remember. Counting always made his head ache. He did not care anyhow. "Let 'er go! I'm enjoying myself! I've got a fat legacy—money lying in the bank—money I haven't earned!" The carefulness of years was destroyed in as many minutes. "That music's simply spiffing!"

Then he glanced up and caught the clean-shaven face bearing

down upon him across the shimmering room like the muzzle of a moving gun. He tried to meet it, but found he could not focus it properly. The same moment he saw that he was mistaken; the man was merely staring at him. Two faces swam and wobbled into one. This movement, and the appearance of coming towards him, were both illusions produced by the alcohol. He drank another glass quickly to steady his vision—and then another...

"I'll call for my bill. Itshtime to go...!" he murmured aloud later, with a very deep sigh. He looked about him for the waiter, who instantly appeared—with coffee and liqueurs, however.

"Dear me, yes. Qui' forgot I or'ered those," he observed offhand, smiling in the man's face, willing and anxious to say a lot of things, but not quite certain what.

"My bill," was what he said finally, "mush b'off!"

The waiter laughed pleasantly, but very politely, in reply. Wiggins repeated his remark about his bill.

"Oh, that will be all right, sir," returned the man, as though no such thing as payment was ever heard of in *this* restaurant. It was rather confusing. Wiggins laughed to himself, drank his liqueur and forgot about everything except the ballet music of Delibes the strings were sprinkling in a silver shower about the hall. His mind ran after them through the glittering air.

"Just fancy if I could catch 'em and take 'em home in a bunch," he said to himself, immensely pleased. He was enjoying himself hugely by now.

And then, suddenly, he became aware that the place was rapidly thinning, lights being lowered, good-nights being said, and that everybody seemed—drunk.

"P'rapsh they've all got legacies!" he thought, flushing with excitement.

He rose unsteadily to his feet and was delighted to find that *he* was not in the least—drunk. He at once respected himself.

"Itsh really 'sgusting that fellows can't stop when they've had 'nough!" he murmured, making his way with steps that required great determination towards the door, and remembering before he got halfway that he had not paid his bill. Turning in a half-circle that brought an unnecessary quantity of the room round with him, he made his way back, lost his way, fumbled about in the increasing gloom, and found himself face to face with the—Head Waiter. The unexpected meeting braced him astonishingly. The dignity of the man had curiously increased.

"I'm looking for my bill," observed Wiggins thickly, wondering for the twentieth time of whom the man's face reminded him; "you haven't seen it about anywhere, I shuppose?" He sat down with more dignity than he could have supposed possible and produced a £5 note from his pocket, the lining of the pocket coming out with it like a dirty glove.

Most of the guests had gone out by this time, and the big hall was very dark. Two lights only remained, and these, reflected from mirror to mirror, made its proportions seem vast and unreal. They flew from place to place, too, distressingly—these lights.

"Half-a-crown will settle that, sir," replied the man, with a respectful bow.

"Nonshense!" replied the other. "Why, I ordered Lancashire hotch-potch, grilled shole, a—a bird or something of the kind, and the wine—"

"I beg your pardon, sir, but—if you will permit me to say so—the others will soon be here now, and—as there will be a specially large attendance, perhaps you would like to make sure of your place." He pocketed the half-crown with a bow, pointed to the far, dim corner of the room, and stepped aside a little to make space for Wiggins to pass.

And Wiggins did pass—though it is not quite clear how he managed to dodge the flying tables. With deep sighs, hot, confused and puzzled, but too obfuscated to understand what it was all about, he obeyed the directions, at the same time wondering uneasily how it was he had forgotten what was a-foot. He wandered towards the end of the hall with the uncertainty of a butterfly that makes many feints before it settles... At a vast distance off the Head Waiter was moving to close the main doors, utterly oblivious now of his existence. He felt glad of that. Something about that fellow was disagreeable—downright nasty. This suddenly came over him with a flood of conviction. The man was more than peculiar: he was sinister... The air smelt horribly of cooked food, tobacco smoke, breathing crowds, scented women and the rest. Whiffs of it, hot and foetid, brought him a little to his senses... Then suddenly he noticed that the big man with the face that was dark and smooth like the muzzle of a cannon, was watching him keenly from a table on the other side where an electric light still burned.

"By George! There he is again, that feller! Wonder whatsh he's smiling at me for. Looking for'sh bill too, p'raps—Now, in a Soup Kishen nothing of the kind—"

He bowed in return, smiling insolently, holding himself steady by a chair to do so. He shoved and stumbled his way on into the shadows, half-mingling with the throng passing out into the street. Then, making a sharp turn back into the room unobserved, he took a few uncertain steps and collapsed silently and helplessly upon a chair that was hidden behind a big palm-tree in a dark corner.

And the last thing he remembered as he sank, boneless, like soft hay, into that corner was that the sham palm-tree bowed towards him, then ran off into the ceiling, and from that elevation, which in no way diminished its size, bowed to him yet again...

It was just after his eyes closed that the door in the gilt panelling at the end of the room softly opened and a woman entered on tiptoe. She was followed by other women and several girls; these, again, from time to time, by men, all dressed in black, all silent, and all ushered by the majestic Head Waiter to their places. The big man with the face like a gun-muzzle superintended. And each individual, on entering, was held there at the secret doorway until a certain sentence had passed his lips. Evidently a password: "It is Saturday night," said the one being admitted, "and we close early," replied the Head Waiter and the big man. And then the door was closed until the next soft tapping came.

But Wiggins, plunged in the stupor of the first sleep, knew none of all this. His frock-coat was bunched about his neck, his black tie under his ear, his feet resting higher than his head. He looked like a collapsed air-ship in a hedge, and he snored heavily.

III

It was about an hour later when he opened his eyes, climbed painfully and heavily to his feet, staggered back against the wall utterly bewildered—and stared. At the far end of the great hall, its loftiness now dim, was a group of people. The big mirrors on all sides reflected them with the effect of increasing their numbers indefinitely. They stood and sat upon an improvised platform. The electric lights, shaded with black, dropped a pale glitter upon their faces. They were systematically grouped, the big man in the centre, the Head Waiter at a small table just behind him. The former was speaking in low, measured tones.

In his dark and distant corner Wiggins first of all seized the carafe and quenched his feverish thirst. Next he advanced slowly and with the utmost caution to a point nearer the group where he could hear what was being said. He was still a good deal confused in mind, and had no idea what the hour was or what he had been doing in the meantime. There were some twenty or thirty people, he saw, of both sexes, well dressed, many of them distinguished in appearance, and all wearing black; even their gloves were black; some of the women, too, wore black veils—very thick. But in all the faces without exception there was something—was it about the lips and mouths?—that was peculiar and—repellent.

Obviously this was a meeting of some kind. Some society had hired the hall for a private gathering. Wiggins, understanding this, began to feel awkward. He did not wish to intrude; he had no right to listen; yet to make himself known was to betray that he was still very considerably intoxicated. The problem presented itself in these simple terms to his dazed intelligence. He was also aware of another fact: about these black-robed people there was something which made him secretly and horribly—afraid.

The big man with the smooth face like a gun-muzzle sat down after a softly-uttered speech, and the group, instead of applauding with their hands, waved black handkerchiefs. The fluttering sound of them trickled along the wastes of hall towards the concealed eavesdropper. Then the Head Waiter rose to introduce the next speaker, and the instant Wiggins saw him he understood what it was in his face that was familiar. For the false beard no longer adorned his lips, the wig that altered the shape of his forehead and the appearance of his eyes had been removed, and the likeness he bore to the philanthropist, Wiggins's late employer, was too remarkable to be ignored. Wiggins just repressed a cry, but a low gasp apparently did escape him, for several members of the group turned their heads in his direction and stared.

The Head Waiter, meanwhile, saved him from immediate discovery by beginning to speak. The words were plainly audible, and the resemblance of the voice to that other voice he knew now to be stopped with dust, was one of the most dreadful experiences he had ever known. Each word, each trick of expression came as a new and separate shock.

"... and the learned Doctor will say a few words upon the *rationale* of our subject," he concluded, turning with a graceful bow to make room for a distinguished-looking old gentleman who advanced shambling from the back of the improvised platform.

What Wiggins then heard—in somewhat disjointed sentences owing to the buzzing in his ears—was at first apparently meaningless. Yet it was freighted, he knew, with a creeping and sensational horror that would fully reveal itself the instant he discovered the clue. The old clever-faced scoundrel was saying vile things. He knew it. But the key to the puzzle being missing, he could not quite guess what it was all about. The Doctor, gravely and with balanced phrases, seemed to be speaking of the fads of the day with regard to food and feeding. He ridiculed vegetarianism, and all the other *isms*. He said that one and all were based upon ignorance and fallacy, declaring that the time had at last come in the history of the race when a rational system of feeding was a paramount necessity. The physical and psychical conditions of the times demanded it, and the soul of man could never be emancipated until it was adopted. He himself was proud to be one of the founders of their audacious and secret Society, revolutionary and pioneer in the best sense, to which so many of the medical fraternity now belonged, and so many of the brave women too, who were in the van of the feminist movements of the times. He said a great deal in this vein. Wiggins, listening in growing amazement and uneasiness, waited for the clue to it all.

In conclusion, the speaker referred solemnly to the fact that there was a stream of force in their Society which laid them open to the melancholy charge of being called "hysterical." "But after all," he cried, with rising enthusiasm and in accents that rang down the hall, "a Society without hysteria is a dull Society, just as a woman without hysteria is a dull woman. Neither the Society nor the woman need yield to the tendency; but that it is present potentially infers the faculty, so delicious in the eyes of all sane men—the faculty of running to extremes. It is a sign of life, and of very vivid life. It is not for nothing, dear friends, that we are named the—" But the buzzing in Wiggins's ears was so loud at this moment that he missed the name. It sounded to him something between "Can-I-believes" and "Camels," but for the life of him he could not overtake the actual word. The Doctor had uttered it, moreover, in a lowered voice—a suddenly lowered voice... When the noise in his ears had passed he heard the speaker bring his address to an end in these words: "... and I will now ask the secretaries to make their reports from their various sections, after which, I understand"—his tone grew suddenly thick and clouded—"we are to be regaled with a collation—a sacramental collation—of the usual kind..." His voice hushed away to nothing. His mouth was working most curiously. A wave of excitement unquestionably ran over the faces of the others. Their mouths also worked oddly. Dark and sombre things were afoot in that hall.

Wiggins crouched a little lower behind the edge of the overhanging table-cloth and listened. He was perspiring now, but there were touches of icy horror, fingering about in the neighbourhood of his heart. His mental and physical discomfort were very great, for the conviction that he was about to witness some dreadful scene—black as the garments of the participants in it—grew rapidly within him. He devised endless plans for escape, only to reject them the instant they were formed. There was no escape possible. He had to wait till the end.

A charming young woman was on her feet, addressing the audience in silvery tones; sweet and comely she was, her beauty only marred by that singular leer that visited the lips and mouths of all of them. The flesh of his back began to crawl as he listened. He would have given his whole year's legacy to be out of it, for behind that voice of silver and sweetness there crowded even to her lips the rush of something that was unutterable—loathsome. Wiggins felt it. The uncertainty as to its exact nature only added to his horror and distress.

"... so this question of supply, my friends," she was saying, "is becoming more and more difficult. It resolves itself into a question of ways and means." She looked round upon her audience with a touch of nervous apprehension before she continued. "In my particular sphere of operations—West Kensington—I have regretfully to report that the suspicions and activity of the police, the foolish, old-fashioned police, have now rendered my monthly contributions no longer possible. There have been too many disappearances of late—" She paused, casting her eyes down. Wiggins felt his hair rise, drawn by a shivery wind. The words "contributions" and "disappearances" brought with them something quite freezing.

"... As you know," the girl resumed, "it is to the doctors that we must look chiefly for our steadier supplies, and unfortunately in my sphere of operations we have but one doctor who is a member... I do not like to—to resign my position, but I must ask for lenient consideration of my failure"—her voice sank lower still—"... my failure to furnish tonight the materials—" She began to stammer and hesitate dreadfully; her voice shook; an ashen pallor spread to her very lips. "… the elements for our customary feast—"

A movement of disapproval ran over the audience like a wave; murmurs of dissent and resentment were heard. As the girl paled more perceptibly the singular beauty of her face stood out with an effect of almost shining against that dark background of shadows and black garments. In spite of himself, and forgetting caution for the moment, Wiggins peeped over the edge of the table to see her better. She was a lady, he saw, high-bred and spirited. That pallor, and the timidity it bespoke, was but evidence of a highly sensitive nature facing a situation of peculiar difficulty—and danger. He read in her attitude, in the poise of that slim figure standing there before disapproval and possible disaster, the bearing and proud courage of a type that would face execution with calmness and dignity. Wiggins was amazed that this thought should flash through him so vividly—from nowhere. Born of the feverish aftermath of alcohol, perhaps—yet born inevitably, too, of this situation before his eyes.

With a thrill he realized that the girl was speaking again, her voice steady, but faint with the gravity of her awful position.

"… and I ask for that justice in consideration of my failure which—the difficulties of the position demand. I have had to choose between that bold and ill-considered action which might have betrayed us all to the authorities, and—the risk of providing nothing for tonight."

She sat down. Wiggins understood that it was a question of life and death. The air about him turned icy. He felt the perspiration trickling on several different parts of his body at once.

An old lady rose instantly to reply; her face was stern and dreadful, although the signature of breeding and culture was plainly there in the delicate lines about the nostrils and forehead. Her mien held something implacable. She was dressed in black silk that rustled, and she was certainly well over sixty; but what made Wiggins squirm there in his narrow hiding-place was the extraordinary resemblance she bore to Mrs. Sturgis, the superintendent of one of his late employer's soup kitchens. It was all diabolically grotesque. She glanced round upon the group of members, who clearly regarded her as a leader. The machinery of the whole dreadful scene then moved quicker.

"Then are we to understand from the West Kensington secretary," she began in firm, even tones, "that for tonight there is—nothing?" The young girl bowed her head without rising from her chair.

"I beg to move, then, Mr. Chairman," continued the terrible old lady in iron accents, "that the customary procedure be followed, and that a Committee of Three be appointed to carry it into immediate effect." The words fell like bomb-shells into the deserted spaces of the hall.

"I second the motion," was heard in a man's voice.

"Those in favour of the motion will show their hands," announced the big chairman with the clean-shaven face.

Several score of black-gloved hands waved in the air, with the effect of plumes upon a jolting hearse.

"And those who oppose it?"

No single hand was raised. An appalling hush fell upon the group.

"I appoint Signor Carnamorte as chairman of the sub-committee, with power to choose his associates," said the big man. And the "Head Waiter" bowed his acceptance of the duty imposed upon him. There was at once then a sign of hurried movement, and the figure of the young girl was lost momentarily to view as several members surged round her. The next instant they fell away and she stood clear, her hands bound. Her voice, soft as before but very faint, was audible through the hush.

"I claim the privilege belonging to the female members of the Society," she said calmly; "the right to find, if possible, a substitute."

"Granted," answered the chairman gravely. "The customary ten minutes will be allowed you in which to do so. Meanwhile, the preparations must proceed in the usual way."

With a dread that ate all other emotions, Wiggins watched keenly from his concealment, and the preparations that he saw in progress, though simple enough in themselves, filled him with a sense of ultimate horror that was freezing. The Committee of Three were very busy with something at the back of the improvised platform, something that was heavy and, on being touched, emitted a metallic and sonorous ring. As in the strangling terror and heat of nightmare the full meaning of events is often kept concealed until the climax, so Wiggins knew that this simple sound portended something that would only be revealed to him later—something appalling as Satan—sinister as the grave. That ring of metal was the Gong of Death. He heard it in his own heart, and the shock was so great that he could not prevent an actual physical movement. His jerking leg drove sharply against a chair. The chair—squeaked.

The sound pierced the deep silence of the big hall with so shrill a note that of course everybody heard it. Wiggins, expecting to have the whole crew of these black-robed people about his ears, held his breath in an agony of suspense. All those pairs of eyes, he felt, were searching the spot where he lay so thinly hidden by the table-cloth. But no steps came towards him. A voice, however, spoke: the voice of the girl: she had heard the sound and had divined its cause.

"Loosen my bonds," she cried, "for there is some one yonder among the shadows. I have found a substitute! And—I swear to Heaven—*he is plump!*"

The sentence was so extraordinary, that Wiggins felt a spring of secret merriment touched somewhere deep within him, and a gush of uncontrollable laughter came up in his throat so suddenly that before he could get his hand to his mouth, it rang down the long dim hall and betrayed him beyond all question of escape. Behind it lay the strange need of violent expression. He had to do something. The life of this slender and exquisite girl was in danger. And the nightmare strain of the whole scene, the hints and innuendoes of a dark purpose, the implacable nature of the decree that threatened so fair a life—all resulted in a pressure that was too much for him. Had he not laughed, he would certainly have shrieked aloud. And the next minute he did shriek aloud. The screams followed his laughter with a dreadful clamour, and at the same instant he staggered noisily to his feet and rose into full view from behind the table. Everybody then saw him.

Across the length of that dimly-lighted hall he faced the group of people in all their hideous reality, and what he saw cleared from his fuddled brain the last fumes of the alcohol. The white visage of each member seemed already close upon him. He saw the glimmering pallor of their skins against the black clothes, the eyes ashine, the mouths working, fingers pointing at him. There was the Head Waiter, more than ever like the dead philanthropist whose life had been spent in feeding others; there the odious smooth face of the big chairman; there the stern-lipped old lady who demanded the sentence of death. The whole silent crew of them stared darkly at him, and in front of them, like some fair lily growing amid decay, stood the girl with the proud and pallid face, calm and self-controlled. Immediately beyond her, a little to one side, Wiggins next perceived the huge iron cauldron, already swinging from its mighty tripod, waiting to receive her into its capacious jaws. Beneath it gleamed and flickered the flames from a dozen spirit-lamps.

"My substitute!" rang out her clear voice. "My substitute! Unloose my hands! And seize him before he can escape!"

"He cannot escape!" cried a dozen angry voices.

"In darkness!" thundered the chairman, and at the same moment every light was extinguished from the switchboard—every light but one. The bulb immediately behind him in the wall was left burning.

And the crew were upon him, coming swiftly and stealthily down the empty aisles between the tables. He saw their forms advance and shift by the gleam of the lamps beneath the awful cauldron. With the advance came, too, the sound of rushing, eager breathing. He imagined, though he could not see, those evil mouths a-working. And at this moment the subconscious part of him that had kept the secret all this time, suddenly revealed in letters of flame the name of the Society which fifteen minutes before he had failed to catch. The subconscious self, that supreme stage manager, that arch conspirator, rose and struck him in the face as it were out of the darkness, so that he understood, with a shock of nauseous terror, the terrible nature of the net in which he was caught.

For this Secret Society, meeting for their awful rites in a great public restaurant of mid-London, were maniacs of a rare and singular description—vilely mad on one point but sane on all the rest. They were Cannibals!

Never before had he run with such speed, agility and recklessness; never before had he guessed that he could leap tables, clear chairs with the flying manner of a hurdle race, and dodge palms and flower-pots as an athlete of twenty dodges collisions in the football field. But in each dark corner where he sought a temporary refuge, the electric light on the wall above immediately sprang into brilliance, one of the crew having remained by the switchboard to control this diabolically ingenious method of keeping him ever in sight.

For a long time, however, he evaded his crowding and clumsy pursuers. It was a vile and ghastly chase. His flying frock-coat streamed out behind him, and he felt the elastic side of his worn boots split under the unusual strain of the twisting, turning ankles as he leaped and ran. His pursuers, it seemed, sought to prolong the hunt on purpose. The passion of the chase was in their blood. Round and round that hall, up and down, over tables and under chairs, behind screens, shaking the handles of doors—all immovable, past gleaming dish-covers on the wheeled joint-tables, taking cover by swing doors, curtains, palms, everything and anything, Wiggins flew for his life from the pursuing forces of a horrible death.

And at last they caught him. Breathless and exhausted, he collapsed backwards against the wall in a dark corner. But the light instantly flashed out above him. He lay in full view, and in another second the advancing horde—he saw their eyes and mouths so close—would be upon him, when something utterly unexpected happened: his head in falling struck against a hard projecting substance and—a bell rang sharply out. It was a telephone!

How he ever managed to get the receiver to his lips, or why the answering exchange came so swiftly he does not pretend to know. He had just time to shout, "Help! help! Send police X... Restaurant! Murder! Cannibals!" when he was seized violently by the collar, his arms and legs grasped by a dozen pairs of hands, and a struggle began that he knew from the start must prove hopeless.

The fact that help might be on the way, however, gave him courage. Wiggins smashed right and left, screamed, kicked, bit and butted. His frock-coat was ripped from his back with a whistling tear of cloth and lining, and he found himself free at the edge of a group that clawed and beat everywhere about him. The dim light was now in his favour. He shot down the hall again like a hare, leaping tables on the way, and flinging dish-covers, carafes, menus at the pursuing crowd as fast as he could lay hands upon them.

Then came a veritable pandemonium of smashed glass and crockery, while a grip of iron caught his arms behind and pinioned them beyond all possibility of moving. Turning quickly, he found himself looking straight into the eyes of a big blue policeman, the door into the street open beside him. The crowd became at once inextricably mixed up and jumbled together. The chairman, and the girl who was to have been eaten, melted into a single person. The philanthropist and the old lady slid into each other. It was a horrible bit of confusion. He felt deadly sick and dizzy. Everything dropped away from his sight then, and darkness tore up round him from the carpet. He remembered nothing more for a long time.

Perhaps the most vivid recollection of what occurred afterwards—he remembers it to this day, and his memory may be trusted, for he never touched wine again—was the weary smile of the magistrate, and the still more weary voice as he said in the court two days later—

"Forty shillings, and be bound over to keep the peace in two sureties for six months. And £5 to the proprietor of the restaurant to pay damages for the broken windows and crockery. Next case...!"

A MADMAN'S DIARY

Lu Xun

Lu Xun (1881–1936), also known as Lu Hsun and Zhou Shuren, was an influential figure in Chinese literature. As a writer and critic, Lu Xun is celebrated as one of the most important cultural commentators of twentieth-century China, known by some as the Father of Modern Chinese Literature.

"A Madman's Diary" (also translated as "Diary of a Madman") was first published as *"Kuangren riji"* in 1918, and was later collected in *Nahan (Call to Arms)* in 1923. The story is heavily inspired by Nikolay Gogol's *"Zapisiki summashedshego"* (1835) a tale of a fictional clerk whose title also translates into "Diary of a Madman". The story—framed through the contents of a diary left behind by the brother of our narrator's friend—exists in the conflicting realities of being the single owner of dangerous knowledge or being caught in the throes of obsessive paranoia. The text's visceral and grotesque descriptions of eating are heightened by the brother-writer's fears of an illicit conspiracy among the "green-faced, long-toothed people" of his community.

The tone of "A Madman's Diary" is thought to be largely influenced by Lu Xun's own growing disillusionment with the structures and conflicts within contemporary Chinese society. In 1926, Lu Xun left his home in Beijing, settling in Shanghai due to political unrest. In Shanghai, Lu Xun became acquainted with the ideas of Marxism and became heavily interested in penning his own political works. Due to its framing device and suggestion of unreliable narration, "A Madman's Diary" becomes an intriguing read to pair with Twain's similarly critical "Cannibalism in the Cars". The translation used here is by Yang Xianyi & Gladys Yang from the Foreign Languages Press edition of *Selected Stories of Lu Hsun*, published in 1960.

Two brothers, whose names I need not mention here, were both good friends of mine in high school; but after a separation of many years we gradually lost touch. Some time ago I happened to hear that one of them was seriously ill, and since I was going back to my old home I broke my journey to call on them, I saw only one, however, who told me that the invalid was his younger brother.

"I appreciate your coming such a long way to see us," he said, "but my brother recovered some time ago and has gone elsewhere to take up an official post." Then, laughing, he produced two volumes of his brother's diary, saying that from these the nature of his past illness could be seen, and that there was no harm in showing them to an old friend. I took the diary away, read it through, and found that he had suffered from a form of persecution complex. The writing was most confused and incoherent, and he had made many wild statements; moreover he had omitted to give any dates, so that only by the colour of the ink and the differences in the writing could one tell that it was not written at one time. Certain sections, however, were not altogether disconnected, and I have copied out a part to serve as a subject for medical research. I have not altered a single illogicality in the diary and have changed only the names, even though the people referred to are all country folk, unknown to the world and of no consequence. As for the title, it was chosen by the diarist himself after his recovery, and I did not change it.

I

Tonight the moon is very bright.

I have not seen it for over thirty years, so today when I saw it I felt in unusually high spirits. I begin to realize that during the past thirty-odd years I have been in the dark; but now I must be extremely careful. Otherwise why should that dog at the Chao house have looked at me twice?

I have reason for my fear.

II

Tonight there is no moon at all, I know that this bodes ill. This morning when I went out cautiously, Mr. Chao had a strange look in his eyes, as if he were afraid of me, as if he wanted to murder me. There were seven or eight others, who discussed me in a whisper. And they were afraid of my seeing them. All the people I passed were like that. The fiercest among them grinned at me; whereupon I shivered from head to foot, knowing that their preparations were complete.

I was not afraid, however, but continued on my way. A group of children in front were also discussing me, and the look in their eyes was just like that in Mr. Chao's while their faces too were ghastly pale. I wondered what grudge these children could have against me to make them behave like this. I could not help calling out: "Tell me!" But then they ran away.

I wonder what grudge Mr. Chao can have against me, what grudge the people on the road can have against me. I can think of nothing except that twenty years ago I trod on Mr. Ku Chiu's* account sheets for many years past, and Mr. Ku was very displeased. Although Mr. Chao does not know him, he must have heard talk of this and decided to avenge him, so he is conspiring against me with the people on the road. But then what of the children? At that time they were not yet born, so why should they eye me so strangely today, as if they were afraid of me, as if they wanted to murder me? This really frightens me, it is so bewildering and upsetting.

I know. They must have learned this from their parents!

III

I can't sleep at night. Everything requires careful consideration if one is to understand it.

Those people, some of whom have been pilloried by the magistrate, slapped in the face by the local gentry, had their wives taken away by bailiffs, or their parents driven to suicide by creditors, never looked as frightened and as fierce then as they did yesterday.

The most extraordinary thing was that woman on the street yesterday who spanked her son and said, "Little devil! I'd like to bite several mouthfuls out of you to work off my feelings!" Yet all the time she looked at me. I gave a start, unable to control myself; then all those green-faced, long-toothed people began to laugh derisively. Old Chen hurried forward and dragged me home.

---

* Ku Chiu means "Ancient Times." Lu Hsun had in mind the long history of feudal oppression in China.

He dragged me home. The folk at home all pretended not to know me; they had the same look in their eyes as all the others. When I went into the study, they locked the door outside as if cooping up a chicken or a duck. This incident left me even more bewildered.

A few days ago a tenant of ours from Wolf Cub Village came to report the failure of the crops, and told my elder brother that a notorious character in their village had been beaten to death; then some people had taken out his heart and liver, fried them in oil and eaten them, as a means of increasing their courage. When I interrupted, the tenant and my brother both stared at me. Only today have I realized that they had exactly the same look in their eyes as those people outside.

Just to think of it sets me shivering from the crown of my head to the soles of my feet.

They eat human beings, so they may eat me.

I see that woman's "bite several mouthfuls out of you," the laughter of those green-faced, long-toothed people and the tenant's story the other day are obviously secret signs. I realize all the poison in their speech, all the daggers in their laughter. Their teeth are white and glistening: they are all man-eaters.

It seems to me, although I am not a bad man, ever since I trod on Mr. Ku's accounts it has been touch-and-go. They seem to have secrets which I cannot guess, and once they are angry they will call anyone a bad character. I remember when my elder brother taught me to write compositions, no matter how good a man was, if I produced arguments to the contrary he would mark that passage to show his approval; while if I excused evil-doers, he would say: "Good for you, that shows originality." How can I possibly guess their secret thoughts—especially when they are ready to eat people?

Everything requires careful consideration if one is to understand it. In ancient times, as I recollect, people often ate human beings, but I am rather hazy about it. I tried to look this up, but my history has no chronology, and scrawled all over each page are the words: "Virtue and Morality." Since I could not sleep anyway, I read intently half the night, until I began to see words between the lines, the whole book being filled with the two words—"Eat people."

All these words written in the book, all the words spoken by our tenant, gaze at me strangely with an enigmatic smile.

I too am a man, and they want to eat me!

IV

In the morning I sat quietly for some time. Old Chen brought lunch in: one bowl of vegetables, one bowl of steamed fish. The eyes of the fish were white and hard, and its mouth was open just like those people who want to eat human beings. After a few mouthfuls I could not tell whether the slippery morsels were fish or human flesh, so I brought it all up.

I said, "Old Chen, tell my brother that I feel quite suffocated, and want to have a stroll in the garden." Old Chen said nothing but went out, and presently he came back and opened the gate.

I did not move, but watched to see how they would treat me, feeling certain that they would not let me go. Sure enough! My elder brother came slowly out, leading an old man. There was a murderous gleam in his eyes, and fearing that I would see it he lowered his head, stealing glances at me from the side of his spectacles.

"You seem to be very well today," said my brother.

"Yes," said I.

"I have invited Mr. Ho here today," said my brother, "to examine you."

"All right," said I. Actually I knew quite well that this old man was the executioner in disguise! He simply used the pretext of feeling my pulse to see how fat I was; for by so doing he would receive a share of my flesh. Still I was not afraid. Although I do not eat men, my courage is greater than theirs. I held out my two fists, to see what he would do. The old man sat down, closed his eyes, fumbled for some time and remained still for some time; then he opened his shifty eyes and said, "Don't let your imagination run away with you. Rest quietly for a few days, and you will be all right."

Don't let your imagination run away with you! Rest quietly for a few days! When I have grown fat, naturally they will have more to eat; but what good will it do me, or how can it be "all right"? All these people wanting to eat human flesh and at the same time stealthily trying to keep up appearances, not daring to act promptly, really made me nearly die of laughter. I could not help roaring with laughter, I was so amused. I knew that in this laughter were courage and integrity. Both the old man and my brother turned pale, awed by my courage and integrity.

But just because I am brave they are the more eager to eat me, in order to acquire some of my courage. The old man went out of the gate, but before he had gone far he said to my brother in a low voice, "To be eaten at once!" And my brother nodded. So you are in it too! This stupendous discovery, although it came as a shock, is yet no more than I had expected: the accomplice in eating me is my elder brother!

The eater of human flesh is my elder brother!

I am the younger brother of an eater of human flesh!

I myself will be eaten by others, but none the less I am the younger brother of an eater of human flesh!

V

These few days I have been thinking again: suppose that old man were not an executioner in disguise, but a real doctor; he would be none the less an eater of human flesh. In that book on herbs, written by his predecessor Li Shih-chen,* it is clearly stated that men's flesh can be boiled and eaten; so can he still say that he does not eat men?

As for my elder brother, I have also good reason to suspect him. When he was teaching me, he said with his own lips, "People exchange their sons to eat." And once in discussing a bad man, he said that not only did he deserve to be killed, he should "have his flesh eaten and his hide slept on."† I was still young then, and my heart beat faster for some time, he was not at all surprised by the story that our tenant from Wolf Cub Village told us the other day about eating a man's heart and liver, but kept nodding his head. He is evidently just as cruel as before. Since it is possible to "exchange sons to eat," then anything can be exchanged, anyone can be eaten. In the past I simply listened to his explanations, and let it go at that; now I know that when he explained it to me, not only was there human fat at the corner of his lips, but his whole heart was set on eating men.

VI

Pitch dark. I don't know whether it is day or night. The Chao family dog has started barking again.

---

* A famous pharmacologist (1518–1593), author of *Ben-cao-gang-mu*, the *Materia Medica*.
† These are quotations from the old classic *Zuo Zhuan*.

The fierceness of a lion, the timidity of a rabbit, the craftiness of a fox...

VII

I know their way; they are not willing to kill anyone outright, nor do they dare, for fear of the consequences. Instead they have banded together and set traps everywhere, to force me to kill myself. The behaviour of the men and women in the street a few days ago, and my elder brother's attitude these last few days, make it quite obvious. What they like best is for a man to take off his belt, and hang himself from a beam; for then they can enjoy their heart's desire without being blamed for murder. Naturally that sets them roaring with delighted laughter. On the other hand, if a man is frightened or worried to death, although that makes him rather thin, they still nod in approval.

They only eat dead flesh! I remember reading somewhere of a hideous beast, with an ugly look in its eye, called "hyena" which often eats dead flesh. Even the largest bones it grinds into fragments and swallows: the mere thought of this is enough to terrify one. Hyenas are related to wolves, and wolves belong to the canine species: The other day the dog in the Chao house looked at me several times; obviously it is in the plot too and has become their accomplice. The old man's eyes were cast down, but that did not deceive me!

The most deplorable is my elder brother. He is also a man, so why is he not afraid, why is he plotting with others to eat me? Is it that when one is used to it he no longer thinks it a crime? Or is it that he has hardened his heart to do something he knows is wrong?

In cursing man-eaters, I shall start with my brother, and in dissuading man-eaters, I shall start with him too.

VIII

Actually, such arguments should have convinced them long ago...

Suddenly someone came in. He was only about twenty years old and I did not see his features very clearly. His face was wreathed in smiles, but when he nodded to me his smile did not seem genuine. I asked him: "Is it right to eat human beings?"

Still smiling, he replied, "When there is no famine how can one eat human beings?"

I realized at once, he was one of them; but still I summoned up courage to repeat my question:

"Is it right?"

"What makes you ask such a thing? You really are... fond of a joke... It is very fine today."

"It is fine, and the moon is very bright. But I want to ask you: Is it right?"

He looked disconcerted, and muttered: "No..."

"No? Then why do they still do it?"

"What are you talking about?"

"What am I talking about? They are eating men now in Wolf Cub Village, and you can see it written all over the books, in fresh red ink."

His expression changed, and he grew ghastly pale. "It may be so," he said, staring at me. "It has always been like that..."

"Is it right because it has always been like that?"

"I refuse to discuss these things with you. Anyway, you shouldn't talk about it. Whoever talks about it is in the wrong!"

I leaped up and opened my eyes wide, but the man had vanished. I was soaked with perspiration. He was much younger than my elder brother, but even so he was in it. He must have been taught by his parents. And I am afraid he has already taught his son: that is why even the children look at me so fiercely.

IX

Wanting to eat men, at the same time afraid of being eaten themselves, they all look at each other with the deepest suspicion...

How comfortable life would be for them if they could rid themselves of such obsessions and go to work, walk, eat and sleep at ease. They have only this one step to take. Yet fathers and sons, husbands and wives, brothers, friends, teachers and students, sworn enemies and even strangers, have all joined in this conspiracy, discouraging and preventing each other from taking this step.

X

Early this morning I went to look for my elder brother. He was standing outside the hall door looking at the sky, when I walked up behind him, stood between him and the door, and with exceptional poise and politeness said to him:

"Brother, I have something to say to you."

"Well, what is it?" he asked, quickly turning towards me and nodding.

"It is very little, but I find it difficult to say. Brother, probably all primitive people ate a little human flesh to begin with. Later, because their outlook changed, some of them stopped, and because they tried to be good they changed into men, changed into real men. But some are still eating—just like reptiles. Some have changed into fish, birds, monkeys and finally men; but some do not try to be good and remain reptiles still. When those who eat men compare themselves with those who do not, how ashamed they must be. Probably much more ashamed than the reptiles are before monkeys.

"In ancient times Yi Ya boiled his son for Chieh and Chou to eat; that is the old story.* But actually since the creation of heaven and earth by Pan Ku men have been eating each other, from the time of Yi Ya's son to the time of Hsu Hsi-lin,† and from the time of Hsu Hsi-lin down to the man caught in Wolf Cub Village. Last year they executed a criminal in the city, and a consumptive soaked a piece of bread in his blood and sucked it.

"They want to eat me, and of course you can do nothing about it single-handed; but why should you join them? As man-eaters they are capable of anything. If they eat me, they can eat you as well; members of the same group can still eat each other. But if you will just change your ways immediately, then everyone will have peace. Although this has been going on since time immemorial, today we could make a special effort to be good, and say this is not to be done! I'm sure you can say so, brother. The other day when the tenant wanted the rent reduced, you said it couldn't be done."

At first he only smiled cynically, then a murderous gleam came

---

* According to ancient records, Yi Ya cooked his son and presented him to Duke Huan of Chi who reigned from 685 to 643 B.C. Chieh and Chou were tyrants of an earlier age. The madman has made a mistake here.

† A revolutionary at the end of the Ching dynasty (1644–1911), Hsu His-lin was executed in 1907 for assassinating a Ching official. His heart and liver were eaten.

into his eyes, and when I spoke of their secret his face turned pale. Outside the gate stood a group of people, including Mr. Chao and his dog, all craning their necks to peer in. I could not see all their faces, for they seemed to be masked in cloths; some of them looked pale and ghastly still, concealing their laughter. I knew they were one band, all eaters of human flesh. But I also knew that they did not all think alike by any means. Some of them thought that since it had always been so, men should be eaten. Some of them knew that they should not eat men, but still wanted to; and they were afraid people might discover their secret; thus when they heard me they became angry, but they still smiled their cynical, tight-lipped smile.

Suddenly my brother looked furious, and shouted in a loud voice:

"Get out of here, all of you! What is the point of looking at a madman?"

Then I realized part of their cunning. They would never be willing to change their stand, and their plans were all laid; they had stigmatized me as a madman. In future when I was eaten, not only would there be no trouble, but people would probably be grateful to them. When our tenant spoke of the villagers eating a bad character, it was exactly the same device. This is their old trick.

Old Chen came in too, in a great temper, but they could not stop my mouth, I had to speak to those people:

"You should change, change from the bottom of your hearts!" I said. "You must know that in future there will be no place for man-eaters in the world.

"If you don't change, you may all be eaten by each other. Although so many are born, they will be wiped out by the real men, just like wolves killed by hunters. Just like reptiles!"

Old Chen drove everybody away. My brother had disappeared. Old Chen advised me to go back to my room. The room was pitch dark. The beams and rafters shook above my head. After shaking for some time they grew larger. They piled on top of me.

The weight was so great, I could not move. They meant that I should die. I knew that the weight was false, so I struggled out, covered in perspiration. But I had to say:

"You should change at once, change from the bottom of your hearts! You must know that in future there will be no place for man-eaters in the world..."

XI

The sun does not shine, the door is not opened, every day two meals.

I took up my chopsticks, then thought of my elder brother; I know now how my little sister died: it was all through him. My sister was only five at the time. I can still remember how lovable and pathetic she looked. Mother cried and cried, but he begged her not to cry, probably because he had eaten her himself, and so her crying made him feel ashamed. If he had any sense of shame...

My sister was eaten by my brother, but I don't know whether mother realized it or not.

I think mother must have known, but when she cried she did not say so outright, probably because she thought it proper too. I remember when I was four or five years old, sitting in the cool of the hall, my brother told me that if a man's parents were ill, he should cut off a piece of his flesh and boil it for them if he wanted to be considered a good son; and mother did not contradict him. If one piece could be eaten, obviously so could the whole. And yet just to think of the mourning then still makes my heart bleed; that is the extraordinary thing about it!

XII

I can't bear to think of it.

I have only just realized that I have been living all these years in a place where for four thousand years they have been eating human flesh. My brother had just taken over the charge of the house when our sister died, and he may well have used her flesh in our rice and dishes, making us eat it unwittingly.

It is possible that I ate several pieces of my sister's flesh unwittingly, and now it is my turn...

How can a man like myself, after four thousand years of man-eating history—even though I knew nothing about it at first—ever hope to face real men?

XIII

Perhaps there are still children who have not eaten men?

Save the children...

April 1918

1960

PIG

Roald Dahl

Roald Dahl (1916–1990) is revered for his marvellously strange children's stories, tales of telekinetic children, anthropomorphic foxes, and amicable giants. Dahl's legacy is laced with odd consumables: witches with a taste for children, unnaturally large fruit, potion-like medicines, "snozzcumbers" and secretive chocolate factories.

His attention to the delightful allure—and disgust—of all things edible is ubiquitous. Strange eating is a thread that runs throughout much of Dahl's works, with his adult fiction approaching food from a far less whimsical, more wicked angle. Whilst his children's stories hint at the captivating nature of fairy-tale-esque giants and witches and their taste for children, his adult tales revel in the odd realities of consumptive ethics. Dahl was a prolific short story writer, penning eighteen collections for adults. Among these tales is "Pig", a short story originally published in the 1960 collection *Kiss Kiss*. The figure of the pig appeared to haunt Dahl, who also wrote a poem titled "The Pig". The poem is an equally eerie work depicting an anthropomorphic pig's philosophical ponderings—and stark realization—of the meaning of life. The story "Pig" considers violence, exoticism, vulnerability, and the dark depths of appetites with an almost existential tone. Reading the short story and poem in tandem, the two pieces show a brooding consideration of the line between human and animal; hinting towards a fundamental flaw that haunts the dinner table's supposed morality code. This story is made all the more impactful when you learn of Dahl's supposed vegetarian diet.

Once upon a time, in the City of New York, a beautiful baby boy was born into this world, and the joyful parents named him Lexington.

No sooner had the mother returned home from the hospital carrying Lexington in her arms than she said to her husband, "Darling, now you must take me out to a most marvellous restaurant for dinner so that we can celebrate the arrival of our son and heir."

Her husband embraced her tenderly and told her that any woman who could produce such a beautiful child as Lexington deserved to go absolutely anywhere she wanted. But was she strong enough yet, he inquired, to start running around the city late at night?

"No," she said, she wasn't. But what the hell.

So that evening they both dressed themselves up in fancy clothes, and leaving little Lexington in care of a trained infant's nurse who was costing them twenty dollars a day and was Scottish into the bargain, they went out to the finest and most expensive restaurant in town. There they each ate a giant lobster and drank a bottle of champagne between them, and after that, they went on to a nightclub, where they drank another bottle of champagne and then sat holding hands for several hours while they recalled and discussed and admired each individual physical feature of their lovely newborn son.

They arrived back at their house on the East Side of Manhattan at around two o'clock in the morning and the husband paid off the taxi driver and then began feeling in his pockets for the key to the front door. After a while, he announced that he must have left it in the pocket of his other suit, and he suggested they ring the bell and get the nurse to come down and let them in. An infant's nurse at twenty dollars a day must expect to be hauled out of bed occasionally in the night, the husband said.

So he rang the bell. They waited. Nothing happened. He rang it again, long and loud. They waited another minute. Then they both stepped back on to the street and shouted the nurse's name (McPottle) up at the nursery windows on the third floor, but there was still no response. The house was dark and silent. The wife began to grow apprehensive. Her baby was imprisoned in this place, she told herself. Alone with McPottle. And who was McPottle? They had known her for two days, that was all, and she had a thin mouth, a small disapproving eye, and a starchy bosom, and quite clearly she was in the habit of sleeping too soundly for safety. If she couldn't hear the front-door bell, then how on earth did she expect to hear a baby crying? Why, this very second the poor thing might be swallowing its tongue or suffocating on its pillow.

"He doesn't use a pillow," the husband said. "You are not to worry. But I'll get you in if that's what you want." He was feeling rather superb after all the champagne, and now he bent down and undid the laces of one of his black patent-leather shoes, and took it off. Then, holding it by the toe, he flung it hard and straight through the dining-room window on the ground floor.

"There you are," he said, grinning. "We'll deduct it from McPottle's wages."

He stepped forward and very carefully put a hand through the hole in the glass and released the catch. Then he raised the window.

"I shall lift you in first, little mother," he said, and he took his wife around the waist and lifted her off the ground. This brought her big red mouth up level with his own, and very close, so he started kissing her. He knew from experience that women like very much to be kissed in this position, with their bodies held tight and their legs dangling in the air, so he went on doing it for quite a long time, and she wiggled her feet, and made loud gulping noises down in her throat. Finally, the husband turned her round and began easing her gently through the open window into the dining-room. At this point, a police patrol car came nosing silently along the street towards them. It stopped about thirty yards away, and three cops of Irish extraction leaped out of the car and started running in the direction of the husband and wife, brandishing revolvers.

"Stick 'em up!" the cops shouted. "Stick 'em up!" But it was impossible for the husband to obey this order without letting go of his wife, and had he done this she would either have fallen to the ground or would have been left dangling half in and half out of the house, which is a terribly uncomfortable position for a woman; so he continued gallantly to push her upward and inward through the window. The cops, all of whom had received medals before for killing robbers, opened fire immediately, and although they were still running, and although the wife in particular was presenting them with a very small target indeed, they succeeded in scoring several direct hits on each body—sufficient anyway to prove fatal in both cases.

Thus, when he was no more than twelve days old, little Lexington became an orphan.

11

The news of this killing, for which the three policemen subsequently received citations, was eagerly conveyed to all relatives of the deceased couple by newspaper reporters, and the next morning the closest of these relatives, as well as a couple of undertakers, three lawyers, and a priest, climbed into taxis and set out for the house with the broken window. They assembled in the living-room, men and women both, and they sat around in a circle on the sofas and armchairs, smoking cigarettes and sipping sherry and debating what on earth should be done now with the baby upstairs, the orphan Lexington.

It soon became apparent that none of the relatives was particularly keen to assume responsibility for the child, and the discussions and arguments continued all through the day. Everybody declared an enormous, almost an irresistible desire to look after him, and would have done so with the greatest of pleasure were it not for the fact that their apartment was too small, or that they already had one baby and couldn't possibly afford another, or that they wouldn't know what to do with the poor little thing when they went abroad in the summer, or that they were getting on in years, which surely would be most unfair to the boy when he grew up, and so on and so forth. They all knew, of course, that the father had been heavily in debt for a long time and that the house was mortgaged and that consequently there would be no money at all to go with the child.

They were still arguing like mad at six in the evening when suddenly, in the middle of it all, an old aunt of the deceased father (her name was Glosspan) swept in from Virginia, and without even removing her hat and coat, not even pausing to sit down, ignoring all offers of a martini, a whisky, a sherry, she announced firmly to the assembled relatives that she herself intended to take sole charge of the infant boy from then on. What was more, she said, she would assume full financial responsibility on all counts, including education, and everyone else could go back home where they belonged and give their consciences a rest. So saying, she trotted upstairs to the nursery and snatched Lexington from his cradle and swept out of the house with the baby clutched tightly in her arms, while the relatives simply sat and stared and smiled and looked relieved, and McPottle the nurse stood stiff with disapproval at the head of the stairs, her lips compressed, her arms folded across her starchy bosom.

And thus it was that the infant Lexington, when he was thirteen days old, left the City of New York and travelled southward to live with his Great Aunt Glosspan in the State of Virginia.

III

Aunt Glosspan was nearly seventy when she became guardian to Lexington, but to look at her you would never have guessed it for one minute. She was as sprightly as a woman half her age, with a small, wrinkled, but still quite beautiful face and two lovely brown eyes that sparkled at you in the nicest way. She was also a spinster, though you would never have guessed that either, for there was nothing spinsterish about Aunt Glosspan. She was never bitter or gloomy or irritable; she didn't have a moustache; and she wasn't in the least bit jealous of other people, which in itself is something you can seldom say about either a spinster or a virgin lady, although of course it is not known for certain whether Aunt Glosspan qualified on both counts.

But she was an eccentric old woman, there was no doubt about that. For the past thirty years she had lived a strange isolated life all by herself in a tiny cottage high up on the slopes of the Blue Ridge Mountains, several miles from the nearest village. She had five acres of pasture, a plot for growing vegetables, a flower garden, three cows, a dozen hens, and a fine cockerel.

And now she had little Lexington as well.

She was a strict vegetarian and regarded the consumption of animal flesh as not only unhealthy and disgusting, but horribly cruel. She lived upon lovely clean foods like milk, butter, eggs, cheese, vegetables, nuts, herbs, and fruit, and she rejoiced in the conviction that no living creature would be slaughtered on her account, not even a shrimp. Once, when a brown hen of hers passed away in the prime of life from being eggbound, Aunt Glosspan was so distressed that she nearly gave up egg-eating altogether.

She knew not the first thing about babies, but that didn't worry her in the least. At the railway station in New York, while waiting for the train that would take her and Lexington back to Virginia, she bought six feeding-bottles, two dozen diapers, a box of safety pins, a carton of milk for the journey, and a small paper-covered book called *The Care of Infants*. What more could anyone want? And when the train got going, she fed the baby some milk, changed its nappies after a fashion, and laid it down on the seat to sleep. Then she read *The Care of Infants* from cover to cover.

"There is no problem here," she said, throwing the book out of the window. "No problem at all."

And curiously enough there wasn't. Back home in the cottage everything went just as smoothly as could be. Little Lexington drank his milk and belched and yelled and slept exactly as a good baby should, and Aunt Glosspan glowed with joy whenever she looked at him and showered him with kisses all day long.

IV

By the time he was six years old, young Lexington had grown into a most beautiful boy with long golden hair and deep blue eyes the colour of cornflowers. He was bright and cheerful, and already he was learning to help his old aunt in all sorts of different ways around the property, collecting the eggs from the chicken house, turning the handle of the butter churn, digging up potatoes in the vegetable garden, and searching for wild herbs on the side of the mountain. Soon, Aunt Glosspan told herself, she would have to start thinking about his education.

But she couldn't bear the thought of sending him away to school. She loved him so much now that it would kill her to be parted from him for any length of time. There was, of course, that village school down in the valley, but it was a dreadful-looking place, and if she sent him there she just knew they would start forcing him to eat meat the very first day he arrived.

"You know what, my darling?" she said to him one day when he was sitting on a stool in the kitchen watching her make cheese. "I don't really see why I shouldn't give you your lessons myself."

The boy looked up at her with his large blue eyes, and gave her a lovely trusting smile. "That would be nice," he said.

"And the very first thing I should do would be to teach you how to cook."

"I think I would like that, Aunt Glosspan."

"Whether you like it or not, you're going to have to learn some time," she said. "Vegetarians like us don't have nearly so many foods to choose from as ordinary people, and therefore they must learn to be doubly expert with what they have."

"Aunt Glosspan," the boy said, "what *do* ordinary people eat that we don't?"

"Animals," she answered, tossing her head in disgust.

"You mean *live* animals?"

"No," she said. "Dead ones."

The boy considered this for a moment.

"You mean when they die they *eat* them instead of *burying* them?"

"They don't wait for them to die, my pet. They kill them."

"How do they kill them, Aunt Glosspan?"

"They usually slit their throats with a knife."

"But what *kind* of animals?"

"Cows and pigs mostly, and sheep."

"Cows!" the boy cried. "You mean like Daisy and Snowdrop and Lily?"

"Exactly, my dear."

"But *how* do they eat them, Aunt Glosspan?"

"They cut them up into bits and they cook the bits. They like it best when it's all red and bloody and sticking to the bones. They love to eat lumps of cow's flesh with the blood oozing out of it."

"Pigs too?"

"They adore pigs."

"Lumps of bloody pig's meat," the boy said. "Imagine that. What else do they eat, Aunt Glosspan?"

"Chickens."

"Chickens!"

"Millions of them."

"Feathers and all?"

"No, dear, not the feathers. Now run along outside and get Aunt Glosspan a bunch of chives, will you, my darling?"

Shortly after that, the lessons began. They covered five subjects, reading, writing, geography, arithmetic, and cooking, but the latter was by far the most popular with both teacher and pupil. In fact, it very soon became apparent that young Lexington possessed a truly remarkable talent in this direction. He was a born cook. He was dextrous and quick. He could handle his pans like a juggler. He could slice a single potato into twenty paper-thin slivers in less time than it took his aunt to peel it. His palate was exquisitely sensitive, and he could taste a pot of strong onion soup and immediately detect the presence of a single tiny leaf of sage. In so young a boy, all this was a bit bewildering to Aunt Glosspan, and to tell the truth she didn't quite know what to make of it. But she was proud as proud could be, all the same, and predicted a brilliant future for the child.

"What a mercy it is," she said, "that I have such a wonderful little fellow to look after me in my dotage." And a couple of years later, she retired from the kitchen for good, leaving Lexington in sole charge of all household cooking. The boy was now ten years old, and Aunt Glosspan was nearly eighty.

V

With the kitchen to himself, Lexington straight away began experimenting with dishes of his own invention. The old favourites no longer interested him. He had a violent urge to create. There were hundreds of fresh ideas in his head. "I will begin," he said, "by devising a chestnut soufflé." He made it and served it up for supper that very night. It was terrific. "You are a genius!" Aunt Glosspan cried, leaping up from her chair and kissing him on both cheeks. "You will make history!"

From then on, hardly a day went by without some new delectable creation being set upon the table. There was Brazilnut soup, hominy cutlets, vegetable ragout, dandelion omelette, cream-cheese fritters, stuffed-cabbage surprise, stewed foggage, shallots *à la bonne femme*, beetroot mousse piquant, prunes Stroganoff, Dutch rarebit, turnips on horseback, flaming spruce-needle tarts, and many many other beautiful compositions. Never before in her life, Aunt Glosspan declared, had she tasted such food as this; and in the mornings, long before lunch was due, she would go out on to the porch and sit there in her rocking-chair, speculating about the coming meal, licking her chops, sniffing the aromas that came wafting out through the kitchen window.

"What's that you're making in there today, boy?" she would call out.

"Try to guess, Aunt Glosspan."

"Smells like a bit of salsify fritters to me," she would say, sniffing vigorously.

Then out he would come, this ten-year-old child, a little grin of triumph on his face, and in his hands a big steaming pot of the most heavenly stew made entirely of parsnips and lovage.

"You know what you ought to do," his aunt said to him, gobbling the stew. "You ought to set yourself down this very minute with paper and pencil and write a cooking-book."

He looked at her across the table, chewing his parsnips slowly.

"Why not?" she cried. "I've taught you how to write and I've taught you how to cook and now all you've got to do is put the two things together. You write a cooking-book, my darling, and it'll make you famous the whole world over."

"All right," he said. "I will."

And that very day, Lexington began writing the first page of that monumental work which was to occupy him for the rest of his life. He called it *Eat Good and Healthy*.

VI

Seven years later, by the time he was seventeen, he had recorded over nine thousand different recipes, all of them original, all of them delicious.

But now, suddenly, his labours were interrupted by the tragic death of Aunt Glosspan. She was afflicted in the night by a violent seizure, and Lexington, who had rushed into her bedroom to see what all the noise was about, found her lying on her bed yelling and cussing and twisting herself up into all manner of complicated knots. Indeed, she was a terrible sight to behold, and the agitated youth danced around her in his pyjamas, wringing his hands, and wondering what on earth he should do. Finally, in an effort to cool her down, he fetched a bucket of water from the pond in the cow field and tipped it over her head, but this only intensified the paroxysms, and the old lady expired within the hour.

"This is really too bad," the poor boy said, pinching her several times to make sure that she was dead. "And how sudden! How quick and sudden! Why only a few hours ago she seemed in the very best of spirits. She even took three large helpings of my most recent creation, devilled mushroomburgers, and told me how succulent it was."

After weeping bitterly for several minutes, for he had loved his aunt very much, he pulled himself together and carried her outside and buried her behind the cowshed.

The next day, while tidying up her belongings, he came across an envelope that was addressed to him in Aunt Glosspan's handwriting. He opened it and drew out two fifty-dollar bills and a letter.

Darling boy [the letter said,] I know that you have never yet been down the mountain since you were thirteen days old, but as soon as I die you must put on a pair of shoes and a clean shirt and walk down to the village and find the doctor. Ask the doctor to give you a death certificate to prove that I am dead. Then take this certificate to my lawyer, a man called Mr. Samuel Zuckermann, who lives in New York City and who has a copy of my will. Mr. Zuckermann will arrange everything. The cash in this envelope is to pay the doctor for the certificate and to cover the cost of your journey to New York. Mr. Zuckermann will give you more money when you get there, and it is my earnest wish that you use it to further your researches into culinary and vegetarian matters, and that you continue to work upon that great book of yours until you are satisfied that it is complete in every way. Your loving aunt—Glosspan

Lexington, who had always done everything his aunt told him, pocketed the money, put on a pair of shoes and a clean shirt, and went down the mountain to the village where the doctor lived.

"Old Glosspan?" the doctor said. "My God, is *she* dead?"

"Certainly she's dead," the youth answered. "If you will come back home with me now I'll dig her up and you can see for yourself."

"How deep did you bury her?" the doctor asked.

"Six or seven feet down, I should think."

"And how long ago?"

"Oh, about eight hours."

"Then she's dead," the doctor announced. "Here's the certificate."

VII

Our hero now sets out for the City of New York to find Mr. Samuel Zuckermann. He travelled on foot, and he slept under hedges, and he lived on berries and wild herbs, and it took him sixteen days to reach the metropolis.

"What a fabulous place this is!" he cried as he stood at the corner of Fifty-seventh Street and Fifth Avenue, staring around him. "There are no cows or chickens anywhere, and none of the women looks in the least like Aunt Glosspan."

As for Mr. Samuel Zuckermann, he looked like nothing that Lexington had ever seen before.

He was a small spongy man with livid jowls and a huge magenta nose, and when he smiled, bits of gold flashed at you marvellously from lots of different places inside his mouth. In his luxurious office, he shook Lexington warmly by the hand and congratulated him upon his aunt's death.

"I suppose you knew that your dearly beloved guardian was a woman of considerable wealth?" he said.

"You mean the cows and the chickens?"

"I mean half a million bucks," Mr. Zuckermann said.

"How much?"

"Half a million dollars, my boy. And she's left it all to you." Mr. Zuckermann leaned back in his chair and clasped his hands over his spongy paunch. At the same time, he began secretly working his right forefinger in through his waistcoat and under his shirt so as to scratch the skin around the circumference of his navel—a favourite exercise of his, and one that gave him a peculiar pleasure. "Of course, I shall have to deduct fifty per cent for my services," he said, "but that still leaves you with two hundred and fifty grand."

"I am rich!" Lexington cried. "This is wonderful! How soon can I have the money?"

"Well," Mr. Zuckermann said, "luckily for you, I happen to be on rather cordial terms with the tax authorities around here, and I am confident that I shall be able to persuade them to waive all death duties and back taxes."

"How kind you are," murmured Lexington.

"I should naturally have to give somebody a small honorarium."

"Whatever you say, Mr. Zuckermann."

"I think a hundred thousand would be sufficient."

"Good gracious, isn't that rather excessive?"

"Never undertip a tax inspector or a policeman," Mr. Zuckermann said. "Remember that."

"But how much does it leave for me?" the youth asked meekly.

"One hundred and fifty thousand. But then you've got the funeral expenses to pay out of that."

"*Funeral* expenses?"

"You've got to pay the funeral parlour. Surely you know that?"

"But I buried her myself, Mr. Zuckermann, behind the cowshed."

"I don't doubt it," the lawyer said. "So what?"

"I never used a funeral parlour."

"Listen," Mr. Zuckermann said patiently. "You may not know it, but there is a law in this State which says that no beneficiary under a will may receive a single penny of his inheritance until the funeral parlour has been paid in full."

"You mean that's a *law*?"

"Certainly it's a law, and a very good one it is, too. The funeral parlour is one of our great national institutions. It must be protected at all costs."

Mr. Zuckermann himself, together with a group of public-spirited doctors, controlled a corporation that owned a chain of nine lavish funeral parlours in the city, not to mention a casket factory in Brooklyn and a postgraduate school for embalmers in Washington Heights. The celebration of death was therefore a deeply religious affair in Mr. Zuckermann's eyes. In fact, the whole business affected him profoundly, almost as profoundly, one might say, as the birth of Christ affected the shopkeeper.

"You had no right to go out and bury your aunt like that," he said. "None at all."

"I'm very sorry, Mr. Zuckermann."

"Why, it's downright subversive."

"I'll do whatever you say, Mr. Zuckermann. All I want to know is how much I'm going to get in the end, when everything's paid."

There was a pause. Mr. Zuckermann sighed and frowned and continued secretly to run the tip of his finger around the rim of his navel.

"Shall we say fifteen thousand?" he suggested, flashing a big gold smile. "That's a nice round figure."

"Can I take it with me this afternoon?"

"I don't see why not."

So Mr. Zuckermann summoned his chief cashier and told him to give Lexington fifteen thousand dollars out of the petty cash, and to obtain a receipt. The youth, who by this time was delighted to be getting anything at all, accepted the money gratefully and stowed it away in his knapsack. Then he shook Mr. Zuckermann warmly by the hand, thanked him for all his help, and went out of the office.

"The whole world is before me!" our hero cried as he emerged into the street. "I now have fifteen thousand dollars to see me through until my book is published. And after that, of course, I shall have a great deal more." He stood on the pavement, wondering which way to go. He turned left and began strolling slowly down the street, staring at the sights of the city.

"What a revolting smell," he said, sniffing the air. "I can't stand this." His delicate olfactory nerves, tuned to receive only the most delicious kitchen aromas, were being tortured by the stench of the diesel-oil fumes pouring out of the backs of the buses.

"I must get out of this place before my nose is ruined altogether," he said. "But first, I've simply got to have something to eat I'm starving." The poor boy had had nothing but berries and wild herbs for the past two weeks, and now his stomach was yearning for solid food. I'd like a nice hominy cutlet, he told himself. Or maybe a few juicy salsify fritters.

He crossed the street and entered a small restaurant. The place was hot inside, and dark and silent. There was a strong smell of cooking-fat and cabbage water. The only other customer was a man with a brown hat on his head, crouching intently over his food, who did not look up as Lexington came in.

Our hero seated himself at a corner table and hung his knapsack on the back of his chair. This, he told himself, is going to be most interesting. In all my seventeen years I have tasted only the cooking of two people, Aunt Glosspan and myself—unless one counts Nurse McPottle, who must have heated my bottle a few times when I was an infant. But I am now about to sample the art of a new chef altogether, and perhaps, if I am lucky, I may pick up a couple of useful ideas for my book.

A waiter approached out of the shadows at the back, and stood beside the table.

"How do you do," Lexington said. "I should like a large hominy cutlet please. Do it twenty-five seconds each side, in a very hot skillet with sour cream, and sprinkle a pinch of lovage on it before serving—unless of course your chef knows of a more original method, in which case I should be delighted to try it."

The waiter laid his head over to one side and looked carefully at his customer. "You want the roast pork and cabbage?" he asked. "That's all we got left."

"Roast what and cabbage?"

The waiter took a soiled handkerchief from his trouser pocket and shook it open with a violent flourish, as though he were cracking a whip. Then he blew his nose loud and wet.

"You want it or don't you?" he said, wiping his nostrils.

"I haven't the foggiest idea what it is," Lexington replied, "but I should love to try it. You see, I am writing a cooking-book and..."

"One pork and cabbage!" the waiter shouted, and somewhere in the back of the restaurant, far away in the darkness, a voice answered him.

The waiter disappeared. Lexington reached into his knapsack for his personal knife and fork. These were a present from Aunt Glosspan, given him when he was six years old, made of solid silver, and he had never eaten with any other instruments since. While waiting for the food to arrive, he polished them lovingly with a piece of soft muslin.

Soon the waiter returned carrying a plate on which there lay a thick greyish-white slab of something hot. Lexington leaned forward anxiously to smell it as it was put down before him. His nostrils were wide open now to receive the scent, quivering and sniffing.

"But this is absolute heaven!" he exclaimed. "What an aroma! It's tremendous!"

The waiter stepped back a pace, watching his customer carefully.

"Never in my life have I smelled anything as rich and wonderful as this!" our hero cried, seizing his knife and fork. "What on earth is it made of?"

The man in the brown hat looked around and stared, then returned to his eating. The waiter was backing away towards the kitchen.

Lexington cut off a small piece of the meat, impaled it on his silver fork, and carried it up to his nose so as to smell it again. Then he popped it into his mouth and began to chew it slowly, his eyes half closed, his body tense.

"This is fantastic!" he cried. "It is a brand-new flavour! Oh, Glosspan, my beloved Aunt, how I wish you were with me now so you could taste this remarkable dish! Waiter! Come here at once! I want you!"

The astonished waiter was now watching from the other end of the room, and he seemed reluctant to move any closer.

"If you will come and talk to me I will give you a present," Lexington said, waving a hundred-dollar bill. "Please come over here and talk to me."

The waiter sidled cautiously back to the table, snatched away the money, and held it up close to his face, peering at it from all angles. Then he slipped it quickly into his pocket.

"What can I do for you, my friend?" he asked.

"Look," Lexington said. "If you will tell me what this delicious dish is made of, and exactly how it is prepared, I will give you another hundred."

"I already told you," the man said. "It's pork."

"And what exactly is pork?"

"You never had roast pork before?" the waiter asked, staring.

"For heaven's sake, man, tell me what it is and stop keeping me in suspense like this."

"It's pig," the waiter said. "You just bung it in the oven."

"*Pig!*"

"All pork is pig. Didn't you know that?"

"You mean *this* is *pig's* meat?"

"I guarantee it."

"But... but... that's impossible," the youth stammered. "Aunt Glosspan, who knew more about food than anyone else in the world, said that meat of any kind was disgusting, revolting, horrible, foul, nauseating, and beastly. And yet this piece that I have here on my plate is without doubt the most delicious thing that I have ever tasted. Now how on earth do you explain that? Aunt Glosspan certainly wouldn't have told me it was revolting if it wasn't."

"Maybe your aunt didn't know how to cook it," the waiter said.

"Is that possible?"

"You're damned right it is. Especially with pork. Pork has to be very well done or you can't eat it."

"Eureka!" Lexington cried. "I'll bet that's exactly what happened! She did it wrong!" He handed the man another hundred-dollar bill "Lead me to the kitchen," he said. "Introduce me to the genius who prepared this meat."

Lexington was at once taken into the kitchen, and there he met the cook who was an elderly man with a rash on one side of his neck.

"This will cost you another hundred," the waiter said.

Lexington was only too glad to oblige, but this time he gave the money to the cook. "Now listen to me," he said. "I have to admit that I am really rather confused by what the waiter has just been telling me. Are you quite positive that the delectable dish which I have just been eating was prepared from pig's flesh?"

The cook raised his right hand and began scratching the rash on his neck.

"Well," he said, looking at the waiter and giving him a sly wink, "all I can tell you is that I *think* it was pig's meat."

"You mean you're not sure?"

"One can't ever be sure."

"Then what else could it have been?"

"Well," the cook said, speaking very slowly and still staring at the waiter. "There's just a chance, you see, that it might have been a piece of human stuff."

"You mean a man?"

"Yes."

"Good heavens."

"Or a woman. It could have been either. They both taste the same."

"Well—now you really do surprise me," the youth declared.

"One lives and learns."

"Indeed one does."

"As a matter of fact, we've been getting an awful lot of it just lately from the butcher's in place of pork," the cook declared.

"Have you really?"

"The trouble is, it's almost impossible to tell which is which. They're both very good."

"The piece I had just now was simply superb."

"I'm glad you liked it," the cook said. "But to be quite honest, I think that was a bit of pig. In fact, I'm almost sure it was."

"You are?"

"Yes, I am."

"In that case, we shall have to assume that you are right," Lexington said. "So now will you please tell me—and here is another hundred dollars for your trouble—will you please tell me precisely how you prepared it?"

The cook, after pocketing the money, launched out upon a colourful description of how to roast a loin of pork, while the youth, not wanting to miss a single word of so great a recipe, sat down at the kitchen table and recorded every detail in his notebook.

"Is that all?" he asked when the cook had finished.

"That's all."

"But there must be more to it than that, surely?"

"You got to get a good piece of meat to start off with," the cook said. "That's half the battle. It's got to be a good hog and it's got to be butchered right, otherwise it'll turn out lousy whichever way you cook it."

"Show me how," Lexington said. "Butcher me one now so I can learn."

"We don't butcher pigs in the kitchen," the cook said. "That lot you just ate came from a packing-house over in the Bronx."

"Then give me the address!"

The cook gave him the address, and our hero, after thanking them both many times for all their kindnesses, rushed outside and leapt into a taxi and headed for the Bronx.

VIII

The packing-house was a big four-storey brick building, and the air around it smelled sweet and heavy, like musk. At the main entrance gates, there was a large notice which said VISITORS WELCOME AT ANY TIME, and thus encouraged, Lexington walked through the gates and entered a cobbled yard which surrounded the building itself. He then followed a series of signposts (THIS WAY FOR THE GUIDED TOURS), and came eventually to a small corrugated-iron shed set well apart from the main building (VISITORS' WAITING-ROOM). After knocking politely on the door, he went in.

There were six other people ahead of him in the waiting-room. There was a fat mother with her two little boys aged about nine and eleven. There was a bright-eyed young couple who looked as though they might be on their honeymoon. And there was a pale woman with long white gloves, who sat very upright, looking straight ahead, with her hands folded on her lap. Nobody spoke. Lexington wondered whether they were all writing cooking-books, like himself, but when he put this question to them aloud, he got no answer. The grown-ups merely smiled mysteriously to themselves and shook their heads, and the two children stared at him as though they were seeing a lunatic.

Soon, the door opened and a man with a merry pink face popped his head into the room and said, "Next, please." The mother and the two boys got up and went out.

About ten minutes later, the same man returned. "Next, please," he said again, and the honeymoon couple jumped up and followed him outside.

Two new visitors came in and sat down—a middle-aged husband and a middle-aged wife, the wife carrying a wicker shopping-basket containing groceries.

"Next, please," said the guide, and the woman with the long white gloves got up and left.

Several more people came in and took their places on the stiff-backed wooden chairs.

Soon the guide returned for the third time, and now it was Lexington's turn to go outside.

"Follow me, please," the guide said, leading the youth across the yard towards the main building.

"How exciting this is!" Lexington cried, hopping from one foot to the other. "I only wish that my dear Aunt Glosspan could be with me now to see what I am going to see."

"I myself only do the preliminaries," the guide said. "Then I shall hand you over to someone else."

"Anything you say," cried the ecstatic youth.

First they visited a large penned-in area at the back of the building where several hundred pigs were wandering around. "Here's where they start," the guide said. "And over there's where they go in."

"Where?"

"Right there." The guide pointed to a long wooden shed that stood against the outside wall of the factory. "We call it the shackling-pen. This way, please."

Three men wearing long rubber boots were driving a dozen pigs into the shackling-pen just as Lexington and the guide approached, so they all went in together.

"Now," the guide said, "watch how they shackle them."

Inside, the shed was simply a bare wooden room with no roof, but there was a steel cable with hooks on it that kept moving slowly along the length of one wall, parallel with the ground, about three feet up. When it reached the end of the shed, this cable suddenly changed direction and climbed vertically upward through the open roof towards the top floor of the main building.

The twelve pigs were huddled together at the far end of the pen, standing quietly, looking apprehensive. One of the men in rubber boots pulled a length of metal chain down from the wall and advanced upon the nearest animal, approaching it from the rear. Then he bent down and quickly looped one end of the chain around one of the animal's hind legs. The other end he attached to a hook on the moving cable as it went by. The cable kept moving. The chain tightened. The pig's leg was pulled up and back, and then the pig itself began to be dragged backwards. But it didn't fall down. It was rather a nimble pig, and somehow it managed to keep its balance on three legs, hopping from foot to foot and struggling against the pull of the chain, but going back and back all the time until at the end of the pen where the cable changed direction and went vertically upward, the creature was suddenly jerked off its feet and borne aloft. Shrill protests filled the air.

"Truly a fascinating process," Lexington said. "But what was the funny cracking noise it made as it went up?"

"Probably the leg," the guide answered. "Either that or the pelvis."

"But doesn't that matter?"

"Why should it matter?" the guide asked. "You don't eat the bones."

The rubber-booted men were busy shackling the rest of the pigs, and one after another they were hooked to the moving cable and hoisted up through the roof, protesting loudly as they went.

"There's a good deal more to this recipe than just picking herbs," Lexington said. "Aunt Glosspan would never have made it."

At this point, while Lexington was gazing skyward at the last pig to go up, a man in rubber boots approached him quietly from behind and looped one end of a chain around the youth's own ankle, hooking the other end to the moving belt. The next moment, before he had time to realize what was happening, our hero was jerked off his feet and dragged backwards along the concrete floor of the shackling-pen.

"Stop!" he cried. "Hold everything! My leg is caught!"

But nobody seemed to hear him, and five seconds later, the unhappy young man was jerked off the floor and hoisted vertically upward through the open roof of the pen, dangling upside down by one ankle, and wriggling like a fish.

"Help!" he shouted. "Help! There's been a frightful mistake! Stop the engines! Let me down!"

The guide removed a cigar from his mouth and looked up serenely at the rapidly ascending youth, but he said nothing. The men in rubber boots were already on their way out to collect the next batch of pigs.

"Oh, save me!" our hero cried. "Let me down! Please let me down!" But he was now approaching the top floor of the building where the moving belt curled over like a snake and entered a large hole in the wall, a kind of doorway without a door; and there, on the threshold, waiting to greet him, clothed in a dark-stained yellow rubber apron, and looking for all the world like Saint Peter at the Gates of Heaven, the sticker stood.

Lexington saw him only from upside down, and very briefly at that, but even so he noticed at once the expression of absolute peace and benevolence on the man's face, the cheerful twinkle in the eyes, the little wistful smile, the dimples in his cheeks—and all this gave him hope.

"Hi there," the sticker said, smiling.

"Quick! Save me!" our hero cried.

"With pleasure," the sticker said, and taking Lexington gently by one ear with his left hand, he raised his right hand and deftly slit open the boy's jugular vein with a knife.

The belt moved on. Lexington went with it. Everything was still upside down and the blood was pouring out of his throat and getting into his eyes, but he could still see after a fashion, and he had a blurred impression of being in an enormously long room, and at the far end of the room there was a great smoking cauldron of water, and there were dark figures, half hidden in the steam, dancing around the edge of it, brandishing long poles. The conveyor-belt seemed to be travelling right over the top of the cauldron, and the pigs seemed to be dropping down one by one into the boiling water, and one of the pigs seemed to be wearing long white gloves on its front feet.

Suddenly our hero started to feel very sleepy, but it wasn't until his good strong heart had pumped the last drop of blood from his body that he passed on out of this, the best of all possible worlds, into the next.

A DIGESTIF:
ON HUMAN LOVE

BERENICE

Edgar cAllan Poe

Edgar Allan Poe (1809–1849) is a key figure in the history of gothic literature. A prolific writer of horror and mystery short stories and poetry, Poe is perhaps best known for poems "The Raven" (1845) and "Annabel Lee" (1849) and stories such as "The Fall of the House of Usher" (1839), "The Murders in the Rue Morgue"(1841), "The Tell-Tale Heart" (1843) and "The Cask of Amontillado" (1846).

"Berenice" debuted in March 1835 in the periodical *Southern Literary Messenger*, a publication Poe himself edited for some time before leaving on grounds thought to be related to his heavy drinking. The story was heavily edited—with several paragraphs of text being removed in a reprint five years later—after the magazine's editor received numerous complaints from readers. The story has inspired several pieces of media since, becoming the basis of a short film in 1954, and a radio play in 1975. An audio version of "Berenice" was narrated by Vincent Price in 1975.

Poe's stories often incorporate traditionally gothic themes of grieving or loss that drives the characters populating his tales to madness. In true Poe style, "Berenice" follows the descent of narrator Egæus into a monomaniacal obsession as his beloved Berenice begins to sicken, her condition deteriorating from a mystery illness. As his betrothed worsens, Egæus begins to develop an infatuation with arguably the most human of uncanny gastronomic objects, the teeth. Perhaps inspired by Poe's own experiences with opium and heavy drinking, "Berenice" considers the strange nature of the human form, and how our very bodies—of ourselves, and those closest to us—can be made newly strange and haunting.

Dicebant mihi sodales, si sepulchrum amicæ visitarem, curas meas aliquantulum fore levatas.—*Ebn Zaiat.*

Misery is manifold. The wretchedness of earth is multiform. Overreaching the wide horizon as the rainbow, its hues are as various as the hues of that arch—as distinct too, yet as intimately blended. Overreaching the wide horizon as the rainbow! How is it that from beauty I have derived a type of unloveliness?—from the covenant of peace, a simile of sorrow? But as, in ethics, evil is a consequence of good, so, in fact, out of joy is sorrow born. Either the memory of past bliss is the anguish of today, or the agonies which *are*, have their origin in the ecstacies which *might have been.*

My baptismal name is Egæus; that of my family I will not mention. Yet there are no towers in the land more time-honored than my gloomy, gray, hereditary halls. Our line has been called a race of visionaries; and in many striking particulars—in the character of the family mansion—in the frescos of the chief saloon—in the tapestries of the dormitories—in the chiselling of some buttresses in the armory—but more especially in the gallery of antique paintings—in the fashion of the library chamber—and, lastly, in the very peculiar nature of the library's contents—there is more than sufficient evidence to warrant the belief.

The recollection of my earliest years are connected with that chamber, and with its volumes—of which latter I will say no more. Here died my mother. Herein was I born. But it is mere idleness to say that I had not lived before—that the soul has no previous existence. You deny it?—let us not argue the matter. Convinced myself, I seek not to convince. There is, however, a remembrance of aerial forms—of spiritual and meaning eyes of sounds, musical yet sad; a remembrance which will not be excluded; a memory like a shadow—vague, variable, indefinite unsteady; and like a shadow, too, in the impossibility of my getting rid of it while the sunlight of my reason shall exist.

In that chamber was I born. Thus awaking from the long of what seemed, but was not, nonentity, at once into the very regions of fairy land—into a palace of imagination—into the wild dominions of monastic thought and erudition—it is not singular that I gazed around me with a startled and ardent eye that I loitered away my boy-hood in books, and dissipated my youth in revery; but it *is* singular, that as years rolled away, and the noon of manhood found me still in the mansion of my fathers it *is* wonderful what stagnation there fell upon the springs of my life—wonderful how total an inversion took place in the character of my commonest thought. The realities of the world affected me as visions, and as visions only, while the wild ideas of the land of dreams became, in turn, not the material of my everyday existence, but in very deed that existence utterly and solely in itself.

Berenice and I were cousins, and we grew up together in my paternal halls. Yet differently we grew—I, ill of health, and buried in gloom—she, agile, graceful, and overflowing with energy; her's, the ramble on the hillside—mine, the studies of the cloister; I, living within my own heart, and addicted, body and soul, to the most intense and painful meditation—she, roaming carelessly through life, with no thought of the shadows in her path, or the silent flight of the raven-winged hours. Berenice!—I call upon her name—Berenice!—and from the gray ruins of memory a thousand tumultuous recollections are startled at the sound! Ah, vividly is her image before me now, as in the early days of her light-heartedness and joy! Oh, gorgeous yet fantastic beauty! Oh, sylph amid the shrubberies of Arnheim! Oh, Naiad among its fountains! And then—then all is mystery and terror, and a tale which should not be told. Disease—a fatal disease, fell like the simoon upon her frame; and, even while I gazed upon her, the spirit of change swept over her, pervading her mind, her habits, and her character, and, in a manner the most subtle and terrible, disturbing even the identity of her person! Alas! the destroyer came and went!—and the victim—where is she? I knew her not—or knew her no longer as Berenice!

Among the numerous train of maladies superinduced by that fatal and primary one which effected a revolution of so horrible a kind in the moral and physical being of my cousin, may be mentioned as the most distressing and obstinate in its nature, a species of epilepsy not unfrequently terminating in *trance* itself—trance very nearly resembling positive dissolution, and from which her manner of recovery was, in most instances, startlingly abrupt. In the meantime, my own disease—for I have been told that I should call it by no other appellation—my own disease, then, grew rapidly upon me, and assumed finally a monomaniac character of a novel and extraordinary form—hourly and momently gaining vigor—and at length obtaining over me the most incomprehensible ascendency. This monomania, if I must so term it, consisted in a morbid irritability of those properties of the mind in metaphysical science termed the *attentive*. It is more than probable that I am not understood; but I fear, indeed, that it is in no manner possible to convey to the mind of the merely general reader, an adequate idea of that nervous *intensity of interest* with which, in my case, the powers of meditation (not to speak technically) busied and buried themselves, in the contemplation of even the most ordinary objects of the universe.

To muse for long unwearied hours, with my attention riveted to some frivolous device on the margin or in the typography of a book; to become absorbed, for the better part of a summer's day, in a quaint shadow falling aslant upon the tapestry or upon the floor; to lose myself, for an entire night, in watching the steady flame of a lamp, or the embers of a fire; to dream away whole days over the perfume of a flower; to repeat, monotonously, some common word, until the sound, by dint of frequent repetition, ceased to convey any idea whatever to the mind; to lose all sense of motion or physical existence, by means of absolute bodily quiescence long and obstinately persevered in: such were a few of the most common and least pernicious vagaries induced by a condition of the mental faculties, not, indeed, altogether unparalleled but certainly bidding defiance to anything like analysis or explanation.

Yet let me not be misapprehended. The undue, earnest, and morbid attention thus excited by objects in their own nature frivolous, must not be confounded in character with that ruminating propensity common to all mankind, and more especially indulged in by persons of ardent imagination. It was not even, as might be at first supposed, an extreme condition, or exaggeration of such propensity, but primarily and essentially distinct and different. In the one instance, the dreamer, or enthusiast, being interested by an object usually *not* frivolous, imperceptibly loses sight of this object in a wilderness of deductions and suggestions issuing therefrom, until, at the conclusion of a day-dream *often replete with luxury*, he finds the *incitamentum*, or first cause of his musings, entirely vanished and forgotten. In my case, the primary object was *invariably frivolous*, although assuming, through the medium of my distempered vision, a refracted and unreal importance. Few deductions, if any, were made; and those few pertinaciously returning in upon the original object as a centre. The meditations were *never* pleasurable; and, at the termination of the revery, the first cause, so far from being out of sight, had attained that super-naturally exaggerated interest which was the prevailing feature of the disease. In a word, the powers of mind more particularly exercised were, with me, as I have said before, the *attentive*, and are, with the day-dreamer, the *speculative*.

My books, at this epoch, if they did not actually serve to irritate the disorder, partook, it will be perceived, largely, in their imaginative and inconsequential nature, of the characteristic qualities of the disorder itself. I well remember, among others, the treatise of the noble Italian, Cælius Secundus Curio, "*De Amplitudine Beati Regni Dei;*" St. Austin's great work, "The City of God;" and Tertullian's "*De Carne Christi,*" in which the paradoxical sentence, "*Mortuus est Dei filius; credibile est quia ineptumest; et sepultus resurrexit; certum est quia impossibile est,*" occupied my undivided time, for many weeks of laborious and fruitless investigation.

Thus it will appear that, shaken from its balance only by trivial things, my reason bore resemblance to that ocean-crag spoken of by Ptolemy Hephestion, which steadily resisting the attacks of human violence, and the fiercer fury of the waters and the winds, trembled only to the touch of the flower called Asphodel. And although, to a careless thinker, it might appear a matter beyond doubt, that the alteration produced by her unhappy malady, in the *moral* condition of Berenice, would afford me many objects for the exercise of that intense and abnormal meditation whose nature I have been at some trouble in explaining, yet such was not in any degree the case. In the lucid intervals of my infirmity, her calamity, indeed, gave me pain, and, taking deeply to heart that total wreck of her fair and gentle life, I did not fail to ponder, frequently and bitterly, upon the wonder-working means by which so strange a revolution had been so suddenly brought to pass. But these reflections partook not of the idiosyncrasy of my disease, and were such as would have occurred, under similar circumstances, to the ordinary mass of mankind. True to its own character, my disorder revelled in the less important but more startling changes wrought in the *physical* frame of Berenice—in the singular and most appalling distortion of her personal identity.

During the brightest days of her unparalleled beauty, most surely I had never loved her. In the strange anomaly of my existence, feelings with me, *had never been* of the heart, and my passions *always were* of the mind. Through the gray of the early morning—among the trellised shadows of the forest at noonday—and in the silence of my library at night—she had flitted by my eyes, and I had seen her—not as the living and breathing Berenice, but as the Berenice of a dream; not as a being of the earth, earthy, but as the abstraction of such a being; not as a thing to admire, but to analyze; not as an object of love, but as the theme of the most abstruse although desultory speculation. And *now*—now I shuddered in her presence, and grew pale at her approach; yet, bitterly lamenting her fallen and desolate condition, I called to mind that she had loved me long, and, in an evil moment, I spoke to her of marriage.

And at length the period of our nuptials was approaching, when, upon an afternoon in the winter of the year—one of those unseasonably warm, calm, and misty days which are the nurse of the beautiful

Halcyon,*—I sat, (and sat, as I thought, alone,) in the inner apartment of the library. But, uplifting my eyes, I saw that Berenice stood before me.

Was it my own excited imagination—or the misty influence of the atmosphere—or the uncertain twilight of the chamber—or the gray draperies which fell around her figure—that caused in it so vacillating and indistinct an outline? I could not tell. She spoke no word; and I—not for worlds could I have uttered a syllable. An icy chill ran through my frame; a sense of insufferable anxiety oppressed me; a consuming curiosity pervaded my soul; and, sinking back upon the chair, I remained for some time breathless and motionless, with my eyes riveted upon her person. Alas! its emaciation was excessive, and not one vestige of the former being lurked in any single line of the contour. My burning glances at length fell upon the face.

The forehead was high, and very pale, and singularly placid; and the once jetty hair fell partially over it, and overshadowed the hollow temples with innumerable ringlets, now of a vivid yellow, and jarring discordantly, in their fantastic character, with the reigning melancholy of the countenance. The eyes were lifeless, and lustreless, and seemingly pupilless, and I shrank involuntarily from their glassy stare to the contemplation of the thin and shrunken lips. They parted; and in a smile of peculiar meaning, *the teeth* of the changed Berenice disclosed themselves slowly to my view. Would to God that I had never beheld them, or that, having done so, I had died!

*

* For as Jove, during the winter season, gives twice seven days of warmth, men have called this clement and temperate time the nurse of the beautiful Halcyon. —*Simonides.*

The shutting of a door disturbed me, and, looking up, I found that my cousin had departed from the chamber. But from the disordered chamber of my brain, had not, alas! departed, and would not be driven away, the white and ghastly *spectrum* of the teeth. Not a speck on their surface—not a shade on their enamel—not an indenture in their edges—but what that brief period of her smile had sufficed to brand in upon my memory. I saw them *now* even more unequivocally than I beheld them *then*. The teeth!—the teeth!—they were here, and there, and everywhere, and visibly and palpably before me; long, narrow, and excessively white, with the pale lips writhing about them, as in the very moment of their first terrible development. Then came the full fury of my *monomania*, and I struggled in vain against its strange and irresistible influence. In the multiplied objects of the external world I had no thoughts but for the teeth. For these I longed with a frenzied desire. All other matters and all different interests became absorbed in their single contemplation. They—they alone were present to the mental eye, and they, in their sole individuality, became the essence of my mental life. I held them in every light. I turned them in every attitude. I surveyed their characteristics. I dwelt upon their peculiarities. I pondered upon their conformation. I mused upon the alteration in their nature. I shuddered as I assigned to them, in imagination, a sensitive and sentient power, and, even when unassisted by the lips, a capability of moral expression. Of Mademoiselle Salle it has been well said, "*Que tous ses pas etaient des sentiments*," and of Berenice I more seriously believed *que tous ses dents etaient des idees. Des idees!*— ah, here was the idiotic thought that destroyed me! *Des idees!*—ah, *therefore* it was that I coveted them so madly! I felt that their possession could alone ever restore me to peace, in giving me back to reason.

And the evening closed in upon me thus—and then the darkness came, and tarried, and went—and the day again dawned—and the mists of a second night were now gathering around—and still I sat motionless in that solitary room—and still I sat buried in meditation—and still the *phantasma* of the teeth maintained its terrible ascendency, as, with the most vivid and hideous distinctness, it floated about amid the changing lights and shadows of the chamber. At length there broke in upon my dreams a cry as of horror and dismay; and thereunto, after a pause, succeeded the sound of troubled voices, intermingled with many low moanings of sorrow or of pain. I arose from my seat, and throwing open one of the doors of the library, saw standing out in the antechamber a servant maiden, all in tears, who told me that Berenice was—no more! She had been seized with epilepsy in the early morning, and now, at the closing in of the night, the grave was ready for its tenant, and all the preparations for the burial were completed.

I found myself sitting in the library, and again sitting there alone. It seemed that I had newly awakened from a confused and exciting dream. I knew that it was now midnight, and I was well aware, that since the setting of the sun, Berenice had been interred. But of that dreary period which intervened I had no positive, at least no definite comprehension. Yet its memory was replete with horror—horror more horrible from being vague, and terror more terrible from ambiguity. It was a fearful page in the record of my existence, written all over with dim, and hideous, and unintelligible recollections. I strived to decypher them, but in vain; while ever and anon, like the spirit of a departed sound, the shrill and piercing shriek of a female voice seemed to be ringing in my ears. I had done a deed—what was it? I asked myself the question aloud, and the whispering echoes of the chamber answered me,—"*What was it?*"

On the table beside me burned a lamp, and near it lay a little box. It was of no remarkable character, and I had seen it frequently before, for it was the property of the family physician; but how came it *there*, upon my table, and why did I shudder in regarding it? These things were in no manner to be accounted for, and my eyes at length dropped to the open pages of a book, and to a sentence underscored therein. The words were the singular but simple ones of the poet Ebn Zaiat:—"*Dicebant mihi sodales si sepulchrum amicae visitarem, curas meas aliquantulum fore levatas.*" Why, then, as I perused them, did the hairs of my head erect themselves on end, and the blood of my body become congealed within my veins?

There came a light tap at the library door—and, pale as the tenant of a tomb, a menial entered upon tiptoe. His looks were wild with terror, and he spoke to me in a voice tremulous, husky, and very low. What said he?—some broken sentences I heard. He told of a wild cry disturbing the silence of the night—of the gathering together of the household—of a search in the direction of the sound; and then his tones grew thrillingly distinct as he whispered me of a violated grave—of a disfigured body enshrouded, yet still breathing—still palpitating—*still alive!*

He pointed to my garments; they were muddy and clotted with gore. I spoke not, and he took me gently by the hand: it was indented with the impress of human nails. He directed my attention to some object against the wall. I looked at it for some minutes: it was a spade. With a shriek I bounded to the table, and grasped the box that lay upon it. But I could not force it open; and, in my tremor, it slipped from my hands, and fell heavily, and burst into pieces; and from it, with a rattling sound, there rolled out some instruments of dental surgery, intermingled with thirty-two small, white, and ivory-looking substances that were scattered to and fro about the floor.

WITCHES' LOAVES

O. Henry

O. Henry is the pseudonym of American writer William Sydney Porter (1862–1910), a prolific writer of fiction, non-fiction and poetry who published hundreds of short stories in his lifetime. His work is known for its attentive detail to the ordinariness of everyday life, existing as realist explorations of the mundane with characteristic wit. Some stories, such as "Witches' Loaves", function as a kind of comedy of errors, complicating the supposed dreaminess of daily encounters that are otherwise featured in his works. O. Henry's first book *Cabbages and Kings* (1904) was published two years after he moved to New York in 1902 and was followed by nine further collections before his death in 1910.

"Witches' Loaves" was included in *Sixes and Sevens* (1911) a collected volume that was published posthumously. The story foregrounds the complicated nature of courtship and romance with dry irony, suggesting the risky business of preconceptions and the consequences of eluded expectations. "Witches' Loaves" takes for its main theme the relationship between food and romance, and the fickle nature of giving as philanthropy. Miss Meacham herself considers the difficulty of navigating affection through food, concluding that unlike with flowers, "there was no language of edibles". By playing on the connection between women's work and witchery, O. Henry's title alludes to a darker motive that the story may initially suggest. Therefore, the tale works to explore the gendered dynamics of food and sharing, the limits of knowing, and the jarring nature of loneliness experienced in a place of giving. This makes comment on the paradigm between the social nature of obtaining nourishment—evidenced through Miss Meacham's bakery—and the experience of consumption as an essentially individual experience, and therefore, isolating act.

Miss Martha Meacham kept the little bakery on the corner (the one where you go up three steps, and the bell tinkles when you open the door).

Miss Martha was forty, her bank-book showed a credit of two thousand dollars, and she possessed two false teeth and a sympathetic heart. Many people have married whose chances to do so were much inferior to Miss Martha's.

Two or three times a week a customer came in in whom she began to take an interest. He was a middle-aged man, wearing spectacles and a brown beard trimmed to a careful point.

He spoke English with a strong German accent. His clothes were worn and darned in places, and wrinkled and baggy in others. But he looked neat, and had very good manners.

He always bought two loaves of stale bread. Fresh bread was five cents a loaf. Stale ones were two for five. Never did he call for anything but stale bread.

Once Miss Martha saw a red and brown stain on his fingers. She was sure then that he was an artist and very poor. No doubt he lived in a garret, where he painted pictures and ate stale bread and thought of the good things to eat in Miss Martha's bakery.

Often when Miss Martha sat down to her chops and light rolls and jam and tea she would sigh, and wish that the gentle-mannered artist might share her tasty meal instead of eating his dry crust in that draughty attic. Miss Martha's heart, as you have been told, was a sympathetic one.

In order to test her theory as to his occupation, she brought from her room one day a painting that she had bought at a sale, and set it against the shelves behind the bread counter.

It was a Venetian scene. A splendid marble palazzo (so it said on the picture) stood in the foreground—or rather forewater. For the rest there were gondolas (with the lady trailing her hand in the water), clouds, sky, and chiaroscuro in plenty. No artist could fail to notice it.

Two days afterward the customer came in.

"Two loafs of stale bread, if you blease.

"You haf here a fine bicture, madame," he said while she was wrapping up the bread.

"Yes?" says Miss Martha, revelling in her own cunning. "I do so admire art and" (no, it would not do to say "artists" thus early) "and paintings," she substituted. "You think it is a good picture?"

"Der balace," said the customer, "is not in good drawing. Der bairspective of it is not true. Goot morning, madame."

He took his bread, bowed, and hurried out.

Yes, he must be an artist. Miss Martha took the picture back to her room.

How gentle and kindly his eyes shone behind his spectacles! What a broad brow he had! To be able to judge perspective at a glance—and to live on stale bread! But genius often has to struggle before it is recognized.

What a thing it would be for art and perspective if genius were backed by two thousand dollars in the bank, a bakery, and a sympathetic heart to—But these were day-dreams, Miss Martha.

Often now when he came he would chat for a while across the showcase. He seemed to crave Miss Martha's cheerful words.

He kept on buying stale bread. Never a cake, never a pie, never one of her delicious Sally Lunns.

She thought he began to look thinner and discouraged. Her heart ached to add something good to eat to his meagre purchase, but her courage failed at the act. She did not dare affront him. She knew the pride of artists.

Miss Martha took to wearing her blue-dotted silk waist behind the counter. In the back room she cooked a mysterious compound of quince seeds and borax. Ever so many people use it for the complexion.

One day the customer came in as usual, laid his nickel on the showcase, and called for his stale loaves. While Miss Martha was reaching for them there was a great tooting and clanging, and a fire-engine came lumbering past.

The customer hurried to the door to look, as any one will. Suddenly inspired, Miss Martha seized the opportunity.

On the bottom shelf behind the counter was a pound of fresh butter that the dairyman had left ten minutes before. With a bread knife Miss Martha made a deep slash in each of the stale loaves, inserted a generous quantity of butter, and pressed the loaves tight again.

When the customer turned once more she was tying the paper around them.

When he had gone, after an unusually pleasant little chat, Miss Martha smiled to herself, but not without a slight fluttering of the heart.

Had she been too bold? Would he take offence? But surely not. There was no language of edibles. Butter was no emblem of unmaidenly forwardness.

For a long time that day her mind dwelt on the subject. She imagined the scene when he should discover her little deception.

He would lay down his brushes and palette. There would stand his easel with the picture he was painting in which the perspective was beyond criticism.

He would prepare for his luncheon of dry bread and water. He would slice into a loaf—ah!

Miss Martha blushed. Would he think of the hand that placed it there as he ate? Would he—

The front door bell jangled viciously. Somebody was coming in, making a great deal of noise.

Miss Martha hurried to the front. Two men were there. One was a young man smoking a pipe—a man she had never seen before. The other was her artist.

His face was very red, his hat was on the back of his head, his hair was wildly rumpled. He clinched his two fists and shook them ferociously at Miss Martha. *At Miss Martha.*

"*Dummkopf!*" he shouted with extreme loudness; and then "*Tausendonfer!*" or something like it in German.

The young man tried to draw him away.

"I vill not go," he said angrily, "else I shall told her."

He made a bass drum of Miss Martha's counter.

"You haf shpoilt me," he cried, his blue eyes blazing behind his spectacles. "I vill tell you. You vas von *meddingsome old cat!*"

Miss Martha leaned weakly against the shelves and laid one hand on her blue-dotted silk waist. The young man took his companion by the collar.

"Come on," he said, "you've said enough." He dragged the angry one out at the door to the sidewalk, and then came back.

"Guess you ought to be told, ma'am," he said, "what the row is about. That's Blumberger. He's an architectural draftsman. I work in the same office with him.

"He's been working hard for three months drawing a plan for a new city hall. It was a prize competition. He finished inking the lines yesterday. You know, a draftsman always makes his drawing in pencil first. When it's done he rubs out the pencil lines with handfuls of stale breadcrumbs. That's better than India rubber.

"Blumberger's been buying the bread here. Well, today—well, you know, ma'am, that butter isn't well, Blumberger's plan isn't good for anything now except to cut up into railroad sandwiches."

Miss Martha went into the back room. She took off the blue-dotted silk waist and put on the old brown serge she used to wear. Then she poured the quince seed and borax mixture out of the window into the ash can.

LOVERS

Silvina Ocampo

Silvina Ocampo (1903–1993) was an Argentinian writer and artist. Whilst Ocampo's writings are extensive, she came to painting first. As a young woman, Ocampo left Buenos Aries for Paris, where she studied art with Giorgio de Chirico—a painter and critic associated with the surrealist movement—and Fernand Leger, a modernist painter and filmmaker. Elements of rich visuals thread throughout Ocampo's writing; the influence of the surrealist style is evident in the specific, dreamy quality of her stories' details. As Ocampo returned to Buenos Aires, her sister, Victoria, founded *Sur*, a magazine and publishing house which featured Jorge Luis Borges—a fast friend and advocate of Ocampo's own writing—as both writer and editor. 1937 saw the publication of Ocampo's first short story collection; *Viaje olvidado* (*Forgotten Journey*). Following this, Ocampo's publications came quickly, with numerous collections of poetry, short stories, and works of translation.

"Amantes" ("Lovers") was first published in Ocampo's fourth short story collection *Las invitadas* (*The Guests*) in 1961. The story follows the "ritual" meeting of two lovers "through the labyrinths of their days". They coalesce weekly—notably, on Sundays—at a bakery, buying and eating cakes that are like exquisite pieces of edible art. The reader's expectations are subverted. As the story progresses, the lovers-meeting narrative is shifted. The lovers are eerily in tune;

connected through their eating, which is incessant, obsessive, but still somehow vacant, maintaining distance. The story is uncanny in the sense of both Freud's ideas of the double and the automaton; a discomforting mirroring between the two lovers is used to illustrate a strange, forbidden kind of passion that articulates itself through the shared, secret pleasure of food.

In his plastic wallet he carried a picture of her dressed as a harem girl. She had a picture of him in his conscript's uniform on her bedside table.

Their families, jobs, the schedule of meals and bedtimes, all conspired against their meeting often, but those sporadic meetings were rituals and always took place in winter. First they would buy pastries, and then, sitting under the trees, they would savor them, like children with a snack.

Uncertainty is a form of happiness that works in lovers' favor. Through the labyrinths of their days, of crackly, seemingly endless phone calls, they would always choose Dahlias Bakery as their meeting place, and always choose Sunday as the day, but only after discarding other possibilities. Instead of a coat she wore a shaggy plaid blanket that always came in handy. By the bakery window they would exchange greetings without looking at each other, making a show of their confusion. Those who don't see each other often don't know what to say, no doubt.

"Perhaps in a very dark room or in a very fast car," he thought, "I would overcome my shyness." "Perhaps I would know what to say to him in a movie theater after the intermission, or while taking part in a procession," she thought.

After this interior dialogue, they went to the bakery, as always, and bought pieces of four different kinds of cake. One looked like the Monument to the Spaniards, cluttered with plumes of whipped cream and glazed fruit in the form of flowers; another looked like some sort of mysterious and very dark lace, with shiny decorations of chocolate and yellow meringue covered with sprinkles; another looked like a broken marble pedestal, less beautiful than the others but larger, with coffee frosting, whipped cream, and pieces of nuts; another looked like part of a box, with jewels inlaid at either end and snow on top. After paying, when the package was ready, they would go to the Recoleta, next to the wall of the old age home, where children hide after breaking the streetlights and beggars go to wash their clothes in the fountains. Next to a frail tree, whose branches act as swings and horses for the children who play in them, they sat down on the grass. She opened the package and took out the cardboard tray where the cream and meringue and chocolate glowed, though already a bit squashed. Simultaneously, as if their movements were projected onto each other (mysterious and subtle mirror!), first with one hand, then with both hands, they picked up the slices of the cake with plumes of whipped cream (the miniature Monument to the Spaniards), and lifted them to their mouths. They chewed in unison and finished swallowing each bite at the same time. In the same surprising harmony they cleaned their fingers on napkins that others had left lying on the grass. The repetition of these movements connected them with eternity.

After finishing the first slice they again contemplated the remaining slices on the cardboard tray. With loving greed and greater intimacy they took the second pieces: the slices of chocolate decorated with meringue. Without hesitating, squinting their eyes, they lifted them up to mouths agape. Baby pigeons open their beaks the same way to receive the food brought by their mothers. With greater energy and speed, but with identical pleasure, they began chewing and swallowing once more, like two gymnasts exercising at the same time. She, from time to time, would turn to watch some passing car that was especially valuable, smelling excessively of gasoline, or very large, or would lift her head to watch a dove, the symbol of love, fluttering clumsily among the branches. He would look straight ahead, perhaps savoring the taste of those treats less consciously than she. The abundant whipped cream dripped on the grass, on the folded blanket, and on some bits of trash nearby. No smile would light up their harmonious lips until they finished the contents of the little tray of yellowish cardboard covered with waxed paper. The last bit of cake, crumbled between thumb and index finger, took a long time to reach their open mouths. The crumbs that fell on the tray, her skirt, and his pants were carefully picked up and lifted with thumb and finger to their lips.

The third slice of cake, even more opulent than the others, looked like the material used to build the older houses in beach resorts. The fourth piece, lighter but more difficult to eat because of its sponge-like consistency coated with sugar, left them with white mustaches and white spots on their lips. They had to stick out their tongues and close their eyes to clean their mouths. If they didn't dare to take large bites they missed the best part of the cake, covered with peanuts disguised as walnuts or almonds. She stretched out her neck and lowered her head; he didn't change his position. The chewing followed a regular rhythm, as if they were keeping time with a metronome.

They knew there were other treats left on the cardboard tray. After that first difficult moment, the rest was easy. They used their hands like spoons. Without chewing, they filled their mouths with cream and sponge cake before swallowing.

After finishing the contents of the tray, she tossed the festooned cardboard away and took a little package of peanuts out of her pocket.

For several minutes, with the studied gestures of a model, she opened the shells, peeled the nuts, and fed them to him; she saved some for herself, putting them in her mouth and chewing in unison with him. Licking their lips, they attempted a shy conversation on the theme of picnics: people who had died after drinking wine or eating watermelon; a poisonous spider in a picnic basket one Sunday that had killed a girl whose in-laws all hated her; canned goods that had gone bad, but looked delicious, had caused the death of two families in Trenque Lauquen; a storm that had drowned two couples who were celebrating their honeymoons with hard cider and rolls with sausages on the banks of a stream in Tapalqué.

When they had finished the food and the conversation, she unfolded the blanket and they covered themselves with it, lying on the grass. They smiled for the first time, their mouths full of food and words, but she knew (as he did) that, beneath the blanket, love would repeat its usual actions, and that hope, flying farther and farther away on fickle wings, would draw her away from marriage.

UNDER THE JAGUAR SUN

Italo Calvino

Italian author Italo Calvino (1923–1985) is known for his prolific work across multiple genres, as a writer of short stories, novels, essays, and collector of Italian fairy tales and folktales. His most popular works include *Cosmicomics* (1965), *If on a winter's night a traveller* (1979) and *Invisible Cities* (1972). Calvino continues to be renowned as one of the greatest Italian writers, with his liminal, fluid approach to genre and attention to "simple" literary forms and styles cementing his works as understated modern classics. Through his clean, sensorial description, Calvino considered the role of territory, homeland, and different forms of transformation and translation—from place to place, from metaphor to meaning, and from self to other. Calvino himself travelled well, constructing the narrative of "Under the Jaguar Sun"—set in Mexico—whilst himself in Paris.

"Under the Jaguar Sun" was first published as "Sapore sapere" (literally "to taste, to know") in Italian magazine *FMR* in the summer of 1982, before being published with two other stories under its current name in 1986. "Under the Jaguar Sun" palpitates with subtle unease, examining the dichotomies of religious and sensory ecstasy. The tale depicts a food-centric pilgrimage to Mexico, with the feverish consumption perhaps critiquing the relationships between tourists and interactions with "exotic" places. Calvino articulates consumption as a phenomenon working across various levels; physical, interpersonal, and international, working to both highlight and collapse boundaries between the known and the new. The story's rich attention to colour, sight, smell, and sound reinforces the two-fold universal issue of consumption—both in terms of tasting and travelling.

"Oaxaca" is pronounced "Wa*h*aka." Originally, the hotel where we were staying had been the Convent of Santa Catalina. The first thing we noticed was a painting in a little room leading to the bar. The bar was called Las Novicias. The painting was a large, dark canvas that portrayed a young nun and an old priest standing side by side; their hands, slightly apart from their sides, almost touched. The figures were rather stiff for an eighteenth-century picture; the painting had the somewhat crude grace characteristic of colonial art, but it conveyed a distressing sensation, like an ache of contained suffering.

The lower part of the painting was filled by a long caption, written in cramped lines in an angular, italic hand, white on black. The words devoutly celebrated the life and death of the two characters, who had been chaplain and abbess of the convent (she, of noble birth, had entered it as a novice at the age of eighteen). The reason for their being painted together was the extraordinary love (this word, in the pious Spanish prose, appeared charged with ultra-terrestrial yearning) that had bound the abbess and her confessor for thirty years, a love so great (the word in its spiritual sense sublimated but did not erase the physical emotion) that when the priest came to die, the abbess, twenty years younger, in the space of a single day fell ill and literally expired of love (the word blazed with a truth in which all meanings converge), to join him in Heaven.

Olivia, whose Spanish is better than mine, helped me decipher the story, suggesting to me the translation of some obscure expressions, and these words proved to be the only ones we exchanged during and after the reading, as if we had found ourselves in the presence of a drama, or of a happiness, that made any comment out of place. Something intimidated us—or, rather, frightened us, or, more precisely, filled us with a kind of uneasiness. So I will try to describe what I felt: the sense of a lack, a consuming void. What Olivia was thinking, since she remained silent, I cannot guess.

Then Olivia spoke. She said, "I would like to eat *chiles en nogada*." And, walking like somnambulists, not quite sure we were touching the ground, we headed for the dining room.

In the best moments of a couple's life, it happens: I immediately reconstructed the train of Olivia's thought, with no need of further speech, because the same sequence of associations had unrolled in my mind, though in a more foggy, murky way. Without her, I would never have gained awareness of it.

Our trip through Mexico had already lasted over a week. A few days earlier, in Tepotzotlán, in a restaurant whose tables were set among the orange trees of another convent's cloister, we had savored dishes prepared (at least, so we were told) according to the traditional recipes of the nuns. We had eaten a *tamal de elote*—a fine semolina of sweet corn, that is, with ground pork and very hot pepper, all steamed in a bit of cornhusk—and then *chiles en nogada*, which were reddish brown, somewhat wrinkled little peppers, swimming in a walnut sauce whose harshness and bitter aftertaste were drowned in a creamy, sweetish surrender.

After that, for us, the thought of nuns called up the flavors of an elaborate and bold cuisine, bent on making the flavors' highest notes vibrate, juxtaposing them in modulations, in chords, and especially in dissonances that would assert themselves as an incomparable experience—a point of no return, an absolute possession exercised on the receptivity of all the senses.

The Mexican friend who had accompanied us on that excursion, Salustiano Velazco by name, in answering Olivia's inquiries about these recipes of conventual gastronomy, lowered his voice as if confiding indelicate secrets to us. It was his way of speaking—or, rather, one of his ways; the copious information Salustiano supplied (about the history and customs and nature of his country his erudition was inexhaustible) was either stated emphatically like a war proclamation or slyly insinuated as if it were charged with all sorts of implied meanings.

Olivia remarked that such dishes involved hours and hours of work and, even before that, a long series of experiments and adjustments. "Did these nuns spend their whole day in the kitchen?" she asked, imagining entire lives devoted to the search for new blends of ingredients, new variations in the measurements, to alert and patient mixing, to the handing down of an intricate, precise lore.

"*Tenían sus criadas,*" Salustiano answered. ("They had their servants.") And he explained to us that when the daughters of noble families entered the convent, they brought their maids with them; thus, to satisfy the venial whims of gluttony, the only cravings allowed them, the nuns could rely on a swarm of eager, tireless helpers. And as far as they themselves were concerned, they had only to conceive and compare and correct the recipes that expressed their fantasies confined within those walls: the fantasies, after all, of sophisticated women, bright and introverted and complex women who needed absolutes, whose reading told of ecstasies and transfigurations, martyrs and tortures, women with conflicting calls in their blood, genealogies in which the descendants of the conquistadores mingled with those of Indian princesses or slaves, women with childhood recollections of the fruits and fragrances of a succulent vegetation, thick with ferments, though growing from those sun-baked plateaus.

Nor should sacred architecture be overlooked, the background to the lives of those religious; it, too, was impelled by the same drive toward the extreme that led to the exacerbation of flavors amplified by the blaze of the most spicy *chiles*. Just as colonial baroque set no limits on the profusion of ornament and display, in which God's presence was identified in a closely calculated delirium of brimming, excessive sensations, so the curing of the hundred or more native varieties of hot peppers carefully selected for each dish opened vistas of a flaming ecstasy.

At Tepotzotlán, we visited the church the Jesuits had built in the eighteenth century for their seminary (and no sooner was it consecrated than they had to abandon it, as they were expelled from Mexico forever): a theater-church, all gold and bright colors, in a dancing and acrobatic baroque, crammed with swirling angels, garlands, panoplies of flowers, shells. Surely the Jesuits meant to compete with the splendor of the Aztecs, whose ruined temples and palaces—the royal palace of Quetzalcóatl!—still stood, to recall a rule imposed through the impressive effects of a grandiose, transfiguring art. There was a challenge in the air, in this dry and thin air at an altitude of two thousand meters: the ancient rivalry between the civilizations of America and Spain in the art of bewitching the senses with dazzling seductions. And from architecture this rivalry extended to cuisine, where the two civilizations had merged, or perhaps where the conquered had triumphed, strong in the condiments born from their very soil. Through the white hands of novices and the brown hands of lay sisters, the cuisine of the new Indo-Hispanic civilization had become also the field of battle between the aggressive ferocity of the ancient gods of the mesa and the sinuous excess of the baroque religion.

On the supper menu we didn't find *chiles en nogada*. From one locality to the next the gastronomic lexicon varied, always offering new terms to be recorded and new sensations to be defined. Instead, we found *guacamole*, to be scooped up with crisp tortillas that snap into many shards and dip like spoons into the thick cream (the fat softness of the *aguacate*—the Mexican national fruit, known to the rest of the world under the distorted name of "avocado"—is accompanied and underlined by the angular dryness of the tortilla, which, for its part, can have many flavors, pretending to have none); then *guajolote con mole poblano*—that is, turkey with Puebla-style *mole* sauce, one of the noblest among the many *moles*, and most laborious (the preparation never takes less than two days), and most complicated, because it requires several different varieties of *chile*, as well as garlic, onion, cinnamon, cloves, pepper, cumin, coriander, and sesame, almonds, raisins, and peanuts, with a touch of chocolate; and finally *quesadillas* (another kind of tortilla, really, for which cheese is incorporated in the dough, garnished with ground meat and refried beans).

Right in the midst of chewing, Olivia's lips paused, almost stopped, though without completely interrupting their continuity of movement, which slowed down, as if reluctant to allow an inner echo to fade, while her gaze became fixed, intent on no specific object, in apparent alarm. Her face had a special concentration that I had observed during meals ever since we began our trip to Mexico. I followed the tension as it moved from her lips to her nostrils, flaring one moment, contracting the next, (the plasticity of the nose is quite limited—especially for a delicate, harmonious nose like Olivia's—and each barely perceptible attempt to expand the capacity of the nostrils in the longitudinal direction actually makes them thinner, while the corresponding reflex movement, accentuating their breadth, then seems a kind of withdrawal of the whole nose into the surface of the face).

What I have just said might suggest that, in eating, Olivia became closed into herself, absorbed with the inner course of her sensations; in reality, on the contrary, the desire her whole person expressed was that of communicating to me what she was tasting: communicating with me through flavors, or communicating with flavors through a double set of taste buds, hers and mine. "Did you taste that? Are you tasting it?" she was asking me, with a kind of anxiety, as if at that same moment our incisors had pierced an identically composed morsel and the same drop of savor had been caught by the membranes of my tongue and of hers. "Is it *cilantro*? Can't you taste *cilantro*?" she insisted, referring to an herb whose local name hadn't allowed us to identify it with certainty (was it coriander, perhaps?) and of which a little thread in the morsel we were chewing sufficed to transmit to the nostrils a sweetly pungent emotion, like an impalpable intoxication.

Olivia's need to involve me in her emotions pleased me greatly, because it showed that I was indispensable to her and that, for her, the pleasures of existence could be appreciated only if we shared them. Our subjective, individual selves, I was thinking, find their amplification and completion only in the unity of the couple. I needed confirmation of this conviction all the more since, from the beginning of our Mexican journey, the physical bond between Olivia and me was going through a phase of rarefaction, if not eclipse: a momentary phenomenon, surely, and not in itself disturbing—part of the normal ups and downs to which, over a long period, the life of every couple is subject. And I couldn't help remarking how certain manifestations of Olivia's vital energy, certain prompt reactions or delays on her part, yearnings or throbs, continued to take place before my eyes, losing none of their intensity, with only one significant difference: their stage was no longer the bed of our embraces but a dinner table.

During the first few days I expected the gradual kindling of the palate to spread quickly to all our senses. I was mistaken: aphrodisiac this cuisine surely was, but in itself and for itself (this is what I thought to understand, and what I am saying applies only to us at that moment; I cannot speak for others or for us if we had been in a different humor). It stimulated desires, in other words, that sought their satisfaction only within the very sphere of sensation that had aroused them—in eating new dishes, therefore, that would generate and extend those same desires. We were thus in the ideal situation for imagining what the love between the abbess and the chaplain might have been like: a love that, in the eyes of the world and in their own eyes, could have been perfectly chaste and at the same time infinitely carnal in that experience of flavors gained through secret and subtle complicity.

"Complicity": the word, the moment it came into my mind— referring not only to the nun and the priest but also to Olivia and me—heartened me. Because if what Olivia sought was complicity in the almost obsessive passion that had seized her, then this suggested we were not losing—as I had feared—a parity between us. In fact, it had seemed to me during the last few days that Olivia, in her gustatory exploration, had wanted to keep me in a subordinate position: a presence necessary, indeed, but subaltern, obliging me to observe the relationship between her and food as a confidant or as a compliant pander. I dispelled this irksome notion that had somehow or other occurred to me. In reality, our complicity could not be more total, precisely because we experienced the same passion in different ways, in accord with our temperaments: Olivia more sensitive to perceptive nuances and endowed with a more analytical memory, where every recollection remained distinct and unmistakable, I tending more to define experiences verbally and conceptually, to mark the ideal line of journey within ourselves contemporaneously with our geographical journey. In fact, this was a conclusion of mine that Olivia had instantly adopted (or perhaps Olivia had been the one to prompt the idea and I had simply proposed it to her again in words of my own): the true journey, as the introjection of an "outside" different from our normal one, implies a complete change of nutrition, a digesting of the visited country—its fauna and flora and its culture (not only the different culinary practices and condiments but the different implements used to grind the flour or stir the pot)—making it pass between the lips and down the esophagus. This is the only kind of travel that has a meaning nowadays, when everything visible you can see on television without rising from your easy chair. (And you mustn't rebut that the same result can be achieved by visiting the exotic restaurants of our big cities; they so counterfeit the reality of the cuisine they claim to follow that, as far as our deriving real knowledge is concerned, they are the equivalent not of an actual locality but of a scene reconstructed and shot in a studio.)

All the same, in the course of our trip Olivia and I saw everything there was to see (no small exploit, in quantity or quality). For the following morning we had planned a visit to the excavations at Monte Albán, and the guide came for us at the hotel promptly with a little bus. In the sunny, arid countryside grow the agaves used for mescal and tequila, and *nopales* (which we call prickly pears) and cereus—all thorns—and jacaranda, with its blue flowers. The road climbs up into the mountains. Monte Albán, among the heights surrounding a valley, is a complex of ruins: temples, reliefs, grand stairways, platforms for human sacrifice. Horror, sacredness, and mystery are consolidated by tourism, which dictates preordained forms of behavior, the modest surrogates of those rites. Contemplating these stairs, we try to imagine the hot blood spurting from the breast split by the stone axe of the priest.

Three civilizations succeeded one another at Monte Albán, each shifting the same blocks: the Zapotecs building over the works of the Olmecs, and the Mixtecs doing the same to those of the Zapotecs. The calendars of the ancient Mexican civilizations, carved on the reliefs, represent a cyclic, tragic concept of time: every fifty-two years the universe ended, the gods died, the temples were destroyed, every celestial and terrestrial thing changed its name. Perhaps the peoples that history defines as the successive occupants of these territories were merely a single people, whose continuity was never broken even through a series of massacres like those the reliefs depict. Here are the conquered villages, their names written in hieroglyphics, and the god of the village, his head hung upside down; here are the chained prisoners of war, the severed heads of the victims.

The guide to whom the travel agency entrusted us, a burly man named Alonso, with flattened features like an Olmec head (or Mixtec? Zapotec?), points out to us, with exuberant mime, the famous bas-reliefs called "Los Danzantes." Only some of the carved figures, he says, are portraits of dancers, with their legs in movement (Alonso performs a few steps); others might be astronomers, raising one hand to shield their eyes and study the stars (Alonso strikes an astronomer's pose). But for the most part, he says, they represent women giving birth (Alonso acts this out). We learn that this temple was meant to ward off difficult childbirths; the reliefs were perhaps votive images. Even the dance, for that matter, served to make births easier, through magic mimesis—especially when the baby came out feet first (Alonso performs the magic mimesis). One relief depicts a cesarean operation, complete with uterus and Fallopian tubes (Alonso, more brutal than ever, mimes the entire female anatomy, to demonstrate that a sole surgical torment linked births and deaths).

Everything in our guide's gesticulation takes on a truculent significance, as if the temples of the sacrifices cast their shadow on every act and every thought. When the most propitious date had been set, in accordance with the stars, the sacrifices were accompanied by the revelry of dances, and even births seemed to have no purpose beyond supplying new soldiers for the wars to capture victims. Though some figures are shown running or wrestling or playing football, according to Alonso these are not peaceful athletic competitions but, rather, the games of prisoners forced to compete in order to determine which of them would be the first to ascend the altar.

"And the loser in the games was chosen for the sacrifice?" I ask.

"No! The winner!" Alonso's face becomes radiant. "To have your chest split open by the obsidian knife was an honor!" And in a crescendo of ancestral patriotism, just as he had boasted of the excellence of the scientific knowledge of the ancient peoples, so now this worthy descendant of the Olmecs feels called upon to exalt the offering of a throbbing human heart to the sun to assure that the dawn would return each morning and illuminate the world.

That was when Olivia asked, "But what did they do with the victims' bodies afterward?"

Alonso stopped.

"Those limbs—I mean, those entrails," Olivia insisted. "They were offered to the gods, I realize that. But, practically speaking, what happened to them? Were they burned?"

No, they weren't burned.

"Well, what then? Surely a gift to the gods couldn't be buried, left to rot in the ground."

"Los *zopilotes*," Alonso said. "The vultures. They were the ones who cleared the altars and carried the offerings to Heaven."

The vultures. "Always?" Olivia asked further, with an insistence I could not explain to myself.

Alonso was evasive, tried to change the subject; he was in a hurry to show us the passages that connected the priests' houses with the temples, where they made their appearance, their faces covered by terrifying masks. Our guide's pedagogical enthusiasm had something irritating about it, because it gave the impression he was imparting to us a lesson that was simplified so that it would enter our poor profane heads, though he actually knew far more, things he kept to himself and took care not to tell us. Perhaps this was what Olivia had sensed and what, after a certain point, made her maintain a closed, vexed silence through the rest of our visit to the excavations and on the jolting bus that brought us back to Oaxaca.

Along the road, all curves, I tried to catch Olivia's eye as she sat facing me, but thanks to the bouncing of the bus or the difference in the level of our seats, I realized my gaze was resting not on her eyes but on her teeth (she kept her lips parted in a pensive expression), which I happened to be seeing for the first time not as the radiant glow of a smile but as the instruments most suited to their purpose: to be dug into flesh, to sever it, tear it. And as you try to read a person's thoughts in the expression of his eyes, so now I looked at those strong, sharp teeth and sensed there a restrained desire, an expectation.

As we reentered the hotel and headed for the large lobby (the former chapel of the convent), which we had to cross to reach the wing where our room was, we were struck by a sound like a cascade of water flowing and splashing and gurgling in a thousand rivulets and eddies and jets. The closer we got, the more this homogeneous noise was broken down into a complex of chirps, trills, caws, clucks, as of a flock of birds flapping their wings in an aviary. From the doorway (the room was a few steps lower than the corridor), we saw an expanse of little spring hats on the heads of ladies seated around tea tables. Throughout the country a campaign was in progress for the election of a new president of the republic, and the wife of the favored candidate was giving a tea party of impressive proportions for the wives of the prominent men of Oaxaca. Under the broad, empty vaulted ceiling, three hundred Mexican ladies were conversing all at once; the spectacular acoustical event that had immediately subdued us was produced by their voices mingled with the tinkling of cups and spoons and of knives cutting slices of cake. Looming over the assembly was a gigantic full-color picture of a round-faced lady with her black, smooth hair drawn straight back, wearing a blue dress of which only the buttoned collar could be seen; it was not unlike the official portraits of Chairman Mao Tse-tung, in other words.

To reach the patio and, from it, our stairs, we had to pick our way among the little tables of the reception. We were already close to the far exit when, from a table at the back of the hall, one of the few male guests rose and came toward us, arms extended. It was our friend Salustiano Velazco, a member of the would-be president's staff and, in that capacity, a participant in the more delicate stages of the electoral campaign. We hadn't seen him since leaving the capital, and to show us, with all his ebullience, his joy on seeing us again and to inquire about the latest stages of our journey (and perhaps to escape momentarily that atmosphere in which the triumphal female predominance compromised his chivalrous certitude of male supremacy) he left his place of honor at the symposium and accompanied us into the patio.

Instead of asking us about what we had seen, he began by pointing out the things we had surely failed to see in the places we had visited and could have seen only if he had been with us—a conversational formula that impassioned connoisseurs of a country feel obliged to adopt with visiting friends, always with the best intentions, though it successfully spoils the pleasure of those who have returned from a trip and are quite proud of their experiences, great or small. The convivial din of the distinguished gynaeceum followed us even into the patio and drowned at least half the words he and we spoke, so I was never sure he wasn't reproaching us for not having seen the very things we had just finished telling him we had seen.

"And today we went to Monte Albán," I quickly informed him, raising my voice. "The stairways, the reliefs, the sacrificial altars..."

Salustiano put his hand to his mouth, then waved it in mid-air—a gesture that, for him, meant an emotion too great to be expressed in words. He began by furnishing us archeological and ethnographical details I would have very much liked to hear sentence by sentence, but they were lost in the reverberations of the feast. From his gestures and the scattered words I managed to catch ("*Sangre... obsidiana... divinidad solar*"), I realized he was talking about the human sacrifices and was speaking with a mixture of awed participation and sacred horror—an attitude distinguished from that of our crude guide by a greater awareness of the cultural implications.

Quicker than I, Olivia managed to follow Salustiano's speech better, and now she spoke up, to ask him something. I realized she was repeating the question she had asked Alonso that afternoon: "What the vultures didn't carry off—what happened to that, afterward?"

Salustiano's eyes flashed knowing sparks at Olivia, and I also grasped then the purpose behind her question, especially as Salustiano assumed his confidential, abettor's tone. It seemed that, precisely because they were softer, his words now overcame more easily the barrier of sound that separated us.

"Who knows? The priests... This was also a part of the rite—I mean among the Aztecs, the people we know better. But even about them, not much is known. These were secret ceremonies. Yes, the ritual meal... The priest assumed the functions of the god, and so the victim, divine food..."

Was this Olivia's aim? To make him admit this? She insisted further, "But how did it take place? The meal..."

"As I say, there are only some suppositions. It seems that the princes, the warriors also joined in. The victim was already part of the god, transmitting divine strength." At this point, Salustiano changed his tone and became proud, dramatic, carried away. "Only the warrior who had captured the sacrificed prisoner could not touch his flesh. He remained apart, weeping."

Olivia still didn't seem satisfied. "But this flesh—in order to eat it... The way it was cooked, the sacred cuisine, the seasoning—is anything known about that?"

Salustiano became thoughtful. The banqueting ladies had redoubled their noise, and now Salustiano seemed to become hypersensitive to their sounds; he tapped his ear with one finger, signalling that he couldn't go on in all that racket. "Yes, there must have been some rules. Of course, that food couldn't be consumed without a special ceremony... the due honor... the respect for the sacrificed, who were brave youths... respect for the gods... flesh that couldn't be eaten just for the sake of eating, like any ordinary food. And the flavor..."

"They say it isn't good to eat?"

"A strange flavor, they say."

"It must have required seasoning—strong stuff."

"Perhaps that flavor had to be hidden. All other flavors had to be brought together, to hide that flavor."

And Olivia asked, "But the priests... About the cooking of it—they didn't leave any instructions? Didn't hand down anything?"

Salustiano shook his head. "A mystery. Their life was shrouded in mystery."

And Olivia—Olivia now seemed to be prompting him. "Perhaps that flavor emerged, all the same—even through the other flavors."

Salustiano put his fingers to his lips, as if to filter what he was saying. "It was a sacred cuisine. It had to celebrate the harmony of the elements achieved through sacrifice—a terrible harmony, flaming, incandescent..." He fell suddenly silent, as if sensing he had gone too far, and as if the thought of the repast had called him to his duty, he hastily apologized for not being able to stay longer with us. He had to go back to his place at the table.

Waiting for evening to fall, we sat in one of the cafés under the arcades of the *zócalo*, the regular little square that is the heart of every old city of the colony—green, with short, carefully pruned trees called *almendros*, though they bear no resemblance to almond trees. The tiny paper flags and the banners that greeted the official candidate did their best to convey a festive air to the *zócalo*. The proper Oaxaca families strolled under the arcades. American hippies waited for the old woman who supplied them with *mescalina*. Ragged vendors unfurled colored fabrics on the ground. From another square nearby came the echo of the loudspeakers of a sparsely attended rally of the opposition. Crouched on the ground, heavy women were frying tortillas and greens.

In the kiosk in the middle of the square, an orchestra was playing, bringing back to me reassuring memories of evenings in a familiar, provincial Europe I was old enough to have known and forgotten. But the memory was like a trompe-l'oeil, and when I examined it a little, it gave me a sense of multiplied distance, in space and in time. Wearing black suits and neckties, the musicians, with their dark, impassive Indian faces, played for the varicolored, shirtsleeved tourists—inhabitants, it seemed, of a perpetual summer—for parties of old men and women, meretriciously young in all the gleam of their dentures, and for groups of the really young, hunched over and meditative, as if waiting for age to come and whiten their blond beards and flowing hair; bundled in rough clothes, weighed down by their knapsacks, they looked like the allegorical figures of winter in old calendars.

"Perhaps time has come to an end, the sun has grown weary of rising, Chronos dies of starvation for want of victims to devour, the ages and the seasons are turned upside down," I said.

"Perhaps the death of time concerns only us," Olivia answered. "We who tear one another apart, pretending not to know it, pretending not to taste flavors anymore."

"You mean that here—that they need stronger flavors here because they know, because here they ate..."

"The same as at home, even now. Only we no longer know it, no longer dare look, the way they did. For them there was no mystification: the horror was right there, in front of their eyes. They ate as long as there was a bone left to pick clean, and that's why the flavors..."

"To hide that flavor?" I said, again picking up Salustiano's chain of hypotheses.

"Perhaps it couldn't be hidden. *Shouldn't* be. Otherwise, it was like not eating what they were really eating. Perhaps the other flavors served to enhance that flavor, to give it a worthy background, to honor it."

At these words I felt again the need to look her in the teeth, as I had done earlier, when we were coming down in the bus. But at that very moment her tongue, moist with saliva, emerged from between her teeth, then immediately drew back, as if she were mentally savoring something. I realized Olivia was already imagining the supper menu.

It began, this menu, offered us by a restaurant we found among low houses with curving grilles, with a rose-colored liquid in a hand-blown glass: *sopa de camarones*—shrimp soup, that is, immeasurably hot, thanks to some variety of *chiles* we had never come upon previously, perhaps the famous *chiles jalapeños*. Then *cabrito*—roast kid—every morsel of which provoked surprise, because the teeth would encounter first a crisp bit, then one that melted in the mouth.

"You're not eating?" Olivia asked me. She seemed to concentrate only on savoring her dish, though she was very alert, as usual, while I had remained lost in thought, looking at her. It was the sensation of her teeth in my flesh that I was imagining, and I could feel her tongue lift me against the roof of her mouth, enfold me in saliva, then thrust me under the tips of the canines. I sat there facing her, but at the same time it was as if a part of me, or all of me, were contained in her mouth, crunched, torn shred by shred. The situation was not entirely passive, since while I was being chewed by her I felt also that I was acting on her, transmitting sensations that spread from the taste buds through her whole body. I was the one who aroused her every vibration—it was a reciprocal and complete relationship, which involved us and overwhelmed us.

I regained my composure; so did she. We looked carefully at the salad of tender prickly-pear leaves (*ensalada de nopalitos*)—boiled,

seasoned with garlic, coriander, red pepper, and oil and vinegar—
then the pink and creamy pudding of *maguey* (a variety of agave),
all accompanied by a carafe of *sangrita* and followed by coffee with
cinnamon.

But this relationship between us, established exclusively through
food, so much so that it could be identified in no image other than
that of a meal—this relationship which in my imaginings I thought cor-
responded to Olivia's deepest desires—didn't please her in the slight-
est, and her irritation was to find its release during that same supper.

"How boring you are! How monotonous!" she began by saying,
repeating an old complaint about my uncommunicative nature and
my habit of giving her full responsibility for keeping the conversation
alive—an argument that flared up whenever we were alone together
at a restaurant table, including a list of charges whose basis in truth
I couldn't help admitting but in which I also discerned the fundamental reasons for our unity as a couple; namely, that Olivia saw and
knew how to catch and isolate and rapidly define many more things
than I, and therefore my relationship with the world was essentially
via her. "You're always sunk into yourself, unable to participate in
what's going on around you, unable to put yourself out for another,
never a flash of enthusiasm on your own, always ready to cast a pall
on anybody else's, depressing, indifferent—" And to the inventory
of my faults she added this time a new adjective, or one that to my
ears now took on a new meaning: "Insipid!"

There: I was insipid, I thought, without flavor. And the Mexican
cuisine, with all its boldness and imagination, was needed if Olivia
was to feed on me with satisfaction. The spiciest flavors were the
complement—indeed, the avenue of communication, indispensable
as a loudspeaker that amplifies sounds—for Olivia to be nourished
by my substance.

"I may seem insipid to you," I protested, "but there are ranges of flavor more discreet and restrained than that of red peppers. There are subtle tastes that one must know how to perceive!"

The next morning we left Oaxaca in Salustiano's car. Our friend had to visit other provinces on the candidate's tour, and offered to accompany us for part of our itinerary. At one point on the trip he showed us some recent excavations not yet overrun by tourists. A stone statue rose barely above the level of the ground, with the unmistakable form that we had learned to recognize on the very first days of our Mexican archeological wanderings: the *chacmool*, or half-reclining human figure, in an almost Etruscan pose, with a tray resting on his belly. He looks like a rough, good-natured puppet, but it was on that tray that the victims' hearts were offered to the gods.

"Messenger of the gods—what does that mean?" I asked. I had read that definition in a guidebook. "Is he a demon sent to earth by the gods to collect the dish with the offering? Or an emissary from human beings who must go to the gods and offer them the food?"

"Who knows?" Salustiano answered, with the suspended attitude he took in the face of unanswerable questions, as if listening to the inner voices he had at his disposal, like reference books. "It could be the victim himself, supine on the altar, offering his own entrails on the dish. Or the sacrificer, who assumes the pose of the victim because he is aware that tomorrow it will be his turn. Without this reciprocity, human sacrifice would be unthinkable. All were potentially both sacrificer and victim—the victim accepted his role as victim because he had fought to capture the others as victims."

"They could be eaten because they themselves were eaters of men?" I added, but Salustiano was talking now about the serpent as symbol of the continuity of life and the cosmos.

Meanwhile I understood: my mistake with Olivia was to consider myself eaten by her, whereas I should be myself (I always had been) the one who ate her. The most appetizingly flavored human flesh belongs to the eater of human flesh. It was only by feeding ravenously on Olivia that I would cease being tasteless to her palate.

This was in my mind that evening when I sat down with her to supper. "What's wrong with you? You're odd this evening," Olivia said, since nothing ever escaped her. The dish they had served us was called *gorditas pellizcadas con manteca*—literally, "plump girls pinched with butter." I concentrated on devouring, with every meatball, the whole fragrance of Olivia—through voluptuous mastication, a vampire extraction of vital juices. But I realized that in a relationship that should have been among three terms—me, meatball, Olivia—a fourth term had intruded, assuming a dominant role: the name of the meatballs. It was the name *"gorditas pellizcadas con manteca"* that I was especially savoring and assimilating and possessing. And, in fact, the magic of that name continued affecting me even after the meal, when we retired together to our hotel room in the night. And for the first time during our Mexican journey the spell whose victims we had been was broken, and the inspiration that had blessed the finest moments of our joint life came to visit us again.

The next morning we found ourselves sitting up in our bed in the *chacmool* pose, with the dulled expression of stone statues on our faces and, on our laps, the tray with the anonymous hotel breakfast, to which we tried to add local flavors, ordering with it mangoes, papayas, cherimoyas, guayabas—fruits that conceal in the sweetness of their pulp subtle messages of asperity and sourness.

Our journey moved into the Maya territories. The temples of Palenque emerged from the tropical forest, dominated by thick, wooded mountains: enormous ficus trees with multiple trunks like roots, lilac-colored *macuilis*, *aguacates*—every tree wrapped in a cloak of lianas and climbing vines and hanging plants. As I was going down the steep stairway of the Temple of the Inscriptions, I had a dizzy spell. Olivia, who disliked stairs, had chosen not to follow me and had remained with the crowd of noisy groups, loud in sound and color, that the buses were disgorging and ingesting constantly in the open space among the temples. By myself, I had climbed to the Temple of the Sun, to the relief of the jaguar sun, to the Temple of the Foliated Cross, to the relief of the *quetzal* in profile, then to the Temple of the Inscriptions, which involves not only climbing up (and then down) a monumental stairway but also climbing down (and then up) the smaller, interior staircase that leads down to the underground crypt. In the crypt there is the tomb of the king-priest (which I had already been able to study far more comfortably a few days previously in a perfect facsimile at the Anthropological Museum in Mexico City), with the highly complicated carved stone slab on which you see the king operating a science-fiction apparatus that to our eyes resembles the sort of thing used to launch space rockets, though it represents, on the contrary, the descent of the body to the subterranean gods and its rebirth as vegetation.

I went down, I climbed back up into the light of the jaguar sun—into the sea of the green sap of the leaves. The world spun, I plunged down, my throat cut by the knife of the king-priest, down the high steps onto the forest of tourists with super-8s and usurped, broad-brimmed sombreros. The solar energy coursed along dense networks of blood and chlorophyll; I was living and dying in all the fibers of what is chewed and digested and in all the fibers that absorb the sun, consuming and digesting.

Under the thatched arbor of a restaurant on a river-bank, where Olivia had waited for me, our teeth began to move slowly, with equal rhythm, and our eyes stared into each other's with the intensity of serpents'—serpents concentrated in the ecstasy of swallowing each other in turn, as we were aware, in our turn, of being swallowed by the serpent that digests us all, assimilated ceaselessly in the process of ingestion and digestion, in the universal cannibalism that leaves its imprint on every amorous relationship and erases the lines between our bodies and *sopa de frijoles huachinango a la vera cruzana*, and *enchiladas*.

July 19, 1982
Paris

A NOTE
ON THE ILLUSTRATIONS

The images featured in this volume are sourced from the following volumes of Isabella Mary Beeton's books of household management, cookery and housekeeping.

Isabella Mary Beeton, *The Book of Household Management, etc.*, S. O. Beeton, 1861.

Isabella Mary Beeton, *The Book of Household Management, etc.*, Ward, Lock, Bowden & Co., 1892.

Isabella Mary Beeton, *Mrs. Beeton's Family Cookery and Housekeeping Book, etc.*, Ward, Lock & Co., 1907.

For more Tales of the Weird titles
visit the British Library Shop (shop.bl.uk)

We welcome any suggestions, corrections or feedback you may have, and will
aim to respond to all items addressed to the following:

The Editor (Tales of the Weird), British Library Publishing,
The British Library, 96 Euston Road, London NW1 2DB

We also welcome enquiries through our Twitter account, @BL_Publishing.